BOSS DADDY

SUZANNE HART

JUST LOVE PUBLISHING

DESCRIPTION

OMG Is this for real?

My dashing, gorgeous ex wants to hire me.

He needs my help to recover his kid.

I can't say no.

So we end up living in the same house and things get complicated.

Is this our second chance?

We were lovers in college till I broke his heart.

But now he's my client and I shouldn't get involved. I should focus on the case.

How can I?

When he touches me with those strong hands in all the wrong places.

Now I'm afraid I'll be the one with a broken heart...

© **Copyright 2019 by Suzanne Hart - All rights reserved.**

In no way is it legal to reproduce, duplicate, or transmit any part of this document in either electronic means or in printed format. Recording of this publication is strictly prohibited and any storage of this document is not allowed unless with written permission from the publisher. All rights reserved.

Respective authors own all copyrights not held by the publisher.

WARNING: This book contains sexually explicit scenes and adult language. It may be considered offensive to some readers. This book is for sale to adults ONLY.

Please ensure this book is stored somewhere that cannot be accessed by underage readers.

CONTENTS

1. Matt	1
2. Kayla	5
3. Matt	10
4. Kayla	15
5. Matt	21
6. Kayla	26
7. Matt	31
8. Kayla	33
9. Matt	37
10. Matt	40
11. Kayla	46
12. Matt	49
13. Kayla	57
14. Matt	62
15. Kayla	66
16. Matt	71
17. Kayla	74
18. Matt	76
19. Kayla	86
20. Matt	91
21. Kayla	98
22. Matt	107
23. Kayla	113
24. Matt	120
25. Kayla	126
26. Matt	140
27. Kayla	143
28. Matt	150
29. Kayla	159
30. Matt	167
31. Kayla	181

32. Matt		187
33. Kayla		192
34. Matt		200
35. Kayla		208
36. Matt		214
37. Kayla		224
38. Matt		227
39. Kayla		235
40. Matt		243
41. Kayla		248
42. Matt		253
43. Kayla		258
44. Matt		268
45. Kayla		278
46. Matt		285
47. Matt		295
48. Kayla		308
49. Matt		318
A note from the author		323
About Suzanne Hart		325
Also by Suzanne Hart		327

ONE
MATT

It went well. It actually went well.

Long after the meeting ended and the boardroom had been cleared, I was left sitting in a seat at the top of the table in complete and utter awe. When I had the plan of starting my software business up, I had no idea it would work. Not only did it work, but it was also going above and beyond any expectations I might have had.

I just landed my biggest client yet – we were partnering up with one of the biggest web development companies in the country. That meant that my company, my tiny little start-up company that was already making me more money than I ever imagined, was about to be one of the biggest names in the industry.

My company was one of the most talked about software developers. Our name was scattered in the headlines as the biggest up-and-coming name in the technological field. I was still struggling to wrap my head around it myself, but it turns out, people went wild for insight from those who had been in service. The idea behind my devices was simple; I wanted the soldiers who were on active duty to be able to let their loved ones know that they were okay even when they were in situations where having their phone on them could endanger them. At the touch of a button, they would get across the message that they were safe.

Of course, it was still in its infancy. I was going off of everything that I had learned while being out in the field – from the types of situations that we could end up in, to the chances of the device falling into the wrong hands. I only hoped that it would be possible one day.

In the meantime, we were working on smaller projects. A whole new line of phones and computers was being released, each of which had the tiny pieces of what I wanted to eventually accomplish. I considered them my prototypes.

Technology was the way of the future. I knew that.

Did I ever think that I was going to have my name all over it at any point in time or that I might someday end up having more than nine digits in my bank account? No, but there I was and that someday had arrived. My mind was blown.

Eventually, I had to force myself to get up and out of my seat. Closing hours were fast approaching, and I knew my secretary had long since clocked out. To my relief, my secretary had left me in peace after the meeting. I had a feeling that she knew I was still reeling. So far, this deal had been the biggest one I'd shaken hands on, but every little one had been just as amazing to me and I needed a few moments to process it all. She seemed to understand that well enough.

It was incredible. The best part was that I could tell the partnering company was happy with my proposal. They knew this could work as well as I did if we simply wrapped up all the loose ends.

I couldn't help but wonder how my grandfather would feel if he knew I had used the majority of the inheritance he had left to me to start up a firm revolving around technology. I could hear his voice now.

"Those computers are a waste of time, if you ask me. Things were never this complicated in my day!"

I smiled at the memory of his face and how it might have contorted and reddened the way that it did when he got overexcited. He may not have approved of the means but I liked to think that he would be proud of my success, regardless. I'd used what he left me to make something of myself.

Of course, that only meant that my entire life had been turned the slightest bit upside down since I had gotten back. My family and I were never the type to wear expensive suits and sully ourselves with the corporate world. Yet there I was, well-dressed, in a particularly tall building that overlooked the city through shiny glass windows.

Sure, I had the option of leaving it all behind and moving out to the countryside but I felt like I was doing a lot of good. I had too many memories of being out there and it hurt to have to think about them. My grandfather left me more than money. He left me an entire ranch. He gave me the family business and I chose to take a very different path for myself.

Climbing into the elevator, I pressed the button that would take me down to the ground floor, breathing in a sigh of relief as the doors of the elevator pinged shut. I didn't think I would ever get past the reprieve of going home after a long day – even if that home did happen to be in a similar building. The penthouse suite was calling my name and I couldn't say that its voice was particularly enticing.

Still, a home with a bed was better than the racks in my

unit. I didn't have to share a bunk with anyone else. One of the nicest things was the knowledge that, unless something unexpected happened, I was guaranteed to get eight hours of uninterrupted sleep if I wanted it.

TWO

KAYLA

To say I was nervous would be an understatement.

The building loomed over me, the epitome of corporate chic. I could see the elevators traveling up and down what had to be at least sixty flours, the silhouettes of men and women making their way up and down the skyscraper. I struggled to imagine that I might soon be one of them.

As if the building needed to add any more of an air of pretentiousness, there was a big water feature standing on the doorstep, echoing with the trickle of what I was sure was meant to be tranquility.

I walked toward it with my head held high. This was a massive opportunity for me. I couldn't let my nerves get the best of me. I caught a glimpse of myself before I entered the building, in its gleaming glass windows, and forced a smile onto my face. I thought that I passed for a professional. No one needed to know it was nothing but a façade.

Between the receptionist on the ground floor, the woman I ended up in the elevator with, and the secretary outside the office, I felt underwhelming. They were all wearing the same sort of suit dress I wore, pinstriped skirts and blazers over button-up blouses, but their hair and makeup were done immaculately whereas mine was not. I had always been a bit of a Plain Jane.

I never thought that my appearance mattered all that much and I had made sure to look neat and presentable, but I never expected to be surrounded by women who took things to the next level.

When I was on the top floor, I walked over to the desk handled by a woman with bold red lips and long lashes. She glanced up at me but her fingers continued tapping on the keyboard in front of her. She had a headset on and I didn't know if I was meant to say anything, so I merely dropped the blue folder I was holding onto her desk. She gazed at me skeptically and then inclined her head toward some empty seats around a coffee table on the far side of the lobby.

I had barely taken a seat before she stood up from behind the desk. She was incredibly tall and resembled a supermodel in high heels that I couldn't imagine being comfortable. She made her way through a set of double doors on the left side of the room and disappeared from my sight.

I wasn't sure how long I sat there, but as each second ticked by, I couldn't help wondering what on earth had possessed me to apply for the job. Of course, I had never expected to actually get called, but I had taken the chance anyway. And I *did* get called. That didn't mean that I had to accept the interview, though.

"He's right through there, Miss Walker," the receptionist said, her voice breaking through my thoughts. Her hair was shiny and blonde and the expression on her face screamed judgment as she sat back down behind her desk and resumed typing.

Then again, maybe I just imagined it. Either way, I wasn't meant to respond. That much was obvious.

With a deep breath, I stood from my chair in the small waiting area and made my way toward the doors that she indicated. They were mahogany, as clean and modern as everything else within sight, and opened easily.

I knew that *he* was at the head of the company, but seeing him still knocked the breath out of me. The office was massive and furnished luxuriously. He sat in a leather chair behind an expensive mahogany desk. Clearly, mahogany was a running theme because the small lounging area on the side of the room nearest to the door also had a mahogany coffee table, surrounded by leather armchairs and a couch. It was obviously for entertaining clients. It was either that or just for show.

The floor-to-ceiling windows were massive and so clean that it seemed like there was nothing there, like I could skydive right off the edge. The view of the city behind him was incredible. But none of that matched the sight of the man in the office.

He looked up from what he was typing and fixed those eyes on me. In spite of myself, I felt something deep within me tighten as his gaze met mine. I gulped and shut the door behind me, walking toward his desk on suddenly shaky legs as he stood up from his chair.

"Kayla?"

His voice hadn't changed much at all. It was still smooth and rich, like heated honey pouring over my every sense. I had to pat down the flames threatening to engulf me, deep within my core.

Clearly, he was surprised to see me. I couldn't blame the guy. It had been over ten years since I last saw him.

"Hello, Mr. Cole."

I had to remind myself that I couldn't use his first name. This was first and foremost an interview, and there was no time for such casualness. Nevertheless, it was hard to miss the surprise that registered on his face before he composed himself.

"Of course," he murmured more to himself than me. He gestured to the empty seat across from him. "Please sit down, Miss Walker."

I nodded and took the seat across from him, trying not to immediately start fidgeting. I put my hands in my lap and gave him a small smile. He returned it and sat back down, but his eyes were still taking me in curiously.

He looked so different. The years had been kind to him. He had been a good-looking man even back then, but now... He no longer had a baby face and his jaw had grown sharper, more chiseled. Whatever he had been doing in the gym had definitely been working for him because he was all muscle. His eyes were what got me. Those eyes still held the same mischievous light that I remembered from all those years ago.

Matt was wearing a suit, dark gray and bordering on black. His jacket was unbuttoned and I could clearly see the way the light-blue, almost white shirt clung to his taut body beneath. I had to stop there. The next thing I knew, my eyes would be on his crotch and all the manliness it held. His pants were probably just as tight, shaped to his masculine form.

God, the way his eyes raked over me gave me goosebumps. They weren't the only things that I wanted raking over my body. *What am I thinking?*

After what seemed like an age, he finally tore them away from me and I released a quiet breath I didn't even realize I'd been holding. He focused at a folder in front of him and began flipping through it. I recognized it as the same blue folder I had given to his secretary – the one full of my details and credentials.

THREE
MATT

When I learned that I would be interviewing someone for the position of the legal representative, the woman who walked through the doors was the last thing I ever expected. My breath hitched at the mere sight of her. I won't even bother mentioning how my cock stirred in my pants.

The longer I stared at her, the more memories came to my mind. She looked just as gorgeous as ever – perhaps even more so since she had grown up. Her hips had filled out and her breasts had somehow gotten bigger. She was all curves and soft flesh, full-bodied and shorter than me.

Even though she was wearing an outfit that almost mirrored every other woman in the building, she wore it somehow differently. Her skirt ended just above her knee, revealing enough leg for me to imagine following it upward, and her blouse stretched over her breasts in the most enticing way. Her heels were subtle and they made no real difference since I still towered over her frame.

Her short brown curls framed her pretty face and I knew she hadn't truly changed a bit. The smile she gave me told me that the clever piece of work who gave our teachers hell in college was still in there.

Boy, did I want to bring her out.

I had to force myself to stare away from her. The way she used my last name instead of my first let me know she wasn't here for a catch-up session. This was all about business.

Professionalism was a must.

Nevertheless, as I gazed down at the impressive list of qualifications and credentials before me, I couldn't help but think that Kayla had come a long way since I had known her. While I had gone off and enlisted, she had stayed behind in the city and built herself up. She worked for some of the most prestigious firms and now she was a freelancer.

My agents and my managers and my financial advisors – okay, yes, everyone – had told me to be certain that I was hiring someone who knew what they were doing. The paperwork before me told me that Kayla Walker definitely knew what she was doing. It was no wonder she had made it into the interview; up until that point, only two others had gotten by the scrutiny of my stern secretary.

"You have a rather impressive history, Miss Walker," I finally said.

I closed the folder and pushed it away from me. I had seen everything I needed to. From there, carrying out an interview was simply a formality; I already knew that I would be giving Kayla the job if she was still interested in being a part of the company once she saw what it was about.

As I met her jade-green eyes, I wasn't sure it was such a good idea to hire her, but I forced that thought to the back of my mind. I could separate business from personal. Who cared if I was imagining how those eyes looked when they rolled to the back of her skull in pleasure?

"Thank you, Mr. Cole. I'm hoping that I will be a good addition to your company."

"Please, call me Matthew," I said.

We could be formal and still use one another's first names. This was foolish and awkward.

She nodded her head slowly. "Okay... Matthew."

Kayla had always been different. All through college, she was the fascination of every boy and even some of the girls. It was no surprise why. She was sharp as a knife, with a quick wit, and an even quicker tongue. No matter where she went, she had a way of standing out in her simplicity. Even then, sitting across from me, I could see that she wore hardly any makeup and her hair was loose and naturally wavy.

Different was what I was searching for in my business, though. I was drawn to different. And there was no denying I was drawn to Kayla at that moment.

I would make any excuse to spend a little more time in her company.

"I guess I should probably get on with this," I said.

She raised her eyebrows.

"The interview process, I mean."

The corners of Kayla's mouth twitched upward in a smirk. "Would I be right in suggesting that Matthew Cole was as unprepared as ever?"

I wasn't sure what brought it out of her, what I had done that suddenly made her feel comfortable enough with me to say it, but it made me grin. The cheeky little minx was still in there.

"Perhaps. This isn't an exam, you know."

"I didn't know that it would be you when I first applied," Kayla admitted. "I was interested in the work the company did and I started doing research. Your name popped up long after I sent the application through."

I arched an eyebrow. I couldn't deny that I was afraid of what that might mean. I was well aware of the fact that a lot of people didn't believe someone like me could graduate college and actually go somewhere in the world.

It didn't help that when I enlisted in the military, I was looked down on. What kind of person went to study business and technology and then ran away to become a soldier? A lot of people thought I would never make it back and I was pretty sure a lot of people didn't care whether or not I did.

"And now that you do?" I asked.

"It only makes me even more impressed. I want to be a part of bringing good to the world. That's what you're doing, right?"

I nodded my head. "That's what I want to do, yes."

"Then let me know what you need me to do for you to make that happen and we'll get this show on the road."

I had to resist the urge to laugh at the way she took charge. She always had a way of doing that. There were some classes that Kayla had led better than the lecturers herself. She was born for it.

That was, unless I took control. If I recalled correctly, she quite liked that.

Before I let my thoughts go completely astray, I opened the drawer on the left side of my desk and pulled out a file full of everything she needed to know. I mentally thanked my financial advisor for once again having me covered. I needn't have worried about anything.

When I passed the file to Kayla, she started flipping through its contents without a word. There was nothing confidential in there but I knew I didn't have to be concerned even if there was. My company had become too big to cross.

I cursed myself mentally at the mere thought. Was I actually considering making sure that no one crossed me, not even Kayla? She hadn't even done anything to say that she would be a threat. This was what the corporate world was doing to me.

Everything had to be defensive. There was no other way around it.

Once she had taken in everything she needed to, Kayla glanced back up at me and I knew from the spark in her eyes that she was on the same page as me. She wanted in. It was a face I was getting used to receiving from the people who heard about my idea.

It was the same look that had caused several companies to make me offers of partnerships, others mergers, and even more, their assistance in exchange for nothing more than to be a part of what I was trying to accomplish.

There was something about Kayla giving me that look that did something else to me though. I swallowed as my mouth suddenly went dry. This woman was going to drive me crazy.

Hell, she only just arrived and she was already driving me crazy.

FOUR

KAYLA

The way he was eyeing me had me squirming in my seat. I passed the file back to him and his fingers brushed across mine, sending tiny charges of electricity pulsing through my system. I licked my lips and instantly regretted it as his eyes followed the movement.

"So," he said. He sounded strangely breathless. Was that just my imagination? "Do I take it you're ready to cover the company's behind?"

I could barely bring myself to nod my head. "We still have a long way to go, don't we?"

"We do, indeed. The company is still growing, but I know this could work. It has so much potential to help so many people."

The gaze on his face was enough to convince me if everything in the ledger had not already done it. He was so passionate about it – that much was glaringly obvious. Judging by everything they had started building and the number of other firms and companies that were practically pledging their allegiance to his, I couldn't blame him.

He had created a system of belief in his idea.

"You can count me in. If you'll have me, that is."

I wanted to be a part of this. And if I got to spend a little more time with Matthew, well, that wouldn't hurt me much either. As if he read my mind, he suddenly stood from his seat and made his way toward the other side of the desk.

Without a thought, I stood from my seat as well. I convinced myself that he was going to shake my hand or something, but he didn't seem to be approaching me for that. I was suddenly confused, wondering what was going on and if I had misread the situation.

Were we done or not? Did I have the job?

"I just have one request," he said.

Matt was standing over me and I didn't know where to look. He leaned back on his desk and I had to stop myself from staring at his body. I had been right about those pants, they *were* shaped to his body, and I'd be damned if I was imagining the bulge at the front of them.

Forcing myself to glance up at his face, which was equally distracting with its nearly perfect bone structure, I asked him. "What is it?"

"Have dinner with me."

Well, I definitely wasn't expecting that. He had this smirk on his face, as if he knew what he was doing to me, and I had to stifle my gasp of surprise. The man was nothing if not confident.

"I don't know if that's appropriate, Matthew."

"Kayla, don't pretend that you haven't been feeling the same tension that I have since the moment you opened that door and walked into my office."

His voice had so much authority in it and I could feel my heart starting to race, hammering wildly on the inside of my chest. There was no point in denying it. He was right and he knew it. He never gave me a chance to answer before continuing anyway.

"I'm not asking for much. I just want you to come over. I'll make us a meal and we can do some catching up."

Before I could give him an answer, Matt reached out toward me and I felt his thumb brush my jawline gently. He tilted my head up to glance at him and my breath caught in my throat at the look in his eyes. There was no mistaking the desire there.

"Do you always get what you want?" I asked breathlessly, knowing full well the answer.

Matt chuckled and the sound was deep and throaty, full of promise.

"As a matter of fact, yes," he murmured. He was leaning in toward me. I could have pulled away if I wanted to, but for some reason, I didn't. Before I knew it, his face was inches away and his lips were hovering over mine. "Yes, I do."

I did the worst thing I could have done, but I couldn't help myself. My mouth had gone dry being in such close proximity to him. I darted my tongue out to moisten my lips and his eyes followed the movement just like they did before.

With a groan, his lips crashed down onto mine. I gasped in surprise, my lips parting beneath his and giving him instant entrance to my mouth. His hand ended up in my hair and I tilted my head back further, my body bowing against his as my eyelids fluttered shut.

The kiss was not gentle or slow. Matt kissed me forcefully, his tongue entering my mouth and fighting mine for dominance. I could feel moisture pooling in my underwear and I desperately craved his touch. He must have known what he was doing to me. There was no doubt in my mind he wanted me just as much, particularly when I felt his other hand move down to cup my bottom and pull me against him.

I could feel the hardness of him despite the annoying layers of material between us, and I rolled my hips against him. He gave a low growl against my mouth in response, gripping on to me tighter still. Deciding not to fight it anymore, I reached for him, my fingers grasping the lapel of his jacket.

There were voices at war inside my mind; one telling the other to stop before this went too far and the other saying it didn't give a fuck because it felt too good.

Suddenly, there was a knock on the door, making my mind up for me. As though I had been doused in cold water, I realized where I was and what I was doing and sprang away from Matthew. I was pretty sure I had pushed him away, in fact.

Matt cleared his throat. He didn't take his heated gaze off of me as he said, "Enter."

I didn't dare turn around. I was sure that what little makeup I had on must be smudged, my hair in disarray where his hand had gripped it, and my cheeks flushed. How was I even supposed to set foot out of the office? I shut my eyes and released a steadying breath, trying to clear my head of all the thoughts racing through it.

It didn't help to close them. I could still see Matt behind closed eyelids, could still picture his face as he stared at me through those deep-brown eyes, could still mentally tear every piece of expensive clothing off of him.

Fuck, I had to get a hold of myself. We weren't hormonal college kids anymore. He was about to be my *boss*, for goodness sake!

"Mr. Cole, your two p.m. is waiting for you in the boardroom."

"Thank you, Lydia," Matt said.

I opened my eyes to see that they were still fixed on me and I felt my insides tighten once more.

"Could you please let them know I will be right with them?"

"Of course," the voice of the receptionist said.

I heard the gentle click of the door closing and heaved a sigh. That was far too close for my liking. What was I thinking?

For all I knew, Matt did this all the time. I wouldn't be surprised with all the gorgeous women walking around the building. I didn't want to be another one of them. No, that wasn't me.

"So, dinner tomorrow evening? It's a Friday so I don't have to wake up early."

I could have said no. I really could have. Ultimately, it was up to me. There was no reason to go to his place, other than the tiny little voice in the back of my mind reminding me that I *wanted* to go.

As much as I could push that voice to the back of my mind, the heat deep within my belly wouldn't be tamed so easily. Trying to reason with myself, I decided that maybe one night wouldn't hurt me. I could get it all out of my system so Matt and I could work together without it hovering over us like some dark cloud filled with sparks of electricity.

If I was being honest with myself, I knew there was no way it was going to be that simple.

Reluctantly, I nodded my head. "Okay."

"Okay?"

Matthew's eyebrows were raised as though he hadn't expected me to say yes all along. I could have rolled my eyes. Instead, I took a step backward from him. Being so close to him was doing my head in. All I could think about was how good it felt to be kissed by him and how hot his body felt against mine. If he touched me again, I didn't think that I could control myself.

"I will see you tomorrow at seven."

This time, he smiled. He took a step toward me but I took another back. We were playing some kind of game of cat and mouse and I did not feel like being the mouse right then.

My new boss accepted this, staying where he was with a knowing grin on his face. Oh, what I would have done to wipe the smirk off of his lips. I swore to myself that I would do it the following evening.

I turned away and started walking toward the door. I paused only to run my fingers loosely through my hair, trying my best to neaten it up. I pulled open the door and walked out of the office with my head held high. Matthew's secretary, Lydia, raised her head briefly to gaze at me curiously and I offered her a polite smile before turning away from her to press the button that brought the elevator up.

FIVE
MATT

For the majority of the following day, I could barely concentrate on my work. I found myself constantly looking down at the time. I would think that hours had passed – it certainly felt that way – only to find that it had been mere minutes since the last time I checked. My mind was fixed on Kayla and the evening I had planned ahead.

The only thing that drew me away from those thoughts was the sound of the phone on my desk ringing. It was unusual for calls to come straight through to me. Lydia would get them first, unless someone had the direct line.

"Hello?"

"Well now, there we go. I finally got this thing to work."

Relaxing back in my chair, I smiled. There was no mistaking the soft, kind voice of my grandmother. Her naturally abrasive nature didn't match that voice at all.

"Hello, Grams. How are you doing?"

"Matthew, my boy, when are you going to pay me a visit?"

I had to resist the urge to chuckle. My grandmother was a no-nonsense woman. She didn't beat around the bush. All of a sudden, I missed her terribly. It had been months since the last time I saw her. I would like to say that we parted on good terms but I could still hear her voice in my head as she yelled after me, her cheeks wet with tears.

Grams, unsurprisingly, was disappointed that I would not be staying with her on the ranch to take over the family business. It was my grandfather's legacy and I was off in the city, miles away from home. She felt as though I was personally betraying them. How could I blame her?

My grandparents raised me out on the ranch, shaped me into the man I had become. Having lost my parents at the early age of four, I couldn't truly remember them all that well. Sometimes I wondered what it would've been like having them around, but my grandmother and grandfather had given me more than I could ever have asked for.

I would be grateful to them always.

"Soon, Grams, I promise. The company is really taking off. If you want, maybe I could even have you fly up here to visit me sometime."

She scoffed on the other end of the line. My grandmother felt much the same about the city as my late grandfather had. "All that pollution will give me more wrinkles."

I couldn't hold the laugh back. "We'll set a date soon, then. I miss the ranch, anyway. How is Mikey doing?"

Mikey was my brother – not by blood. Like me, he had lost his parents young. Unlike me, he didn't have any other family members who could take him in. The poor kid was only fifteen when he got hooked on drugs. If it weren't for my grandparents being as kind as they were, he likely would have been on a one-way path to the big house.

They never went easy on him though. He had to go cold turkey on all the hard stuff and as soon as the sweats had stopped making him scream out in the middle of the night, he was put to work herding the cattle and helping maintain the fences. He hated it at first but quickly took to the animals.

Eventually, he got so good at taking care of them when they were injured or sick that he was the first one we called. Last I heard, he was studying to be a vet. I wondered if he had opened up his own practice yet.

I hadn't seen Mikey the last time I went to the small town I grew up in. I barely saw anyone. I was in and out like a phantom, lurking at the back of my grandfather's funeral. I hadn't wanted to be there longer than necessary. I was gone when he died and I hated myself for it.

On top of that, I was pretty sure that Mikey resented me for not being around too. He probably hated that I went off to the city rather than taking up the reins of the ranch. I wouldn't be surprised, nor could I truly blame him.

"Mikey is doing all right. He's on an internship at the moment."

"An internship?"

"Yeah, down at ol' Doc Simmons. Waste of his time, if you ask me, but what do I know?"

Doc Simmons was the local vet. "Well, I guess he has to learn under someone higher if he wants to know how to do the job properly."

Grams snorted. "He might want to learn under someone who knows how to do it properly then."

I wasn't sure what to say to that. I couldn't speak for Doc Simmons's skills as a vet. I had never had to go to him. Mikey usually handled all the animals on the ranch.

"I'll take your word for that."

"You better. How is city life treating you? Have you found a girl up there?"

Unbidden, the image of Kayla with her hair in a mess

and her full lips swollen from my kisses crept into my mind. The corners of my mouth twitched upward at the memory of the way she had rolled her hips against me. *Really not helping me distract myself from her, Grams.*

"Nah," I said. "I'm too busy doing all this work and stuff."

"Matthew, I want more grandkids. You better plan on giving me some."

I gulped. *More.*

As if she could read my thoughts on the other end of the line, Grams spoke again, this time in a gentler voice. "How is Kevin? Have you seen him at all? Or even Jenna?"

My heart ached at the mention of his name. I hadn't seen either of them in a month. Of course, being away from them was nothing new, but it hurt a lot more knowing that they were just a short drive away and I still couldn't go and see my little boy.

Kevin was my son – a soon-to-be eight-year-old boy. Jenna was my, as of recently, ex-wife. The divorce papers had been settled only a month before but we had been separated for years before then. It was all a formality by the time I signed the paperwork. As much as I wanted to, I could not hate Jenna for leaving me. I spent so much time away on deployment, and when she started seeing my son's English teacher, there was nothing I could say or do.

What was done was done.

The one thing I could hate her for, though, was taking sole custody of my son. Okay, maybe hate was a strong word. I didn't hate her. It just hurt like a bitch. While I was on duty, the absence had been difficult for Jenna, and I got that. I honestly did. I still didn't see why that meant she had to prevent me from spending time with Kevin though.

"Matthew?" My grandmother's voice broke me out of my reverie.

"Sorry, Grams. I gotta go. It's getting busy here at the office."

"Matt," she said, trying to hold on to me.

"I'll call you soon," I interrupted, "I love you."

I hung up the phone before she had a chance to respond.

SIX
KAYLA

My alarm rudely interrupted one of the most pleasant dreams that I'd had in a while. I was riding a horse, out on a farm, and the freedom of having the wind blow through my hair was something I had long since forgotten. Back in my bed, however, my arm swung out and switched the alarm off.

I would have loved to stay in bed all day. Perhaps I could have closed my eyes and found my way back to the dream. My second alarm went off a moment later, beeping loudly to remind me I had some paperwork waiting and groceries to pick up.

With a yawn, I stretched out my limbs and swung my legs off of my bed. I groggily dragged myself toward the kitchen and set about making myself a cup of coffee. Within the first few sips, I was starting to feel like a capable human being again. That didn't mean I was looking forward to the work that awaited me.

Still, I had to get around to it eventually.

The papers were there to help me cut off all of my loose ends. It had been a while since I acted as an official consultant for a firm but I had yet to sign off a lot of the cases I had already wrapped up. Until they were closed, my contracts with the firms were still in effect – which meant that I couldn't actually accept a new job.

All the papers couldn't go into a box in a back room with the *case closed* label until I stamped all of them with my special seal of approval, otherwise known as my signature. I couldn't technically end my terms of employment until they were submitted.

One of the worst parts of being a lawyer, at least for me, was the paperwork. It was so tedious and yet so necessary. My faraway dream was a silly one but all I wanted was to be able to hire an assistant who could do the bulk of it for me one day.

That morning, I woke up to two emails from addresses I didn't recognize. One was from Lydia, Matthew's secretary, and one was from him.

Lydia emailed me my new contract but I had decided to hold off on signing it thus far. I would wait until after speaking to Matthew. I wasn't even sure what had happened the previous day. It didn't seem like an interview had taken place, but at the same time, I felt as though Matt had brought me on board with his company. The dinner with him would help me clear everything up.

If I was going to start working for him, I wanted no confusion before agreeing.

There was a small voice in the back of my mind that told me it was impossible to have no confusion between Matt and me. I actually wanted to disagree with it but I was beginning to wonder if applying to his company was such a good idea. Could I truly work with someone I wanted so badly?

The mere thought of Matt made my heart race. Things

hadn't changed between us, not really. Somehow, we always found our way back to one another.

In college, we eventually had to cut things off because every time we got together, we ended up in bed. Don't get me wrong – it was great, God, it was more than great. Unfortunately for Matthew, I had come to the conclusion that my studies were more important and had cut him off completely. I would never forget the look on his face when I told him it was over.

Back then, it was definitely more than sex. He made me feel like no one ever had. If I was honest with myself, nothing had trully changed there. Ten years later, and I had never met another man who could make my knees weak like he could.

I sighed as I remembered the way my legs had shaken when I saw him the previous day. He definitely wasn't a boy anymore and it seemed the man in Matt had an even stronger pull on me. He certainly had a firmer grip if his hand on my ass was anything to go by.

Sitting in my study, I didn't even realize how turned on I was until I was squirming in my seat, rubbing my thighs together to soothe the ache between my legs. Just the thought of him was doing things to me! How was I supposed to keep a level head when I went to his place for dinner?

Reminded of him, I checked the email Matt had sent me.

Kayla,

Please find my address linked below. It's the penthouse suite.

I look forward to seeing you this evening.

Regards,
Matt

I even read his email in his deliciously smooth voice. His address was an attached location. Of course, he lived in the penthouse. I had to resist the urge to roll my eyes. He had turned into quite the rich city boy, hadn't he?

Then again, perhaps he had always been a city boy.

There was no point trying to continue my work. I just couldn't keep my mind off him. I started to pack up the papers, separating the complete forms from those that weren't.

At the bottom of it all, there were several papers from orphanages and foster homes from all over the state. A lump formed in my throat as I froze on them. They were the real reason I was still in the city, but I was beginning to feel like I was following a trail that had gone cold a long time ago.

Keeping them out, I shut the rest of my work away in two respective boxes titled *complete* and *incomplete*. I was relieved to see that the *incomplete* file had gotten much smaller. Not that I needed reminding, but seeing the papers laid out for me helped.

I couldn't give up now. He was still out there somewhere.

I had to keep believing that. I didn't know what I would do if I lost hope.

∽

By six, I was just about ready. I put some effort into styling my hair and it sat on top of my head in a deliberately messy bun, loose curly tendrils framing my face. That same face was looking back at me from the mirror with color in her cheeks, extra-pink lips, and thick, dark lashes.

I didn't know what to wear. It wasn't like we were going to a restaurant and even if he had been taking me to one, I wasn't the type of person who had fancy dresses hiding in my cupboard. I settled on a simple red summer dress that clung to my figure, flaring out at the waist and dotted with black and yellow flowers. It ended halfway down my thighs, showing more leg than I had to the interview. The only place it was really tight was around my chest. With a low neckline, I was keenly aware of the way my breasts looked in it.

For the first time in months, I put earrings on to go with the gold heart-shaped locket that I always wore around my neck. I held on to it for a moment, closing my eyes as I remembered them. Inside was a picture of both my parents – the last thing that I had left of them, along with the locket that my father had once given my mother. I liked to think that they were there with me, watching over.

Tears prickled at my eyes and I decided it was time to leave.

The cab was already waiting for me by the time I got outside.

I still wasn't sure what exactly I was going to do when I got to Matthew's. Whatever it was, I knew I had to at least try to keep my wits about me. There was no denying that I wanted the man but I wasn't the kind of girl who could just, well, get it out of my system.

And I was pretty sure Matt wasn't the kind of man who could give me more than that.

SEVEN
MATT

I left the office early. It had been many years since I'd cooked dinner for a woman and I wanted it to be good. To my chagrin, I found I absolutely wanted to impress Kayla. I felt like a little boy with a crush. Oddly enough, Kayla had always had that effect on me. Even when we'd been in college, she had the ability to make me feel like a carefree teenager.

Before I got home, I stopped off at the grocery store to shop for all the ingredients I needed. Two hours later, and I was freshly showered with a pair of jeans and a black shirt, opting for casual. Pretty soon, I had managed to prepare a meal that had even my mouth watering. My apartment smelt scrumptious. I found myself grinning at the thought of Kayla's face.

The menu included a simple couscous salad; a main of rosemary braised lamb, roast potatoes, and sweet carrots on the side; and the dessert was a crisp peppermint tart because it was quick and easy. I may or may not have remembered that Kayla's favorite chocolate when we'd been in college was peppermint crisp. Every time she was stressed about an exam, she always bought herself mint chocolate to calm down.

I could remember the way she tasted when I kissed her after she ate one of those chocolates. Shaking the thoughts out of my mind before they got out of control, I checked on the lamb. It was so tender, it was practically melting off the bone. I couldn't wait to serve it.

I made a mental note to thank my grandmother for all the fantastic meals she had cooked for us over the years. She was the typical grandmother who made sure you were well-fed whenever you were in her house. When I was still a boy, cooking with Grams was one of the things that had slowly started to bring me out of my shell after the loss of my parents.

Of course, I couldn't remember any of that, but she'd told me once I was older.

It had served me well living on my own and it had helped me better when I had a family. I hoped it would serve me well that evening. It wasn't until I was in the kitchen and preparing our meal that I realized just how much I missed being able to cook for someone else.

I had low music playing in the background and I found myself whistling along as I made the food. The tart had just gone into the fridge when I heard the buzz of the intercom. I glanced at the clock to see that it was seven p.m.

My heart started to race as I pressed the button to let her in.

I had to stop myself from glancing in the nearest mirror to make sure that I looked okay. What was happening to me? No woman had ever made me so nervous before.

EIGHT

KAYLA

The first thing that caught my attention when I walked through the door was the fact that Matt was wearing an apron. I smirked at him. It looked so out of place on his big, muscular frame.

I couldn't linger on that for too long as the second thing I noticed became apparent. My belly grumbled hungrily as I walked past Matt and into his huge apartment. The place smelled absolutely amazing. I had no idea what was for dinner but I couldn't wait to eat.

"You look..." Matt stared at me and my cheeks warmed under his scrutiny. They moved over the length of my body and back up again until he was staring into my eyes. Why did I feel so naked all of a sudden? "Ravishing."

"You don't look too bad yourself."

I tried to sound casual but he was so attractive and my voice came out husky. The top button of his shirt was undone and I could see a glimpse of the tan skin beneath. All I could think about was unbuttoning the rest of them and revealing more of his body.

"It smells amazing in here," I said, forcing myself to look away.

I glanced around the apartment – my eyes anywhere but on that hunk of a man. It was surprisingly well-decorated. I couldn't help but notice it was missing a feminine touch. There were a few things that I would have added here and there like a throw or a flowerpot...

Wow, Kayla. Easy there. Hold your horses.

"Food is just about ready so we can eat soon."

I turned around and he was holding out a glass of red wine for me, gripping his own in his opposite hand. I took mine gratefully and immediately had a sip. Maybe the wine would calm my nerves. Then again, the way Matt was looking at me told me it was unlikely.

He looked at me like I was what he planned on having for dinner.

"Uhm, so, Lydia sent through the contract this morning," I said, trying my hand at conversation.

"Did she now? I assume everything is to your agreement?"

Matt took a step toward me and I stood my ground. I felt like prey again, but my clit was throbbing in anticipation. I didn't know how much longer I could play this game.

The room was bursting with sexual energy.

I didn't think Matt wanted a response from me. Either way, I couldn't get my tongue to formulate any words. I was too busy staring at his mouth, remembering the way it had felt against mine, and how I yielded to his kisses.

"I never imagined that you would still be here," he suddenly said.

"What do you mean?"

"You always seemed like the kind of girl who was going to go away, travel the world, and try all of these exotic things. I know from your résumé how hard you've worked over the last few years, but it just surprises me."

I shrugged. I didn't want to get into that. It wasn't like I had the money to go gallivanting around the world, anyway.

"I have my reasons for staying."

Matt raised his eyebrows. "What might those be?"

I glanced down at the floor, biting down on my lower lip. I couldn't tell him. There would be no point. Besides, I didn't need someone else judging me for a decision I had made years ago.

Normally, I would have made a quick quip, asking him why he was still here but I already knew the answer to that question. It was admirable. And unlike me, he had left – he'd gone and enlisted in the military.

I simply moped about.

"Okay, don't tell me then. But will you please stop biting your lip like that?"

That got my attention again. I looked back up at him and his eyes were stormy. I sucked in a breath.

Matt put his glass down on the coffee table and when he reached out to take mine, I didn't stop him. He took another step toward me and then he was close enough that I could feel the heat emanating off of him. The little voice inside my head was back, begging me to stop him.

"Matt..." I whispered. "We shouldn't."

"Why not?"

He reached out toward me and his fingers grazed my cheek. He tucked a loose strand of hair behind my cheek. It took everything in me not to lean into his touch.

"What do you want from me?"

"Right now? I want to ravish you."

I tilted my head back to look up at him. "And what about after that? Am I meant to simply be your employee and nothing more? Do you want me to forget that any of this ever happened?"

Matthew's eyes searched mine but I was not going to back down.

"Because if that's the case, then we may as well stop it before it does. I'm not going to forget."

"Kayla." Matt sighed and ran a hand through his hair. It looked so soft and I wanted to lose my own fingers in it, but that wasn't an option. Not unless he told me he could give me more. "I'm not in an easy position. You don't understand. If I was to get involved with someone, it would be splashed all over the papers."

I winced as if he'd slapped me. That stung. "So, what? Are you ashamed of people seeing you with me or something?"

"What? Of course not!"

"Then what is it, Matthew?"

"It's... complicated, okay?"

My cheeks were heated and tears threatened to spill over my waterline. I could feel Matt's eyes on my face but I couldn't bring myself to meet them.

"Look," I started. "I never expected you to give me more. But I don't think I can do this without it. I need more."

Matt sighed again and then said the last thing I expected him to say. "And you deserve more."

"But you're not going to give it to me, are you?"

This time, I forced myself to look up at him. He had a pained expression on his face. It said everything it needed to before he even spoke.

"I can't, Kayla..."

NINE
MATT

Fuck.
I didn't even know how it was happening, but suddenly, Kayla was walking toward the door and I knew there was nothing I could say or do about it. I knew what she wanted but I couldn't give her that. Hell, I couldn't even say we could *try* a relationship.

The press would have a field day. The idea of a relationship had never truly occurred to me but the moment Kayla mentioned it was the moment I knew that it was what I wanted. If there was one woman I wanted more with, it was her.

Besides, we somehow always found our way back to one another and if that wasn't a sign, I didn't know what was.

It wasn't just the press that I was worried about though – it was Jenna.

How could I possibly explain to Kayla all the history that I had with my ex-wife? She barely knew the man that I'd become. If I piled all that baggage onto her before we even got together, before she had a chance to find out who I was, I just knew in my gut that it wouldn't bode well for any relationship.

Kayla was opening the front door. To my surprise, she gave me one last glance over her bare shoulders and I could see that her eyes were watery.

"Kayla, please don't go."

"Goodbye, Matthew."

She walked out of my apartment and the door shut behind her. It didn't even slam, but blew closed with a gentle click. I think a slam might have been more bearable.

I found myself flopping onto the couch with a groan. Things had escalated so quickly and I wasn't sure how. All I knew was that seeing her in that little dress, watching her voluptuous breasts heave with each breath, and how cute her butt looked as she swayed into my apartment had sent all the blood rushing straight to my groin.

That was my problem. I couldn't think with my head. I had to let my cock lead the way.

And it might have just cost me something really good, but now I would never know.

I was so angry with myself that I felt like breaking something. It didn't matter what. I didn't care whether it was the two glasses on the table in front of me, still filled with wine, or my knuckles against a wall.

The food was still waiting for us. I couldn't believe I had screwed up so badly. Kayla had barely walked into the apartment and I was already making moves on her. I had no one to blame but myself.

Suddenly, my phone started vibrating on the kitchen counter.

With a sigh, I pulled myself up off of the couch and walked over to answer it.

"What?" I snapped into the mic.

"Uh, is this Matthew Cole?"

"Yes. I'm Matthew Cole."

"Sir, I'm sorry to be the bearer of bad news, but I'm calling to inform you that Jenna Cole has passed away."

I'd never understood what the phrase *blood ran cold* meant up until that moment. That was precisely what it felt like. Everything inside me turned to ice and my heart felt like it was beating slower than usual.

I swallowed. I couldn't have heard that right. Jenna couldn't be dead.

"Sir, are you still there?"

"How?" I asked breathlessly.

"She had an aneurysm, sir. It was caused by a brain tumor."

A brain tumor? No... That couldn't be right.

"Like, cancer?" I asked.

"Yes, sir. Your wife was stage four, terminal."

I gulped. "Ex. She was my ex-wife."

"Oh, yes. I'm sorry."

The person on the other end of the line sounded so indifferent. They weren't there to comfort me or offer a sympathetic shoulder. My whole world felt like it had come out from beneath my feet.

I sank to the floor, resting my back against the counter behind me, and ended the call. I expected to be crying or something but there were no tears. I didn't even know what I was feeling. I felt numb.

There was one thought and one thought only that mattered. A single name was playing itself over and over in my mind. At that moment, it was the only important thing in the world – not me, not my company, not Kayla.

Kevin.

TEN

MATT

Life on the ranch was a world apart from life in the city. I had forgotten all about the quiet. The constant whir of people surrounding me, streets that were never devoid of cars, and the general hustle and bustle of the corporate world were all absent out there.

It was quite surreal to be back and I wasn't sure if that was a good or a bad thing yet.

It had been a week since the news of Jenna's death. My ex-wife was no longer with us. To say it was a shock would have been an understatement. I didn't know how to feel about it. In fact, I was pretty sure I hadn't even begun to process the news properly.

The first thing that I'd done in my haze was drive all the way to her house. The housekeeper, a Dominican woman who didn't speak much English, answered the door. Her name was Crystal. It was clear that she was shocked to see "Mister Matt."

I paid her no mind. "Is Kevin here?"

"Si." Crystal nodded her head. Her accent was as thick as I remembered. "He is upstairs in his room."

With that, I stepped into the house. Crystal protested, saying something in Spanish that I didn't quite understand. Based on the tone of her voice, I would say that she didn't want me in the house. I ignored her. I only had one thing in mind.

My son's bedroom was the first door on the left. I remembered the house like the back of my hand. It hadn't changed much since the last time I'd been there – since I'd lived there. I pushed the door handle open and burst into the room. Kevin was sitting on the floor, playing with some toys. He raised his head and stared at me with wide eyes. They were innocent eyes. I was suddenly struck with an overwhelming feeling of guilt.

My son had no idea that his mother had just passed away. He was innocently playing with toys in his room like he would have been on any other day. He didn't have a care in the world.

At the sight of me, his brow furrowed. "Daddy?"

I sprang into action at the sound of his voice. I knew where everything was and Jenna had not moved the room around as far as I could see. Hardly anything had changed in my son's room. I could see a few new toys were added to his collection and he had a bigger schoolbag. It was lying on the floor near the door. I knew it would be there. Kevin always dropped his bag beside the door when he got back from school – no matter how many times Jenna moaned at him to pick it up and put it where it belonged.

I tugged open the wardrobe and dug around the shelf at the top. There were a few small duffel bags there. We stored them for beach and camping trips. Admittedly, it had been a very long time since we'd taken either of those, but the bags were still there. After pulling out one of the bigger bags, I began darting around my son's bedroom. He stared at me, his hands frozen in midair, a toy in each one. The housekeeper had followed me up the stairs and she stood in the doorway, peering into the room.

"Senor Matt!" she cried out. "You cannot do this. What are you doing? You must leave Kevin's things alone!"

I knew that she knew I wasn't allowed to be there. Jenna spoke Spanish impeccably. I had no doubt that she told Crystal not to let me anywhere near the house, let alone my son's bedroom. I didn't care at that moment. Jenna wasn't around anymore.

Within minutes, the bag was full of all the clothes I thought Kevin might need. I shoved past Crystal and into my son's bathroom, which was also the guest bathroom, to grab some of his toiletries. When that was done, I made my way back into the bedroom.

It had taken everything out of me not to wrap my arms around my little boy the moment I saw him. He seemed so much bigger since the last time I had seen him. I felt like I'd been missing out on his whole life and there was nothing I could do about it. I did it then, though. I got down on my haunches in front of him. When I pulled Kevin into my arms, hugging him tightly, he started to push me away.

I would be lying if I said it didn't hurt. It stung like a bitch to have Kevin push me away like that. I used to be so close to my boy.

"Kevin, I need you to listen to me, okay?" I was no longer holding him, but we were face to face. "I need you to pick some of your favorite toys. Daddy is taking you away from here."

At that, Crystal gave a high-pitched screech. It was so loud that it hurt my ears and I winced. She raced out of the room and I could just barely make out the words she said. They were thrown in between the string of Spanish words.

"Miss Jenna! I call Miss Jenna! You cannot do this, Mister Matt!"

The dark thought came to my mind before I could stop it. The housekeeper could call Jenna all she wanted, but it didn't matter. My ex-wife wouldn't be answering the phone. I felt even guiltier as soon as I thought it.

I could see the panic on my son's face. I knew it would be there. I knew he wouldn't want to go with me. I didn't even know why I was there. None of my thoughts were making sense. All I knew was that my little boy's mom died and he didn't even know it yet. I wanted to be with him when he found out. Truthfully, I wanted to be the one to tell him as much. That was my right, wasn't it? I was Kevin's father. It was my responsibility to be with him when this happened. I needed to take care of him. It was my job to make sure he understood what all this meant.

In hindsight, I probably shouldn't have rushed into it. I reasoned with myself that death made people do strange things. I was definitely still in shock. That much was for sure. All I could think about was my son.

My training had kicked in. I was acting with the speed of lightning.

"I don't want to go with you!" Kevin yelled. He stood up suddenly, throwing the toys he'd had in his hands onto the ground. "I don't want to go with you!"

My heart ached at those words but it didn't matter. It wasn't his choice. I was his parent and he was going to go with me whether he wanted to or not. With a sigh, I picked up the toys he'd been playing with. I grabbed a few of the smaller ones that were on the floor around him. I spotted his teddy bear on the bed and grabbed that too. After zipping up the duffel bag, I put it over my shoulder. I surveyed the small blue room one last time, making sure there was nothing else Kevin would need.

Once I was sure I had everything, I picked him up. Kevin had no intention of going quietly. He started to cry, screaming and kicking his legs out. I bent to pick up his schoolbag before I started carrying my son down the stairs, ignoring his protests.

There was a part of me that felt like what I was doing was wrong, but I pushed that thought away. A much larger picture dominated my mind. I couldn't help but picture someone else telling my little boy the news. The image tore at my heartstrings and the pain in my chest was enough to keep me going.

By the time we reached the front door, Crystal had reappeared. She didn't seem to be in the mood to protest anymore. I caught a glimpse of her face and saw that it was solemn.

"You know?" I asked.

Crystal nodded her head slowly. "Mister Matt, I am so sorry."

Kevin must have sensed that something was up because he was no longer screaming. He was staring between me and Crystal, his small brow furrowed in confusion as he tried to figure out what was going on. "What's wrong?"

I could have sworn I saw tears in Crystal's eyes as she reached for my son. At first, I tried to pull back from her. Seeing that she wasn't trying to take him from me, however, I stood still. She put her hand on my son's cheek, stroking it softly with her thumb. And at that moment, Crystal reminded me that she had been taking care of my son since before he could walk. Whenever his mom and dad weren't around, she was there for him. She made sure he ate, slept, and bathed all at the right times. She was practically Kevin's third parent. She pressed a gentle kiss to my son's forehead. That was enough to make my boy start crying again. He was loud and he held his arms out for Crystal, but she didn't take him from me.

She nodded her head at me. "Go now, Mister Matt."

I did. Without another word, I carried Kevin to the car. I opened the boot, threw the bags in, and then walked over to the backdoor. It was difficult to strap Kevin in with all his kicking and screaming, but I somehow managed. As I pulled back to close the door, the look on my son's face made me shrink a little. If I didn't know any better, I would have described it as contempt.

Pushing away the feeling again, I got into the driver's seat and started the car up. I could have taken us to the airport but I had no idea where Jenna kept Kevin's passport. Instead, I decided to take a very long drive.

The ranch was quite a few hours away.

ELEVEN

KAYLA

It had been a week since I walked out of Matt's apartment. In the chaos that followed, I was suddenly glad I'd walked out on him. At the time, it felt awful. Since then, I had learned that it was all for the best.

I still couldn't get past the fact he had a son. I didn't even know he was once married, let alone that he had a son! There was no denying it though. The worst part of it all wasn't that I clearly didn't know the man I'd gone to college with. It was the fact I'd found out I didn't know him by seeing his face splashed across the tabloids. And alongside Matt's handsome face, his stories were splashed across the papers too.

I'd gone to get my morning coffee from the popup store just down the block when I saw him. His face was pasted across several newspapers and magazines lining the newspaper rack. On his shoulder was a little boy, quite obviously crying his eyes out.

The headlines were all dramatic and similar. They all said one thing. A woman named Jenna Cole — apparently, she'd kept her ex-husband's last name — had passed away of a terminal illness. She was the ex-wife of none other than the CEO of the biggest up-and-coming software company in the country. Naturally, the headlines felt the need to mention the fact that he was a billionaire. She was Matt's ex-wife. A few of the headlines didn't even bother stating that they were divorced. I'd stared at those few words in shock, my blood running cold at the idea that I might have been messing around with a married man.

I put down a dollar and took the cheapest paper available. It was only when I started reading the column that I learned they were no longer together. Relief flooded my system. At least I didn't have to live with the guilt that I'd been making out with and coming on to a married man.

Then again, the feeling was short-lived.

I felt like I barely knew him at all. None of the information in the article had come up when I researched him. I wanted to know all about the man behind the company I was working for and I'd found none of this. If I had, I never would have ended up making out with him in his office, let alone going to his apartment for dinner that last night I'd seen him.

According to the article, Matt got married straight out of college. I couldn't bring myself to feel jealous because I was the one who'd ended things. For all I knew, I could have ended up getting married to him right after college. But no, I had to go and be selfish.

As I already knew, he joined the military. I couldn't help but think about how difficult that must have been for his wife. The article proved my suspicions. It was so difficult for Jenna that she divorced him due to his continuous absence. My heart went out to Matt as I continued reading. Jenna filed for divorce while he was on deployment. Was that even allowed? I felt like that shouldn't be.

The worst part was that the two of them had a son together. It wasn't Jenna's death that was the scandal, it turned out. In the divorce settlement, Jenna had gotten full custody of their son. His name was Kevin and there were several photos of him in the article. He looked like a beautiful little boy, though I thought that he looked nothing like Matt with his green eyes. The scandal was that Matt had gone straight to their house and taken his son. He decided that it was a good idea to do this right after the death of his ex-wife. I couldn't believe it. It seemed crazy and very unlike Matt.

The man I knew wasn't one who acted on impulse. I wondered what on earth had gotten into him or if I even knew the man at all anymore. Closing the paper, I stared at the picture on the front page. The little boy was crying and Matt looked so... forlorn. I hadn't seen him look so lost before.

Yet again, my heart went out to him. But I couldn't stop myself from thinking that I had done the right thing when I walked out of his apartment. As much as it hurt to admit, the headlines proved that much. It wasn't a good idea for things to go any further between us. After all, it was becoming increasingly clear to me that I didn't know him.

How was that any foundation to build a relationship on?

TWELVE
MATT

I planned Jenna's funeral.

That was what I was supposed to say. If you asked me, I would say that the officials planned the funeral with the help of my grandmother. Honestly, most of what I had to do was answer questions. What car did we want, what decorations, what catering service. Stuff like that. I answered the questions in a sort of numb way and before I knew it, the day had arrived.

Despite everything that we'd been through, she had not changed that wish. I was the one who was set with the task of planning the funeral and it was in my hometown. Incidentally, it was her home town too, but that was beside the point.

It was all finally starting to dawn on me when it came to the day. I think I was starting to accept the fact she had passed away. If nothing else, the wake proved that much. I was the first person to see the body. I had to be. I made sure that everything was ready by the time eleven a.m. rolled around. The casket was open and, looking down into it, I could have sworn that Jenna was asleep. I knew better though. She was gone.

The longer I stared down at her, the more aware I became. At first, she looked as pretty as she had in life. The person who dressed Jenna had applied makeup to her face. With a half-smile, I thought that she would have hated the shade of pink that they'd chosen for her. The wrinkles around the corners of her eyes were prominent and I could see that her cheeks were hollow.

Those weren't effects of aging or even death itself. No, I realized, those were the effects of her illness. It had gotten to her in her final days and I hadn't been around to witness any of the major changes, but I could see them then and there. In spite of myself, my hand found hers and I gave it a gentle squeeze. It felt fragile and weak in a way it never had – not to mention cold.

Tears prickled at my eyes and it wasn't long before they began spilling over the rim of my waterline. At first, I didn't even know I was crying. My cheeks were hot and the rivulets of saltwater dripped off of my jawline. Raising a hand, I wiped them away. I knew that we weren't close anymore but that didn't make it any easier. I wished Jenna had told me what she was going through. I would have made more of an effort. It was obvious that she was happy without me in her life, in Kevin's life. But surely, she wouldn't have minded having a little more support? She had to have known that she was sick – and how bad it was.

She had to have known that I would have been there for her if she had only told me.

Resentment boiled in the pit of my belly and I pushed it away as hard as I possibly could. I couldn't afford to think so negatively. It was her right to keep me out of her life – even if I would never understand why she needed to keep me out of Kevin's – and that was what she'd chosen to do. There was no point in thinking badly of her for wanting to live her life the way she wanted to, especially not now that her life was over. All I could do now was take care of our son and make sure that I did right by her.

Joining the military had ruined our relationship and there was no one else to blame. It was my own fault. I wished I could take it all back, but it was far too late for that.

When it was time for the funeral to begin, there were several people around who I didn't know. They were people she'd known after our marriage ended. I noticed quite a few of them were teachers. It made sense for her to be in those sorts of circles since she'd been seeing a teacher herself.

There were many people who I *did* know, though. One such person was her best friend, Casey. I made my way over to her. Casey was pretty in a tomboy sort of way, but that day, she was wearing a black dress that showed off a womanly figure. She'd been speaking to one of the people I didn't recognize and when her eyes landed on me, she gasped.

"Matt," she murmured.

"Hey, Case," I said softly.

I knew that there was a certain code between women. I wasn't sure which category I fell into. Was I meant to be avoided at all costs? Did Casey hate me because she was obligated to hate me? After everything, did any of that matter anymore?

Casey answered all my unspoken questions by hugging me. She was much shorter than I was and her embrace was welcomed. She was warm and she smelled like flowers - real flowers, not the false scent that came with expensive perfumes. It was fresh and natural, reminding me of her. It was a good way to describe Casey. She had always been fresh and natural. She was the tether that Jenna always needed whenever she felt like she was losing her mind. Casey would pull Jenna back down to the earth so that she didn't float away.

"I'm so sorry," Casey said into my ear.

"Me too," was all I could say back.

There was so much more that I wanted to tell Casey, but I didn't know where to begin. She was tasked with the horrible job of giving the eulogy, but I knew that it would be beautiful. Jenna wouldn't have wanted anyone else to do it.

When she finally pulled back, we weren't alone anymore. Anything that I wanted to say to my ex-wife's best friend disappeared. It was all on the tip of my tongue but I couldn't find it anymore. James, my ex-wife's lover, stood in front of me. The English teacher was shorter than I was and he looked up at me. He wore an expression of disdain on his face. His hair was thinning and several grey strands were lining it. Casey seemed to sense the tension between us.

"I'll leave you two alone." She gave my arm a gentle touch before she walked away. I saw her make her way to the back of the room where Jenna's casket stood.

"James," I said curtly.

"Matthew."

It wasn't often that people used my full name. In fact, it happened so rarely that I sometimes forgot it was my name. You'd have a hard time trying to get my attention by calling me Matthew on most days.

"Where is Kevin?" James asked.

Kevin was with his great-grandmother. They were probably on their way here at that very moment. Of course, that wasn't what I told James. For some inexplicable reason, the mere sight of James angered me. I didn't want to tell him. As far as I was concerned, it was none of his business.

"He's around here somewhere."

The longer I looked at him, the more I was struck with the odd urge to punch James – right there and then. That was all I wanted. I didn't even understand *why* I was so angry. Sure, this man had started seeing my wife before we were yet divorced, but that wasn't entirely his fault. All three parties were to blame.

Before I could punch him and before he could answer, we were interrupted. I heard the distinct voice of Grams from somewhere close behind me and I knew that my son had arrived. Without a word to James, I walked away and made my way toward the front of the room.

Kevin came into my sight almost immediately. He was one of the only children present. He was wearing a black suit that was tailored for him only the day before. He looked up at me and my chest ached. I had never seen Kevin look sadder than he did at that moment. I made my way over to him and got down on my haunches. I didn't try to hug Kevin. The past few days had been tense and no good would have come of that. It was quite clear that my son resented me. Ever since I explained to him that Jenna was gone, his attitude had changed completely and, for a child, he had a surprising amount of coldness to his personality. It seemed to be reserved for me.

I fixed his tie instead. I was at a loss of what to do.

The rest of the day seemed to pass me by in a bit of a blur. Even though the service was beautiful, I felt like I was simply going through the motions. I allowed the congregation to lead the way, blindly following their actions. My eyes kept landing on my son.

It was harder to hate James once I saw the way that he interacted with Kevin. I was never near enough to hear what they were saying, but Kevin was far more willing to speak to James than he was to me. That wasn't to say that they were close or anything. No, I thought that Kevin seemed to be distant with James too.

Then again, perhaps I simply imagined things to make myself feel better.

By the time the procession began making their way to the cemetery, I felt like I was starting to accept things. What was happening was real. The numb feeling I'd been hiding behind was all but gone. It was replaced with hurt, anger, and fear. Most of all, I was sad.

When we got to her grave, I was one of the men who lowered the casket into the ground. James was another. There was no animosity between us at that moment. We were both grieving and saying goodbye to a woman we loved. I wasn't in love with her and I hadn't been for a very long time, but Jenna would always have a special place in my heart as my first woman and the mother of my child.

"Grams!" I heard Kevin's soft voice say once I stepped away from the grave.

I was glad, if nothing else, that Kevin and Grams got along. They had not seen each other since Kevin was very young. That was all thanks to Jenna. To say it hurt would be laughable. It was like a kick to my gut – especially since my grandparents had always loved Jenna. I thought that she felt the same. Then again, I didn't know if she regretted her actions at all. For all I knew, she missed my grandparents too.

I didn't know what followed his statement. The buzz of the people around us was too loud. He was drowned out. Thankfully, my grandmother could hear him.

What happened next was what broke the dam.

My son, my sweet boy, walked over to his mother's grave and dropped his favorite teddy bear. It landed alongside the coffin topper, a rosary of her choosing. She wore it around her neck every single day. The teddy bear bounced once before falling on its side, one eye staring up at us from Jenna's grave. There was something incredibly significant about this moment and I knew I would never forget that teddy bear's face looking up at us with dark, beady eyes before the dirt started pouring into the hole in the ground, covering its white fur.

When Kevin walked back over to me, he reached up to take my hand and squeezed it in his tiny fingers. Somehow, I felt like my son was even stronger than I was in that instant. He was holding me together with his small hands. Our hands were linked all through the eulogy. I barely heard a word that Casey said, but I could see the effect her words had on the crowd. I didn't need to hear it to know that every word she said was spoken with love.

~

It was only once the service was over that James came to me. There was a taller, older man beside him. The other man was thin and frail but I got the feeling that he was meant to intimidate me.

"I need to have a word with you, Matthew," James said.

Nearly everyone had left. I had personally thanked each and every person for coming. Needless to say, I was feeling pretty drained by the time everything was over. Behind James, my grandmother was waiting with my son. Kevin looked tired, too. I knew the kid would crash pretty soon.

"What is it, James?"

"I think it's something you'll want to discuss behind closed doors."

I raised my eyebrows but I didn't argue. I wasn't sure how I could. "I'll be right back, Grams."

She nodded at me. I knew there was an empty room on the upper floor of the funeral home. I gestured for the two men to follow me up the stairs. There were pictures of Jenna and her pretty smile pasted to every spare inch of wall in the house. The funeral directors had arranged that. They felt her loved ones should see her when she was at her happiest. For me, it was hard to look at her in general, let alone when she was smiling and laughing for the camera. None of us would ever get to see her that way again.

Once we were behind a closed door, I turned to them. "Well? What is it?"

James looked at the elderly man expectantly. I felt a twinge of annoyance. The elderly man opened his suit jacket and pulled out an envelope. It had already been opened and he slid a piece of paper out of it. He handed it to me.

I looked from the two men to the paper. "What is this?"

"I think you should read it, Matthew," James said.

Overwhelmed once more with the urge to punch him, I opened up the neatly folded paper. My blood ran cold as I saw the title. It was Jenna's will. My heart started to race a little faster as I read it. At first, none of it seemed relevant to me. Jenna hadn't left me anything. That was no surprise. I didn't expect her to leave me anything.

Something else I didn't expect, though, was that she would take something away from me. But there it was. In bold, black ink.

Jenna had given James full guardianship over our son.

THIRTEEN
KAYLA

My first day back at work was different. At first, I wasn't even sure if I still had a job after everything that had happened at Matt's place. I decided, after no one tried to contact me to tell me my contract was terminated, that I did. Normally, I didn't have to go into the office, but that morning Lydia sent me an email. It took me a second to remember that she was Matt's secretary. There was a scheduled meeting with the company's board. It seemed like it was pretty urgent. The email was one of the most official ones I'd seen, considering it was all done on short notice.

I sent back my confirmation. Thankfully, it was one of those mornings where I had my life together, for once. I was already up and about by the time Lydia sent the email and I was dressed professionally. I'd had other plans for the morning but they would have to wait.

After calling myself a cab, I made my way to the office. When I stepped up to the skyscraper, I felt a lot more confident than the last time I'd been there. Though some of that was probably fueled by the anger I felt. I was still pissed off with Matt. It had been over a week and I'd heard nothing from him.

The women that I passed no longer intimidated me. We were all dressed like clones of one another and unlike the last time, I had made an effort to put on a little bit of makeup. My hair looked nice too.

Okay, fine, I'd admit it. I might have dressed up a little bit. There was a chance I might see Matt at the meeting and despite everything, I still wanted him to look at me.

When I got to the top floor, Lydia stood. "Hello, Kayla. How are you?"

I told Lydia I was well but even though she'd asked the question, she didn't genuinely seem interested in my answer. She had a ledger in her hands and she was already walking down a hallway I hadn't noticed before. It led us past Matt's office. It was clear that I was expected to follow.

When we got to the boardroom, it knocked the breath out of me. The entire room was made up of glass. The walls were glass, the doors were glass, and it overlooked the city out of floor-to-ceiling windows. The view was spectacular. I didn't think anyone with vertigo would be so inclined to agree with me.

A long mahogany table took up the bulk of the room. There were several men seated around the table. The seat at the top was empty and I felt my heart sink. I got the distinct feeling it was Matt's seat. And he wouldn't be joining us for the meeting.

I pushed the thoughts of him away. I didn't even know why I was so disappointed. There was nothing between us anymore. He was my boss. Nothing more.

There was only one other woman besides Lydia and me. She gave me a polite smile as I took a seat next to Lydia. I smiled back. The secretary slid the ledger across the table toward a tall, slim man. He had curly blonde hair piled on top of his head and his eyes were hidden behind a pair of rather dirty glasses.

He reached for the ledger and opened it up.

"Right," Lydia said. "As you all know, Mr. Cole is taking a sabbatical from the company."

What? That was news to me.

"The next few months have already been planned out carefully. Mr. Cole wants them to take place. Nothing will change." She paused and everyone at the table nodded. I felt very much out of the loop. No one had told me any of this. "The partners from the latest merger will be in charge of all public appearances. They will be standing in on behalf of the CEO."

I could only blink all this new information in. When had all this happened? Where was Matt? What did this mean for me?

As if Lydia could read my mind, she spoke again; "As for the rest of us, we continue to do our jobs as if he was still here. Some of you are new here and others are not required to come into the office every single day."

Lydia paused, looking directly at me. I couldn't help but feel like she knew something was going on between Matt and me. Well, she needn't have worried. That was all over.

"The only reason that you're here is so you know what is happening with the company," Lydia continued.

The man with the dirty glasses cleared his throat. He didn't speak until he was sure Lydia finished with everything she had to say.

"Thank you, Lydia," he murmured. "I must apologize for the short notice. We didn't receive the official news that Mr. Cole would be taking leave until this morning."

Oh. Well, that explains that. I nodded my head and stopped when I saw that I was the only one doing it.

"My name, for those of you who don't know, is Douglas Jones. I'm one of Mr. Cole's financial advisors. I felt it important that all of you be kept in the loop as you all handle fairly large sectors of the company."

Mr. Jones closed the ledger and I met his eyes. They seemed to see through me and I looked away quickly. I couldn't understand why this meeting was making me feel so uncomfortable. I was usually a lot more professional than this.

"We're going to go through the plans with you this morning," Lydia said. "This ledger is full of the itinerary. You will all be going home with a copy."

I knew that I should have kept my mouth shut but I was too curious not to ask. "Where is Mr. Cole?"

All the eyes at the table were on me. Mr. Jones's gaze lingered on me for the longest time. I felt the same feeling once more; that he could see right through me. Had Matt told him about us?

"I'm afraid that is none of our concern, Miss Walker."

That shut me right up. I felt like I'd been dismissed. With a curt nod, I looked back down at the table. I pulled a notebook and pen out of my bag and set them down in front of me. He was right. We were there to work.

As Mr. Jones took us through the company's plans for the next few months, I couldn't stop my thoughts from straying to Matt. I kicked myself for it. I knew I shouldn't even care. In fact, I wasn't sure why I *did* care.

A million questions came to mind and two of them topped all the others. Was I ever going to see him again? More importantly, was he okay, wherever he was?

I had to push them away. I had a job to do. Besides, with

Matt gone, there was nothing to distract me from my own mission. As soon as the meeting was done, I would get back on track. I remembered the papers sitting beneath a box in my study at home.

They were waiting for me.

FOURTEEN

MATT

The rage coursing through my veins felt like fire. I knew that if it weren't for that lawyer, I would have punched James right then and there. The desire to knock him out had been building all damn day.

I felt utterly fucking betrayed by Jenna. I couldn't believe what I was reading. There was no mistaking it. I let my eyes run up and down the last few lines again and again. My ex-wife was trying to keep me away from my son, even in her death.

Funny enough, it was James that I was angry with. Beyond the fact that he was trying to take Kevin away from me, I was stunned. How dare he do it on the day of her funeral? That was the part that bothered me the most. He waited for everyone to leave just so that he could confront me with a few legal papers. I wasn't even sure they applied.

"This is absolute bullshit," I said. "I don't believe it. Jenna's will hasn't even been released yet."

"As you can see, Matthew, that is a copy of her will."

James's voice was calm, but the way he used my full

name aggravated me. I could feel my fists clenching and unclenching at my sides.

I could do it. I really could. It wouldn't take much. He would be down on the floor in no time. I could fetch Kevin and get the fuck out of there.

Instead, I ground my teeth together. I knew that it wasn't me. Ever since I'd gotten back from the military, anger had become one of my strongest emotions. I was quick to punch first and ask questions later. I had to control myself if I wanted to keep my son.

And I did want to. I truly did.

"I'm not buying any of this, James. You are not taking my boy from me."

"You don't have a choice." James sighed. He was using the tone of voice one might if they were speaking to a child in the middle of a temper tantrum.

I thought that it wasn't far off but it only served to annoy me further.

"I do. This isn't official until her will is released. We'll talk about it then."

"I'm taking Kevin home with me whether you like it or not, Matthew."

The other man took a step closer to me and I raised my eyebrows. Was this guy trying to intimidate me? "Fuck you, James."

"Fuck me? Fuck you, Matthew! Who do you think you are?"

"I'm his fucking father! Me! Not you!"

"Some father. You haven't even been there for your son. Do you even know the first thing about him?"

Were we actually going to pretend that it was my fault? I wanted to be there for him. Every damn day, all I'd wanted was to spend time with my boy.

The lawyer watched all of this but he didn't say anything. I didn't blame the old man. He looked far too frail to be getting caught between two angry men. My grandmother, on the other hand, had no such qualms. I heard her voice calling out at the door before she knocked.

"What's going on in there?" she asked.

"Come in, Grams," I said.

The door opened and my grandmother burst into the room. I could tell that she was angry just by looking at her. "What the hell is going on up here? We can hear you guys swearing at each other from downstairs. Keep your voices down."

The way she said "we" was very deliberate. She was telling us that *Kevin* could hear us shouting at one another. I felt my cheeks redden with chagrin. James obviously felt the same way I did because he hooked a finger in his collar and pulled it off his neck, gulping. My guess was that he was growing pretty hot.

Without another word, I passed the paper to my grandmother. She gave us each one more cursory glance before she started reading the letter. I could see her expression changing from angry to confused. When she looked back up at me, her jaw dropped open.

"What is this?" Her voice was barely a whisper. The question wasn't directed at me, but the other two men.

"I'm sorry, ma'am," the lawyer spoke for the first time, "but this isn't any of your business."

"Excuse me? This man is my grandson. Do you know what that makes that little boy out there?" She didn't wait for an answer. Her lips were pursed. "He is my great-grandson. I have *every* right."

"Actually," the lawyer started.

My grandmother gave him a withering gaze and he

decided better of it. I could almost see him shrinking as he looked at my grandmother. I felt my chest swell with pride.

Everyone in that room was an adult. But there was no one who could make you feel young like my grandmother could. The other two men awkwardly stepped from side to side. They looked like two kids who were caught doing something naughty.

"I don't want to see or hear about this, do you understand me?"

"Ma'am –" James started but my gran cut him off.

"I said, I don't want to hear it. This is Jenna's *funeral*." Her voice was a hiss. I wasn't sure I'd ever seen my grandmother so angry. "How dare you?"

I watched the Adam's apple in James's throat as he swallowed. I could almost hear the gulp. "I'm sorry," he whispered.

"You'd better be." My grandmother shoved the paper against James's chest and he took it from her. "We'll talk when the will is officially, *legally* released." With that, she turned away from all of us and walked right back out of the room. I knew I was expected to follow her, so I did. We were on the staircase when I heard James muttering beneath his breath.

"Damn country folk," he'd said.

If it weren't for the sight at the bottom of the staircase, I would have done something. Kevin was looking up at us, waiting with one of the funeral directors. I instantly felt bad at having left him on his own.

I couldn't risk doing anything. There was no way I was going to lose my son. I had a lot of time to make up for and I wasn't going to spoil it. And I didn't plan on making my kid hate me before I got the chance.

FIFTEEN
KAYLA

I stood outside a small house on the outskirts of town. A cute white picket fence enclosed the property. I could see several toys strewn across the garden, dolls and miniature race cars alike. There was a makeshift tire swing hanging from the large oak in the corner of the garden. It was clear that children lived there.

With a deep breath, I opened the little white gate and made my way up the cobblestone path that led to the front door. There was a rocking chair standing on the porch and a welcome mat with faded letters sat at an angle. I rang the doorbell.

A few moments later, the door opened and a plump woman with red hair stood before me. She had a bowl in her hand and she was mixing some kind of batter.

"Hello?" She said.

"Hi. Are you Mrs. Williams?"

The woman nodded her head. "The one and only. What can I do for you?"

"Uhm. This is going to sound weird, but I was

wondering if I could talk to you about your kids. You see, I'm kind of looking for someone."

Mrs. Williams furrowed her brow and stepped aside. "Why don't you come on in, dear?"

I knew all about Mrs. Williams. Her name was Sasha. She was a foster mom for six children, four girls and two boys. Unfortunately, the papers I had were outdated and I wasn't even sure she was still taking care of all of them.

She led me into a living area. There were more toys strewn all over the place, stuffed animals, a Barbie doll, and a building block set. I could feel my heart starting to race.

"Take a seat, dear. I'll be right with you. I just want to put this in the kitchen." She raised the bowl. She was about to walk out of the room but paused in the doorway. "Would you like something to drink? It's hot out. I could bring some fresh fruit juice."

I found myself smiling. "That would be lovely."

When she was gone, I looked around the room. There were no photos anywhere. I supposed that I couldn't blame them for that. I didn't think I'd be able to keep photos of kids, knowing that they might not always be with me. I sat down on one of the sofas and it sank beneath me.

Photos wouldn't have helped me much, anyway. I didn't know what he looked like. All I had was a social security number to go on, along with a place and date of birth.

Before long, Mrs. Williams returned to the living area. She had taken off the stained apron and I could see that she was wearing a floral sundress. She was carrying a tray with two glasses and a jug of juice. She set the tray down on the table, poured some juice for both of us, and then sat down in the armchair across from me.

"Right. There we are. How can I help you, Miss...?"

"Walker. Kayla Walker. You can call me Kayla, though."

"Okay, Kayla. I'm Sasha." She smiled at me and took a sip from her glass. "But I believe you already know that."

I nodded my head. "I do."

Rather than speak, I decided to let the papers do the talking for me. I dug into my handbag and pulled them out. They were seriously crinkled from all the times that they'd been folded and refolded. I couldn't count the number of times I had read the papers. I could probably recite all the information on them by heart.

I handed the papers to Sasha and watched as she read them.

"Oh... Is this what I think it is?" she finally said.

I couldn't bring myself to speak. I simply nodded my head.

"Well, I'm honestly sorry to tell you, honey... He's not here." She leaned forward and handed me the papers back. "But I think I might know where you can look."

"What?"

I perked up at that. This was the closest that I'd gotten to a lead. I had been to so many foster homes that I was beginning to lose hope. No one knew anything. Every single person I'd spoken to had been another dead end.

Sasha gave me a smile. "You go on and drink your juice. I'm going to go and get my books."

I had no idea what her books were, but I obliged. I picked up my glass and took a sip. The juice was some kind of a tropical blend and it was chilled. It was refreshing and tasted more like mangoes than anything else.

I was trying as hard as I could not to let my thoughts get ahead of me but it was difficult. I was starting to get hopeful. I might be able to find him.

The feel of my phone buzzing from inside my handbag made me start. I opened the zipper and pulled the phone out. I didn't bother checking the number on the screen before answering.

"Hello?"

"Kayla? Hi."

"*Matt?*" His voice was like a jolt to my system, even as manic as it sounded.

"Yeah. Look, I'm sorry. Uh. I need your help." He sounded flustered. It was quite unlike him.

"What's going on?"

"Someone is trying to take my son away from me. I don't know what to do. I didn't know who else to call."

"That's quite all right. Breathe."

He did. I heard him exhale into the microphone, like static on the line.

"Good," I said. "Now, what do you need?"

"Could you come down here?"

I raised my eyebrows. "Down where?"

"To me. To the ranch. I want to hire you as my lawyer."

"You kind of already did that, Matt."

"No, I hired you as my company's legal representative. I want to hire you as *my* lawyer. I know if anyone can get around this, it's you."

"Matt, I don't know about that..."

"I do. Please. I need your help."

I sighed. What was I supposed to do?

Before I had a chance to answer, Sasha walked back into the room. She had a small cardboard box in her hands and she set it down on the table in front of me, right beside the tray. She sat back down across from me and waited for me to finish my call.

I mouthed a quiet, "Sorry" but she simply waved me off with a kind smile.

"Kayla? Are you still there? Will you do it?"

There was no way that I could say no to him. I knew what he was going through all too well. "Okay," I said.

"Okay? As in, you'll do it?"

"Yes," I said softly, knowing that there was no turning back once I agreed. Besides, a rather large part of me just wanted to see him again. "I will."

I could almost hear the relief in Matt's voice the next time he spoke. I could imagine him running his fingers through his thick, soft hair the way he did when he was relieved. I closed my eyes, trying to shut the images of his face out of my mind.

"I'll book the next flight out of the state for you," he said. "I'll see you soon. Don't worry about the company. I'll cover everything."

Of course, he would. It was hard not to roll my eyes. "I'll see you soon."

With that, I hung up the phone. I was ready to dive into the cardboard box with Sasha.

SIXTEEN
MATT

I paced up and down my study. It was my new office. I wasn't sure what else to do at that point. I'd just gotten off the phone with Kayla and I was still nervous. In fact, I felt even more nervous than before. Hearing her voice again had done things to me. I was sure that I would be fine but I never expected to be filled with such longing. She sounded so calm and I would have done anything to stay on the phone with her. It would have been great to just chat but there was too much going on.

In spite of everything that was going on, I found myself looking forward to seeing Kayla again. I absolutely wanted to see her again. I wanted to do more than that, but that was beside the point.

I knew I'd fucked up the last time I saw her. I was never going to stop kicking myself for it. I wondered if there was any way that we could fix things, but I somehow doubted it. Besides, my name was splashed over practically every newspaper in the country by then. My whole story had been told from the one-sided view of some money-hungry journalist.

Why would Kayla want to hear about my side of things?

I knew I wouldn't. I decided to sit back down before I wore the wood down. My gran had already told me off several times. I opened my laptop and brought up my emails.

The least that I could do was make sure things were handled for Kayla. I emailed James as coolly as I could. It was rather difficult for me not to swear at the English teacher in the form of text but I resisted the urge. It seemed I was resisting the urge to do a lot of harm whenever it came to James. I asked him to send me a copy of all of the relevant documents.

I had a feeling that my son's ex English teacher would be only too happy to supply me with all the necessary paperwork. He was cocky enough to believe he had the case in the bag. There was no doubt that James thought he was proving something with those papers.

Once that was done, I logged onto the booking site to order Kayla's plane tickets. The next flight was later that evening. I hoped it would be enough time for her to pack everything she needed. I just couldn't afford to wait until the next day. Every day, I was closer to having to give up my son.

I emailed the copy of the tickets to Kayla.

Rather than be left alone with my thoughts, I decided to go through all of my emails. There were hundreds waiting for me. There was nothing new about that. Apparently, when you were a CEO, you got a lot of attention. Most of them were from the partners and my advisors.

I skipped right past all of those and went straight to Lydia's. My secretary was the most important person to email me. As I expected, she had a full summary of everything that was going on with the company. I didn't even need to bother with all the other emails when I had her. She had gone so far as to email me transcripts of every meeting.

Bless her soul, I thought. I was incredibly lucky to have her as a secretary.

I emailed her a quick thank you and then read through all of the information. Everything was running smoothly. In lieu of my absence, the partners were going to be handling all of the releases. I was kind of sad about it, to be honest. I wanted to be there. I felt like I was missing out. I had built this empire and it was going to have to keep going up without me.

Despite that sad feeling, however, I found that I was happy to be home. I'd missed being in the countryside. Sure, the view from my penthouse and even my office were incredible. But nothing beat the wide-open spaces of nature.

I had a lot of work to get to on the ranch. There were a few fences that needed maintaining. For the most part, Grams had been able to handle the animals. It was the manual labor that I needed to handle. I supposed she wouldn't have known how to direct the ranch hands.

My brother was nowhere to be found. I hadn't seen him since I got back. It made me think that I was quite right about how he felt about me. My brother resented me for leaving for the city as much as my gran had.

It seemed like I was disappointing people from every direction.

SEVENTEEN

KAYLA

I sat at the airport with my boarding pass in my hand. I wasn't sure how I'd even gotten there. What was I doing?

When Matt sent me the tickets and the location of the ranch, I had to do a double-take. I had not been to the state in many years. I avoided it at all costs. So when I saw where the ranch was, I couldn't help but calculate the distance from my parents' farm. For all I knew, Matt and I grew up only a few miles apart from one another.

We were from the same hometown. I'd always known that, but I made an effort not to think about my roots. Things hadn't exactly ended on a good note. There were plenty of reasons for me not to go back there.

My parents had home-schooled me, so it wouldn't have come as a shock. I didn't have much of a social life until I hit college, with the exception of my high school boyfriend.

My parents didn't even know about him. I had met him on one of our trips into town. He was just a sales boy at the local market and he'd packed our groceries. My parents were pretty strict about who I was allowed to hang out with and so, I had hidden his existence from them.

I laughed at the idea of bringing Matt home to them. They would have freaked out. My hand found the locket on my necklace and I held onto it tightly. I felt closer to my parents whenever I held onto that locket, with their faces inside. Maybe they would have been right to freak out.

I wanted to believe that Matt was a good man but I wasn't even sure who he was anymore. I was dropping everything just to go out into the middle of nowhere and help him. What did that say about me?

There were only twenty minutes left until it was time for me to board. I was listening to the sound of the announcements on high alert. It would be just like me to miss my flight. While I waited, I ran through the list of things I'd packed in my mind. I barely had the time to pack for the trip but I was sure that I had everything I might need. I wasn't sure how long I was going to be out on the farm.

I didn't need the papers, but they were the first things that I packed. I was pretty damn sure I wasn't going to have much time to follow up on leads. Still, they were too important to leave behind, especially with Sasha's additions. Mrs. Williams had given me a whole different path to follow and the best part of that it was all recent.

With Sasha's help, I felt like I might have a chance of finding the boy.

EIGHTEEN
MATT

I drove to the airport myself. The blue pickup truck was the same one that my grandparents had given to me for my sixteenth birthday. Back then, it was a wreck that needed some major fixing but I was just the man to put her back together. With a little tender loving care, she was practically good as new.

It felt pretty good to be back in that car, back on those roads, back in my hometown. It was like I'd never even left. I fell back into the steps of my teenage self. Despite everything that was going on, I was feeling pretty damn free.

In time, I hoped that Kevin might feel the same way about my hometown. I felt like being surrounded by nature might do him some good. After all, this was the place that both his parents grew up. Once he was ready to speak to me, I was going to explain that to him. For the moment, however, I was struggling to be patient. I had something up my sleeve though, a plan to make him come around to me.

The second I pulled into the airport parking lot was when the nerves hit me. Only moments before, I had been perfectly fine with the idea of seeing Kayla again. It wasn't until I was waiting for her flight that it kicked in. The last time I'd seen her, she had been very angry with me. And, idiot that I was, I had let her walk out of my apartment. I should have gone after her. I should have told her what I really wanted. But it was all too complicated and she deserved better than that. If we'd been together, I could only imagine how the media would have twisted the story of my ex-wife's death.

Kayla didn't need to have the drama of having her name in the newspapers just because she was dating me. I knew that she felt it wasn't up to me to decide, but for the past few months, this had been my life. I had tried so hard to keep my personal life out of the public eye and, finally, the inevitable had happened. If anything proved that there was no way to keep things quiet, it was Jenna's passing.

I walked into the airport and made my way toward the terminal where she would be. I only sat down because I felt like a freak being the only one standing in the waiting area. I spotted her within moments. Her flight must have landed early.

The sight of her made my heart beat a little faster. She looked as beautiful as ever and she'd just been on a flight for several hours. How was that even possible?

Without a glance in my direction, she made her way to the luggage check to pick up her suitcases. I got up and practically sprinted toward her. I had to remind myself that running wasn't allowed in airports.

"Hey stranger," I said.

Kayla spun on her heel and faced me. Her eyes had a sort of twinkle in them. I wanted to reach out and take her into my arms, but I couldn't do that. Nevertheless, the look on her face was enough to get my thoughts racing.

It was impossible not to remember the way she felt in

my arms, the way she yielded to my kisses. She was a strong woman and could hold her own. But underneath all that, I could remember that she was soft and delicate.

"Matt," she said, "I didn't know you were going to pick me up."

I shrugged and smiled. It was probably the first real smile to grace my lips in quite a while. To my surprise, Kayla gave me a small smile back.

"I wasn't going to pick you up, but well, here I am." I saw the bags piling up behind her and there was a queue of people waiting to collect their luggage behind us. "Which one's yours?"

Kayla pointed at two purple suitcases still making their way down the conveyer belt. I walked along it and grabbed them before they could reach the end. I slung both of them over my shoulders and instantly regretted it as a sharp pain rang out through my upper back.

"What the heck did you pack in these things?" I asked.

Kayla gave a short giggle. It was the cutest, most unexpected noise, and I glanced over at her, shocked. She had that same small smile still on her lips.

"Stuff," she said.

I figured that was all the answer I was going to get and started walking toward the airport doors. The sooner I could dump the bags into the back of my pickup truck, the better. Kayla followed close behind me. I watched her out of the corner of my eye. I had to admire the woman for dressing smart. Her toned legs were encased in a pair of blue jeans that cupped her butt in the best possible way, making me want to reach out and squeeze the pert flesh between my fingertips. The thought alone was enough to make my cock stir, threatening to come to life. She donned a tank top that revealed a fair amount of cleavage and her pale skin jiggled the slightest bit with each step that she took. It was driving me crazy not to watch her every move, my mouth watering for a taste of her. She wasn't even wearing heels. I was so used to women from the city wearing heels everywhere they went. Yet there was Kayla, wearing a pair of boots fit for the country.

I was surprised to see they weren't brand new, either. They looked quite worn. Then I remembered we both grew up in the same home town.

"Are those from when you lived out here?" I asked.

At first, she looked confused, but she saw me staring down at her boots. "Oh. Yeah. They are."

"You kept them after all this time? I always thought you hated the country."

We'd reached the truck by the time she answered. I dropped her bags in the back, glad to see that neither of them had a 'fragile' sticker. I walked around the truck to pull open the passenger door for her and then sprinted to the other side.

I started up the ignition.

"I don't hate the country at all. I love it."

My eyebrows shot up. I found myself trying to remember everything she'd said about home, but it was difficult. Every time the topic came up in the past, she was pretty determined to avoid it entirely.

I looked over at her, but she was staring out of the window, away from me. Suddenly, it felt awkward to try to converse with her. I guessed I couldn't blame her for not wanting to speak to me. I was lucky she was so friendly when she saw me inside.

Reluctantly, I pulled the truck out of the parking lot and turned into the road. I had accepted that we wouldn't be speaking for the duration of the ride and I was right. Kayla remained silent throughout the drive. I couldn't help but notice her looking around, though. She was enthralled by her surroundings.

Usually, I would have taken the back roads because I liked the view, but it was quicker to drive through the town. I didn't want to leave Kevin home alone any longer than necessary. The thought of James popped into my head, unbidden. I knew it was paranoid, but I didn't want to give him any ammunition to take my son away from me. I was pretty sure that leaving your kid alone in a strange environment for a long time counted.

Kayla seemed interested in the town, turning her head to look at certain buildings.

"I guess it's been a long time since you saw this place, huh?"

"More than eight years," Kayla said. Her voice was soft and she still wasn't looking at me. "It feels like a lifetime ago."

For some reason, Kayla sounded sad. I wasn't sure what to do about it. I wanted to ask what it was that made her so sad, but I didn't feel like it was my place. I looked from her to the road again. I had to stop at the traffic lights up ahead. Her hands were folded in her lap, slender and dainty. Before I could second-guess myself, I reached out and took one of her hands in my own.

To my surprise, Kayla didn't pull her hand away immediately. She finally looked over at me and I could see the confusion written on her face. I squeezed her hand gently and she squeezed back before looking back out of the window. She never pulled her hand away. The light turned green and I drove forward again. I held her hand all the way back to the ranch.

When we pulled up to the ranch, Kayla gasped.

There was an archway at the entrance of the driveway. Above it, wrought-iron letters spelled out *The Cole Ranch*. The road was gravel and if I didn't have four-wheel drive, I probably wouldn't have been able to drive up it. At least not without some difficulty. On either side of us, the pastures were fenced off by neat wooden slats. A few of them were dented and the white paint was beginning to chip away here and there. That came with age and weather. I planned on handling that now that I was back in town.

Kayla sat forward in her seat, looking over the land. There were acres and acres of green grass, both ahead of us and on either side of us. Further out, the horses and cattle began to come into sight. A few of the men rounded up some of the steers. The house stood tall and proud ahead of us. There were two old-fashioned wooden barns in the background. The ranch had state-of-the-art stables. There were cabins on the back of the property where the ranch hands lived.

I guessed it wasn't exactly what Kayla had in mind when I mentioned that we had a ranch.

"Okay, I was not expecting this," Kayla admitted, confirming my guess. She was staring at me with wide green eyes.

I grinned at her. By this point, my truck was pulling into the driveway just outside the house. A double garage opened up ahead of me and I pulled in beside my gran's station wagon. I wondered who was going to come out and greet us. The garage couldn't have opened up on its own, after all.

Unfortunately, I had to let go of Kayla's hand, but I gave

it one last squeeze, even though the moment was already gone. I stepped out and walked around the other side so I could open her door. By the time I got there, she was already shutting it behind her, standing outside the truck. Instead, I reached into the back and pulled her bags out. This time, I was more prepared for how much they weighed before I pulled them onto my shoulders.

"Do you need help with those?" Kayla asked. Her eyebrow was arched cheekily. I was sure there was a smirk playing at the corners of her mouth as she looked at me.

"No, I'm quite fine. You can go on ahead." I inclined my head in the direction of the open garage door. She walked ahead of me, giving a shrug of her slim shoulders.

I would be lying if I said I didn't check her out. I desperately wanted to peel the tight jeans she wore off of her body but instead, I watched the way they cupped her toned behind, emphasizing it with each step that she took. I had to force myself to look away from her but not before my mind started to wander.

I could hear my gran's voice before I walked out of the garage. The door swung shut behind me with a smooth electronic buzz. My gran hugged Kayla.

"Thank you so much for coming out here. Matt said if anyone could help us, it would be you."

Kayla looked over at me accusingly, but I could see by the way the corners of her lips twitched that she tried not to smile. "Did he now?"

I gave a sheepish shrug. "It's the truth."

My gran looked between us. There was a strange expression on her face. It was one I recognized. I'd only seen her wear that face a few times in my life. There were two occasions more memorable than any others. The first was when I got caught cheating on my geography paper, or so the teacher thought. The second was when I brought Jenna home. Both times, I got the feeling my grandmother was able to see right through me.

I hoped this wasn't one of such times, but I already knew it was. I avoided her eyes. "Kayla, this is Grams. But I believe you've already met."

Kayla smiled at my gran. "It's lovely to meet you."

"And you, dear." Grams looked up at me. "Mikey arrived while you were out."

"Mikey's here?"

My grandmother's expression darkened slightly. "He's inside."

I was eager to put down Kayla's bags, so I walked past my gran. The stairs up to the front door creaked under the weight of those suitcases. The front door was open. I was so excited to see my brother that I didn't bother checking to see if Kayla was following me. I figured my grandmother could handle that.

"Mikey?" I called, looking around.

He stepped out of the living room on my left.

Mikey looked like he'd put on a bit of weight since the last time I saw him, but not in a bad way. He looked healthier. His cheeks were chubby but they were also pink with color. His chestnut hair had seen better days. His hairline was receding, even though he was only in his early thirties. Then again, my brother had a pretty stressful start in life. Suddenly, I felt guilty. It had been years since I last saw him – since the last time that I was reintegrated. The last time I was in town, I deliberately avoided him. My grandfather died and I was too caught up in my own grief. I avoided everyone I knew. The only person I saw was my gran.

"Hey," I said. My throat seemed to go dry at the sight of him.

"Hello," Mikey said. "It's been a while."

I clenched my jaw. I wasn't sure what to say. You could have sliced the tension in the room with a knife. The air was thick with it. At the most inopportune moment, Kayla walked in through the door behind me. I turned as she bumped into me from behind. She seemed to sense that she'd interrupted something because she backtracked slightly.

My hand automatically reached for her, ready to stop her from stumbling and falling. The small of her back was warm against my hand and for the briefest of moments, I wanted to pull her petite form against mine and press my lips to hers. I had to take a deep breath to clear my thoughts as I forcibly removed my hand from her body, sure that she wasn't going to drop.

"Oh. I'm sorry."

I watched as Kayla's pale cheeks turned a lovely pale shade of pink when she looked up at me.

I wondered if she'd felt the intensity of the moment as I had. Did she feel the same way I did?

"Who's this?" Mikey asked. His eyebrows were raised.

"I'm Kayla." Kayla extended her arm, offering Mikey her hand. She was as polite as ever. The tension still crackled in the air. With a glance in my direction, Mikey took her hand and shook it firmly.

"Kayla, this is my brother Mike."

"Oh," Kayla murmured.

As she stepped back, I tried to remember if I'd ever told Kayla that I had a brother. I was sure I'd mentioned it somewhere along the way. The truth was, I didn't speak about Mikey often. I loved him, even though we weren't blood, but Mikey had a messy history and I didn't like to go into it.

It was something that few people outside of the family knew about. I was pretty sure he didn't either.

"Mikey," I said, turning to my brother. "Kayla is here to help us with the case."

"What case?"

"The case to keep Kevin." It was my grandmother who spoke. She had finally joined the party. We all stood awkwardly in the entrance hall. "It seems that Jenna has left us with a bit of a situation. Matty might lose his son. And Kayla here is an excellent lawyer."

"Holy shit."

I couldn't help but grin as my brother looked between the three of us. "You can say that again."

NINETEEN

KAYLA

"No, you cannot!" Myra yelled. "You boys had better watch your language. This is still my roof, you know."

"Sorry, Grams," the two men said in unison.

Myra was their grandmother. She'd introduced herself to me before Matt walked out of the garage when we arrived. I had to stifle a giggle as both the men dipped their heads, looking apologetic. Matt's grandmother knew how to handle him even if I didn't. Maybe I could ask her for some pointers.

"You better be. Now, Matt, why don't you show Kayla to her room? The poor girl must be tired after her flight." I didn't have the chance to tell her that I wasn't tired because the flight was only a few hours long. She had already turned to Mike. "Mikey, I think you better take a walk to cool off or something."

Mike looked over at Matt and me before nodding his head. He walked past us, out onto the porch. It seemed Myra didn't have anything more to say to us because she followed Mike out of the house.

I wasn't sure why Myra had reacted that way. As far as I was concerned, Mike hadn't really done anything wrong. His reaction seemed pretty tame to me. If it was my nephew, I would have lost my shit. I wasn't even related to Matt's son and I was angry on his behalf. Uttering a single curse word wasn't a bad idea, if you asked me.

"That went well," I said.

I wasn't sure why I said it. It felt odd to remain silent. Everything felt awkward and forced. It had since the moment Matt showed up at the airport, except for the part where he'd held my hand. It still tingled with his touch.

"Well, you just met the last living relatives I have," Matt answered darkly. "Come on. Your room's up here."

I didn't get the chance to look around the house but I'd seen enough to know it was beautiful. The foyer opened up onto a staircase. Everything was wood, smooth and rich in a deep red. There was a living room to the left and the door on the right was shut. Beside the staircase was a long, carpeted hallway. Matt was already walking ahead of me, up the stairs. I followed.

When Matt asked me to come out to the ranch, this place was nothing like I expected. I thought there would be rickety barns, but it looked like they had state-of-the-art stables. The fencing was immaculate and there was greenery as far as I could see.

The house itself was massive and as lovely on the inside as it was on the outside. I would bet anything that there was a fireplace or two. My heart started racing the moment I saw the horses being herded in as we drove up, and it just kept getting better.

We stopped at the third door on the left. There was only one landing.

"This is your room," Matt said as he opened the door.

He walked in and set my luggage down at the end of the bed. He went to draw the curtains and the room was bathed in sunlight. "You have your own bathroom. We have staff to take care of the cleaning and all that. So if you need anything else, just let me know."

Of course, they had staff to take care of things for that. I knew that Matt came from a wealthy family, but I didn't realize just how wealthy. He was a billionaire CEO but I was starting to see that he was probably used to living lavishly.

The ranch wasn't quite what I had in mind when I thought of Matt – I'd admit that. One of the main reasons I'd ended things between us was because I saw him as a preppy city boy. I'd always thought of myself as more down to earth than that. I could never have imagined that we'd lived so close to one another. The farm my parents owned was only a few acres away. It was probably somewhere behind the large pastures they had. Though my family was poorer than Matt's, we had probably grown up in very similar ways.

I looked around the room. A double bed stood against the back wall. It was complete with an oaken headboard and matching nightstands on either side of the bed. There was a large wardrobe on the opposite side of the room. There was a door that I presumed led to the en-suite bathroom. The windows were floor-to-ceiling and they offered me a perfect view of the fields. There was also an armchair near the window. It seemed to be the perfect reading spot.

"It's beautiful," I murmured. "All of it. This place is amazing."

I wasn't inspecting him. I was gazing past him, out of the window. I found it difficult to look at Matt. I had since the moment he came to fetch me from the airport.

He was as handsome as ever but something was different. He seemed to be a little more relaxed. There was a five o'clock shadow on his jaw and his hair was thicker and curlier. I guessed that was the country air. He wasn't wearing a suit or an expensive pair of jeans. No, Matt looked like a cowboy. He had a pair of dirty boots on and worn blue jeans and a black t-shirt. His shirt revealed toned forearms and muscular biceps. His skin was golden, but he'd always been tanned. The only thing missing was a cowboy hat.

God, the thought of Matt wearing a cowboy hat made my knees go weak.

There was no way for me to stop all the feelings flooding my system whenever I looked at Matt. My heart started to race and my mouth went dry and my stomach tightened. As if it knew that I was thinking about him, my hand started to tingle again. It wasn't like I needed reminding that we'd held hands for most of the drive up to the ranch.

Matt stepped toward me, his boots loud on the wood. I forced myself to look up at his face. I bit down on my lower lip and then stopped, releasing the soft flesh, as his eyes followed the movement. The bed was right behind him and I couldn't help but imagine him on it. It was hard not to picture us in it, particularly when his eyes gazed at me so intently.

"So..." I cleared my throat, but I didn't know what to say. I just wanted to get my mind off of the wild images going through my head. "Where's your room?"

Matt smirked down at me when I met his eyes. "I'm just down the hall."

Okay. That definitely didn't help me get my mind off of things. It only made me think of visiting his room in the middle of the night. The idea of sneaking into Matt's room had me thinking all manners of things. I thought of him in his bed with the covers pulled up to his waist. I knew that the trail of dark curls leading downward would barely be concealed.

Whoa, Kayla, I thought. *You're getting a tiny bit carried away there.*

It felt like he'd stepped closer to me, but he hadn't moved. He was within arm's reach. I wanted to reach up to him, to pull his face down to mine, but I couldn't do that. My heart raced in my chest as he stared at me.

Finally, after what seemed like an age, Matt took a step forward. He was inches away from me. I had to force myself to look away from his eyes.

Looking down at the floor, I took a deep breath. "Uhm, I should probably get to work."

"Of course," Matt said. "Make yourself at home. If you need anything, give me a shout."

"I will."

"I've left all the papers in the top drawer of the nightstand on the left."

And just like that, the moment was gone. Matt walked past me, toward the door. My eyes followed him and he turned back at the door to give me a curious look. He looked like he wanted to say something but must have thought better of it. I watched as he turned on his heel and walked down the stairs, his back to me.

I was left in silence.

TWENTY

MATT

The following morning, I was woken by the sound of roosters crowing. My curtains were closed but it was still dark outside. The dawn had barely arrived. I wasn't even sure if we had roosters on the ranch. It could have been another farm or some stray birds on the outside of the fence. Still, that was the sound that woke me in the countryside. Who needed an alarm clock?

I had hardly gotten a wink of sleep. It was mostly due to the knowledge that Kayla was down the hall from me. It was the closest I'd been to her since the night that she walked out of my apartment in the city. Every small sound and creak the house made – and believe me, there were many – made me wish she was making her way to my room.

Unfortunately, that didn't happen. Kayla didn't visit me in the middle of the night, but that didn't stop me from wanting her. I couldn't help it. I knew she felt the same way. The way she'd bitten her lip the previous day, the look on her face when she met my eyes, the way her small hand had felt in mine...

I had to stop myself there. She may have felt the same

way, but Kayla made it clear she didn't want to be with me. I doubted very much that anything had changed. She avoided me for the rest of the afternoon, if that was anything to go by.

My gran made us a roast chicken with spring vegetables for dinner the previous evening. She called everyone down like she used to when I was a boy. Sitting at the table were my gran, my brother, Kayla, Kevin, and me. The seat at the head of the table looked empty without my grandad there, but this was the closest to a family gathering we'd had in a long time. The table was set beautifully.

The good feelings kind of ended there. The dinner was quiet and awkward – at least where I was concerned. I felt as though everyone but my gran was angry with me. And even Grams probably had a lot to say to me. I think the only reason she held back was because she was happy to have me back.

For most of the meal, I was silent.

Mikey was pretty quiet too. He paid more attention to his food than anything else. He didn't eat any of the meat. In my absence, Mikey had gone vegetarian. I supposed I couldn't blame the guy. He worked with animals on a daily basis. There was no way that I could ever do it, but I admired him for his decision. Grams was the one who told me that he no longer ate meat. I'd have been lucky if Mikey told me something about his personal life. We had hardly spoken since I introduced him to Kayla.

Speaking of the beautiful brunette, she seemed content to avoid my eyes. I kept thinking back to the moment we'd shared in her room. I still hadn't figured out why she asked where my room was. I didn't know why her cheeks were pink by the time I walked out of her room. Did she know that the way she bit her lip drove me crazy? It made me think about biting her lip myself and the sounds she might make if I did it.

Fuck, she'd been in my hometown for less than twenty-four hours and she was already taking over every thought and feeling. It was the city all over again. From the moment she walked into my office for that interview, I could think of little else.

I had to remember why she was there. Kevin. He was the most important thing.

All through the meal, my son kept looking over at me. But each time I caught him, he looked back down at his plate. I wanted to tell him to eat more. The poor boy had hardly anything on his plate and it didn't look like he wanted to eat the little that was there. I thought that telling him what to do might upset him further.

There was so much to say to him that I didn't know where to begin. What did you say to your son when you were pretty sure he hated you? I loved him. I had never stopped loving him. More than anything, I wanted to right the wrongs of the past and I wasn't sure how to do that.

I'd resolved to spend as much time as possible with him while I could. I hoped being out here might make him feel better. I'd always felt that raising a child in the city was wrong. When I was a boy, I was surrounded by dirt and animals. That was the way I wanted to raise him.

Jenna was the one who preferred being in the city. The only reason I stayed out there was because I wanted to be close to Kevin – even though I wasn't allowed to see him. And while I was there, I decided to make something of myself. Never in my life did I think that would be in a big skyscraper but there I was. I was doing something that was going to be good for others. But at the end of the day, the city was never the place for me.

I knew that Kayla, and probably many others, thought that I was born and bred for the city. It didn't help that I dressed in expensive suits or that I lived in the penthouse suite. Few people knew those weren't my decisions. I was following advice. Apparently, a CEO was expected to dress and behave in a certain manner. I went along with it purely because I didn't know any better.

The fact of the matter was, as a CEO, I could have been my own boss. If I wanted to walk into the company wearing a cowboy hat, I could have. It had taken me a while, but I was starting to realize I didn't need to let other people tell me what to do.

Of course, I would probably still take all of Douglas's advice to heart. That man didn't *tell* me what to do. He made helpful suggestions here and there. They were usually all for my own good. He always let me make the decision whether or not to follow his advice. I wondered what he would say now.

I was tempted to call Douglas. I didn't think it would be wise, though. I was pretty sure he would have an earful of advice. He would know what I could do about the situation with Kayla. He would know how I could get Kevin to come around to me. He would know what to say or do where James was concerned.

Hell, he was the one who suggested I leave the company in the hands of my partners. That was what they were there for, after all. If I wasn't going to trust other people with my company, Doug said, I shouldn't have added their names to the plaque.

And he had been right. My company was thriving without me. It was going where I wanted it to. If I was honest, it was better this way. I never wanted to be behind the helm of the company. I didn't know that I could trust other people to handle my vision for me. My name was on the plaque and everyone would know the idea was mine. I would be called before things went ahead without my say. Douglas was the one who showed me that I could let go and still be involved at the same time.

So far, so good.

Before I met Douglas, I'd gone to my granddad for all the advice I sought. I was closer to him than Grams in that way. I loved her to bits and we bonded over a lot, but it was Gramps who helped me fix up the pickup truck. It was Gramps who taught me what it meant to be a father and a family man. It was Gramps who inspired me to join the military. It was Gramps who told me what to do when I was accused of cheating on a test in high school. It was Gramps who suggested I go to college when all I wanted was to stay and work on the farm.

I missed him terribly. It felt like it was just yesterday when I heard the news. If it hadn't been for my granddad passing away, I would still be in the military. I'd come home because it felt wrong to leave again. At the same time, I never truly came home.

Perhaps that was why my gran was so angry with me. I imagined it was one of the reasons Mikey was so upset with me. I knew my brother had other reasons, too. At first, I was sure that my brother couldn't possibly be upset with me because of the inheritance. As time went on, however, I was pretty sure he was angry with my granddad and me.

When he died, Gramps left me a ton of money. It was because of that sum that I was able to start my software company. It was his inheritance to me. Grams got a share and Mikey got a share. A few smaller shares went to some of the workers who'd been around for as long as I could remember. To Gramps, they were family. And every single person who was family got something when he died.

I got the biggest thing of all. Gramps left me the ranch. When I came back to town for his funeral, on compassionate leave, I might add, my grandmother told me she expected it. He'd told her that he didn't want to leave the ranch to anyone else. I think it was his last hope of getting me to come back home.

The thought felt like a kick to my gut. If that was the case, I felt like I'd let my grandfather down immensely. Having the ranch left to me didn't make me come back to it. In fact, it did the opposite. I wasn't sure why I'd gone back to the city. I guessed it was the same reason I avoided people when I came back to town for my grandfather's funeral.

I felt like I was being crushed by the pressure. The townspeople knew me as a rebellious teenager, someone who had earned himself a scholarship to college against all odds, and then a man who joined the military. Most of all, they knew me as the grandson of Myra and Sam Cole. Everyone's eyes were on me, waiting to see what I would do next. My shoulders were heavy with the expectations people had of me.

It was a small town. My grandfather's ranch was prestigious and his reputation preceded him. It was no secret my grandfather had left the ranch to me. There was no such thing as a secret in a small town. I was practically a celebrity.

To make matters worse, I'd gone and become a billionaire, kidnapped my own son, and lost a wife. The first words my grandmother uttered at the sight of me were, "Now you've gone and done it. The whole town is buzzing."

With a sigh, I shut my eyes and fell back onto the pillows.

I wasn't quite ready to wake up just yet. The sun was beginning to rise outside my window. I could see the pink glow of the sky between the thin gap of my curtains.

When I was a boy, I would have hopped out of bed and begun the work immediately. There was always work or something to do on the ranch. My grandfather would have thrown me in with the ranch hands. Things weren't that different now but they seemed to manage well enough without me. I wanted to have more of a structured schedule going but that would take time.

It was summer and that meant maintenance would need to be done. The ranch hands had already started on the irrigation chores. All we had to do was make some repairs here and there, working on ditches and pipes. Even though there was no one around to manage them – something Gramps always did – the guys knew what needed to be done. I'd seen them moving the cattle from pasture to pasture just the day before. It was the only way to make sure the animals didn't overgraze certain areas.

I found it funny how my brain remembered everything that needed to be done. I was sure that once I joined them again, my hands would remember just what they had to do, too. In a way, I was pretty excited to start work. I always wanted to take over the ranch one day. This was my second chance.

Maybe a good way to bond with Kevin was to show him the ropes. I was about his age when my grandfather started teaching me. It was nearly time for the first cut of hay. Kevin could help me prepare for the day.

Yeah, I told myself. I would show my boy how to be a rancher.

Who knew? Maybe one day I could pass the ranch down to Kevin. That would be something.

TWENTY-ONE

KAYLA

I was up at the crack of dawn. There must have been roosters on the ranch. By that point, the sound was so foreign to me outside of film and radio that I lay in bed. feeling thoroughly confused. It took a while for my sleep-addled brain to register what was making the noise.

As a girl, the roosters were my wake-up call. They were a call to action. We had many of them, alongside hens. That sound went off before the sun came up and it was my cue to prepare for the day. The first thing I would do was go feed the animals. I would collect the eggs and milk the cows. As an adult, it was like a shock to my system.

I hopped out of bed with newly awakened energy. I drew my curtains to find that the sky was still grey. In the distance, I could just barely make out the line of light on the horizon. The sun hadn't come up yet but I didn't care. I couldn't stay in bed any longer.

Every memory of my childhood was beginning to flood back to me. I was bouncing with a new drive that I didn't know how to describe. My body wanted me to get back into the groove of doing farm chores. Unfortunately, I couldn't do that. It wasn't my place. The idea of going downstairs or outside before anyone else was up felt awkward.

Matt may have said I was welcome to make myself at home, and his grandmother had said the same thing, but I wasn't ready to make myself *that* comfortable just yet. Instead, I decided it would be best for me to dive into the work I had been given. Being back in my hometown felt like a vacation. I had to remind myself I was there for a reason.

I had spent the previous afternoon unpacking my suitcases. I wasn't sure how long I was going to stay on the ranch, but there was no way I was going to be living out of a suitcase. There was more than enough space for all my clothes in the wardrobe.

The first thing I did was pull out a pair of jeans and a loose, pink tank-top. I got dressed before making my bed. Matt told me they had staff to take care of everything but I didn't care. Making my bed in the morning was just one of the ways that I started my day. I didn't think I could ever get used to the idea of someone else doing it for me. I even made my own bed when I stayed in hotels.

I wish I could say that I looked at all the papers the day before but I didn't. Despite the flight only being a few hours long, I found that Myra had been right. I was exhausted. I flopped onto the big bed in the center of the room and sank into the soft mattress. Before I knew it, I'd fallen asleep. The next thing I knew, there was a cowbell being rung and Myra was calling everyone to dinner.

I couldn't complain about dinner. I'd had no company since college and even when I was in college, I'd kept to myself. Most of the girls in my dorm went out to the clubs or with their boyfriends during those years. I was used to eating on my own, but that didn't mean that it was something I enjoyed doing. Sitting around the table and eating a home-cooked meal reminded me of my childhood. It felt almost like having a family again, even if it did seem a little tense and awkward.

For most of the meal, I found myself wondering why things were so tense between Matt and his brother. I couldn't help but notice Myra was a bit nervous too. She didn't strike me as a tense woman.

I felt like she was using me as a distraction. Instead of concentrating on the obvious issues in her family, she was very chatty with me. I can't say I was particularly good conversation. I was still sleepy from my unexpected nap. Not to mention, I was trying hard not to look at Matt. He had clearly showered before dinner and I could still see the crystals of water in his hair. He even smelled good from where I was sitting – which was right beside him.

Rather than let my curiosity get the better of me, I dove into the nightstand on the left side of the bed. There was a thin folder in the drawer. I pulled it out and emptied its contents out onto the bed in front of me.

Matt did not leave anything to chance by the looks of things. He made copies of every message shared between James and him. He had thrown in the emails shared between Jenna and him. He had copies of the divorce settlement, the custodial agreement, and the one that he had initially filed for. There was the copy of the unofficial will, the offender in this entire case. The more I saw, the angrier I got.

I was beginning to think I might not be the right person for the job. It was going to be damn near impossible for me to work for Matt when I was so obviously attached to him. I had to put my emotions away if I was going to be of any use to him at all.

By the time I was done reading through all the papers, I

realized I was going to have to ask him for more. Neither he nor James seemed to have the official letter of guardianship. Further than that, I needed Kevin's papers. Both men, and in fact, the recently deceased Jenna seemed to have forgotten there was a little person in the middle of all of this. Kevin had as much a say as they did. In fact, depending on how he felt about the whole situation, he had the most say.

It was a few hours later that I gazed out of the window. I heard voices from somewhere outside. There were pinks and oranges streaked across the sky, looking for all the world like someone's gorgeous painting. Shining over the green fields, they were beautiful. The ranch hands were already out and about. That was to be expected. I stood from the bed and walked over to the window, sighing as I noticed the horses. I could hear them whinnying and neighing from where I stood.

They were beautiful. I wondered if I would be allowed to go horse-riding while I was on the ranch. It sure wouldn't hurt. If there was one thing that would make the day worth it, it was that. Just seeing the horses tugged on my heart-strings.

Would my body even remember how to ride a horse?

～

To my surprise, Myra started ringing the cowbell at around eight a.m.

The day before taught me that I was expected to go downstairs, so I packed all the papers into the folder. I'd barely opened the door when I bumped into Matt. The force of his body against mine would have been enough to knock me right over but his hands were there. One of them landed on my lower back and I felt every limb stiffen.

"Sorry," I muttered.

"It looks like some things never change."

Matt released me once he was sure I could stand up on my own two feet. He was grinning at me but I found it difficult to concentrate on his face. For some reason, he was topless. He was all muscles and tanned skin and lined abdomen. It made my mouth go dry and my belly tighten.

"Kayla? You okay?"

"Hmmm?" I hummed, looking up at his face.

He still had that grin on his face. I realized what he said. It was quite a few seconds too late, but I laughed. Some things never changed. How many times had I bumped into Matt in the halls of college? How many times had he seen me spill something? How many times had he watched me trip over my own two feet?

"Right! Yeah. I'm still a klutz."

His grin grew even wider.

"*Why* are you not wearing a shirt?" The question left my lips before I knew it. It was a silly question.

"I... uh... I was on my way to get a shirt. I messed batter on the one I was wearing."

I raised my eyebrows. Batter?

"I was helping Grams make pancakes for breakfast," Matt said, answering my unasked question.

Matt was making pancakes? Wait, Matt helped make breakfast? If it was any good, I had the feeling that I was going to start making an effort to be downstairs in the mornings. I would pay to witness him in the kitchen. I mean, especially if he got topless while cooking.

Wow, Kayla, I thought to myself. *Way to objectify your boss.*

I felt my cheeks warming the longer I stared at him. That was what I was doing. I was staring. I ran a hand through my hair, thanking my lucky stars that I'd taken the time to ram a brush through my curls. I tore my eyes away from him.

"I should, uh, get downstairs."

"I should get a new shirt," Matt said.

I could hear the laughter in his voice and I smiled, in spite of myself. There he went again. He had an extraordinary talent of making me feel like a teenager. In the best way. It was hard to stay angry with him. And believe me, I was trying.

As I walked down the stairs, resisting the urge to look back at his half-naked body, I was beginning to wonder just why I'd been so angry with him in the first place. He was revealing this whole new person to me. And it wasn't the same person I thought I'd walked out on.

Myra and Kevin were in the dining room. I could hear the scraping of cutlery against plates and followed the sound. The table was laden with all sorts of foods. Honestly, I hadn't seen a complete breakfast in a while. There were fried eggs, scrambled eggs, bacon, and pancakes within my immediate sight.

"Good morning, Kayla!" Myra said. She was way too chipper that early in the morning. "Have a seat. I hope you're hungry."

Actually, I was suddenly starving. The food smelled so good. I sat in the same chair as the night before. "This looks so good, Myra. What's the occasion?"

Myra furrowed her brow, looking over at me. "There's no occasion. We always have breakfast together in this house."

She didn't say it in a mean way. In fact, she sounded

kind of confused. I had no complaints. It sounded like a pretty good idea to me. "So, we're going to have breakfast like this every morning?"

"I don't think it will be quite the selection, but yes." She glanced over at Kevin and then lowered her voice conspiratorially. "Between you and me, I think Matty got a little excited and went overboard."

"Excited?"

"To have you here, of course. I can't blame the man, really. He failed to mention how beautiful you are."

I stared at Myra with wide eyes, realizing what she was implying. "Oh, Myra, no. Matt and I... We're not –"

"Okay, I'm back. I'm dressed. I'm batter-free!"

Matt dropped down into the seat beside mine with a grin on his face. His cologne hit my nose and I took an involuntary breath. Myra raised a mug to her lips, sipping her coffee and watching me over the rim of her cup. I had a feeling that our conversation was far from over. I hoped that she didn't get too ahead of herself.

The man beside me didn't seem to notice anything amiss. He reached across the table and began loading his plate with food. He grabbed a little bit of everything. He had a mountain on his plate by the end of it. He was already halfway through his second flapjack by the time he noticed me staring at him.

"What?" he mumbled through a mouthful of food.

I burst out laughing. The image was comical. "Nothing, nothing."

"Are you sure you've got enough food there, Matt? You know we aren't going to run out any time soon, right?"

Matt looked over at his grandmother and then back down at his plate. He shrugged his shoulders and finished chewing his food before he answered Myra. "It's all so good, okay? It's been a long time since I had a family breakfast."

You and me both, I thought. I looked around the table. My parents were always too busy to do breakfast. My dad would rush off to work in the mornings and my mom could be found milking the cows. The last time we'd had breakfast as a family was when I was a little girl. I could barely remember it.

The green-eyed boy sitting at the table hadn't said anything yet. I noticed that his plate was empty. I noticed he hadn't eaten much the previous evening either. He was staring down at his lap.

"Hey, Kevin," I said softly. "What do you think looks best here?"

Kevin looked up at me with wide eyes. Beside me, Matt froze. I knocked my knee against his beneath the table. He glanced at me and I looked at his plate pointedly. He seemed to get the message because he started eating again. His grandmother was much quicker with the ball. She did not seem to be paying any attention to me at all. But I knew better.

I shrugged, smiling at Kevin. "You look like you have good taste. I thought you might be able to recommend something to me."

"I..." Kevin paused. He looked around the table, furrowing his brow. He looked kind of adorable, actually. "The pancakes looked delicious. My dad made them."

If I wasn't sitting right next to him, I probably wouldn't have heard Matt's intake of breath. It was soft enough that no one else at the table heard it, including Kevin. I gave the boy a smile.

"They do look pretty good, huh? Are you going to have some with me?"

Kevin's eyes flicked toward his dad. To his credit, Matt had his eyes on his plate. He was still eating, though at a slower pace. I pretended that I didn't notice the flicker.

"I guess I could try one or two," Kevin finally mumbled.

"Good."

I grabbed my fork and used it to pick up two pancakes, before dropping them onto my plate. Kevin followed my lead. I was happy to see that he took three. He seemed at a loss of what to do next. I'd scooped a bit of butter onto my pancakes. It was satisfying watching it melt.

"Hey, Kevin," I started, "do you like maple syrup on your pancakes?"

Kevin nodded vigorously. The syrup was in front of Myra. I stood from my seat and reached for it. Kevin stood up to grab it from me. "Hold it with both hands."

Kevin did as I said, carefully holding the ceramic jug. The syrup was still warm and he poured a generous amount over his pancakes before setting it back down on the table. He looked back up at me, but I made sure I was looking away from him. Out of the corner of my eye, I saw him shove a huge forkful of pancake into his mouth. I was smiling as I started eating. He made a good recommendation. They were delicious.

I felt Matt's elbow knock against mine. I raised my head to look at him. He had a solemn expression on his face, so unlike any other I had seen before.

"Thank you," he whispered low enough that only I could hear it.

TWENTY-TWO

MATT

After breakfast, I suggested that Kevin join me on the ranch. I wanted to show him around. I knew he didn't genuinely feel up to it but with some gentle prodding from Kayla, he nodded and followed me out the front door.

We had been at the ranch for a little over a week. Kevin hadn't really been eating much since the very first day. I was terrified he was going to start losing weight. I even thought that he might have lost some weight as it was. That was all in my head. It hadn't been long enough for him to lose weight. He'd eaten more that morning than any other. I had Kayla to thank for that.

The first thing I did was take Kevin to the stables.

"So what do you think of this place, buddy?" I asked.

He walked beside me, our boots crunching on the dirt. He had his head down and his hands were shoved into the pockets of his jeans. He looked so much older than his years. He shrugged.

"Do you like it?"

"I don't know. It's okay, I guess." He sounded like he

had something else to say so I waited. "When are we going to go home?"

"Well, I was wondering if you might like to stay here."

"What do you mean?"

"You know. This could be our new home."

Kevin didn't answer me at first. We continued walking. The stables were empty when we reached them, but that was fine. I only wanted to show him the stable itself. I thought Kevin was too young to start riding the horses. I could have handled putting him on a pony but we didn't have any just yet. Breeding season was nearly over. The foals would be ready to be delivered soon.

I would wait until then.

"What about school?" Kevin asked.

"There's a school here. There's a whole town. I could take you to see them tomorrow if you want."

"I don't want to go to school here."

A lump formed in my throat. I gulped it down. I wasn't sure I was ready for this conversation yet. But I was the one who brought it up. I guess I thought that he might be more open to the idea. Maybe it was just too soon. His mother had only just died, after all.

"It could be fun," I said softly. I turned to my son. He was hovering near the door of the barn. "You know, the mares are going to give birth soon."

"There are going to be baby horses?"

I smiled. "They're called foals. And yes. There are going to be a few of them around."

"Do you think I could ride them?"

"Would you like that?"

Kevin looked up at me. I felt like he was studying me. I would give anything to look at his thoughts. As soon as he was involved, Kevin seemed to lose interest. He looked back down at his feet. I knew instantly that it was a habit he'd picked up from his mother. Jenna loved looking down at the ground whenever she was upset.

I got down on my haunches in front of Kevin. "You know that you can tell me anything, right?"

Kevin sighed. "I don't want to talk about anything."

"Not even Mom?"

My heart was racing. I'd been avoiding this topic. It wasn't healthy for either of us to keep skirting around it. Kevin was still a kid. He needed to get it out of his system.

"She was sick. I knew it was going to happen. She told me it was going to happen." Kevin paused, his face red with emotion. He was breathing heavily. "Unlike you. You just showed up out of nowhere and took me away. I didn't even ask for any of this."

Breathe, I told myself. The thing about parenthood was that nobody ever told you how to handle situations like that. My ex-wife knew she was sick. She never told me that. I guess it was impossible for her to hide the truth from Kevin.

I had seen the hospital records. I had gotten the medical history. I knew everything there was to know. I wasn't supposed to know but I was finally taking advantage of all that my money had to offer.

"It's okay to be sad about it, Kev," I said gently. I reached out to touch his shoulder but he pulled back before I could. "You know, it's even okay to be angry about it."

"I'm not angry at Mom. I'm angry at you."

As I watched, tears welled in Kevin's eyes. They were threatening to spill over the edge of his waterline. He swiped them away with the back of his hand before that could happen.

"It's okay to be angry at me, too, kid," I said. It was. It hurt, but it was.

"Well, I am! You weren't there! You just left us!"

Kevin pushed me away from him. He caught me off-guard and I fell back onto my ass. I was stunned. "Kevin..."

But my son didn't want to hear anything else I had to say. Before I knew it, he had turned on his heel. He ran out of the barn as fast as his little legs could carry him. It took me a second to catch my breath. But then I was on my feet. I hopped up and ran after him. I was in time to see his back as he headed into the house.

"Fuck," I muttered.

I was faced with a sudden urge to punch something. Nothing was going according to plan. It hadn't since the day Jenna died. I wasn't even sure what I was doing on the ranch anymore.

What was I thinking? My son lost his mom. Like an idiot, I went and dragged him into the middle of nowhere. I took him away from everyone and everything that he knew. For all I knew, he would be better off in the city. James would take care of him. His English teacher knew him better than I did by that point in time.

"Fuck, fuck, fuck!"

"I don't think that's such a good idea, man."

The voice came from behind me. I spun around so fast that I nearly landed on the ground again. Mikey was standing there. He hadn't been at breakfast that morning. I wasn't sure that he was still on the ranch. Apparently, he was.

"The ranch hands will hear you," he elaborated.

"Who cares?" I snapped. "Why do you care?"

Mikey raised his eyebrows, putting his hands up in surrender. "Whoa, man. I'm not so sure I'm the one that you're angry with."

"And what if I am? You're angry with me."

At first, he didn't say anything. I thought he might argue with me. I didn't think I would be able to handle it if he did. We both knew he was angry with me and he had been for a long time.

"What did you expect, man?" he asked, heaving a sigh. His belly expanded with it. "You just left us. You became some hotshot in the city. Gramps died and you were nowhere to be seen."

I shoved my hands into my pockets. I suddenly didn't want to be having this conversation, either. Yet again, I was starting things I wasn't ready to handle just yet.

"Man, he left you this whole place and you just abandoned it. I would have *killed* to be the head of this place. But no, you got it." Mikey snorted derisively. "Hey, I guess I should have expected that. You were his *real* son."

"Don't even go there, Mikey."

"Why not? It's the truth, right?"

I clenched my jaw. It was easier not to answer. Mikey was looking for a fight. I couldn't give in. We were not teenagers anymore. I was too angry to be getting into that can of worms.

Rather than say anything else, I turned around and began walking toward the house. I concentrated on the sound of the dirt beneath my feet. Mikey was right behind me. I could hear his footfalls, heavier and faster. He was running.

Don't do anything stupid, Mike. Don't do anything stupid.

The thought barely crossed my mind before I felt his hands on me. He caught up faster than I had expected. I was only walking, after all. He pushed my shoulders forward. I whipped around to face him.

"What the fuck, man?"

"You don't get to just run away from this. Not this time."

He looked furious. His jaw was clenched and his hands were shaking at his sides. I hadn't seen him in such a state in years. In fact, the last time that I'd seen him look that bad was a few months after my grandparents took him in.

"Mikey... Are you... You're not..."

I struggled to find the words. How was I supposed to ask? Instead, I tried to get a good look at his face. I couldn't tell. It had been years since the last time I saw him. He looked almost like a completely different person.

"Forget about it," he suddenly said.

With that, Mikey shoved past me. He knocked his shoulder into mine with more force than necessary, especially since there was more than enough space for him to pass me. I stood where I was, frozen. I could hear his footsteps as he walked up the stairs. The front door was open but he slammed it behind him. I jumped at the sound, my heart racing. Every nerve was standing on end.

If I had known anything about it, I might have sniffed the air around him. It might have helped put my suspicions to rest. As it was, I didn't do that. I simply let him walk past me and into the house. And even if I had, I had no idea how to tell anyway.

TWENTY-THREE
KAYLA

After having such a lovely breakfast, I decided to head up to my room and get back to work. It was so peaceful on the ranch that I had to keep reminding myself I was there to do a job. The peacefulness was short-lived.

It felt like it was only a few moments after Matt took Kevin to the stables that I heard the sound of yelling. At first, I wasn't sure who was yelling at whom. I was sitting on the bed with my legs crossed and papers scattered all around me – yes, I know, I was a terribly organized worker. I was never one for gossip, but even I had to fight my curiosity. I wanted to stand up and head over to the window, to see what was going on. I forced myself to stay where I was seated.

Needless to say, it was not easy to continue working when the voices got louder. I was able to ignore them until I heard the sound of Kevin's voice. It was so unexpected that I froze. That was when I stood up. I walked over to the window in time to see Kevin running from the big old barn toward the house.

A moment later, Matt followed him out of the barn.

From my window, I could see most of the ranch. My vision stopped short of the front door because of the alcove hanging over the porch. It was hiding Matt from my sight, along with whoever he was fighting with next. I only heard the voices of two men and the words they yelled at one another were drowned out by the sound of the wind, becoming distorted as they traveled through the air up toward my window.

Downstairs, I heard the sound of feet running along the wooden floors. I went over to my door and tugged it open the smallest amount, peeking through the small gap. I couldn't see anything but I was sure that it was Kevin.

I wanted to go out to him but I didn't feel that it was my place. My heart went out to the little boy. At the same time, it went out to Matt. I had been watching him interact with Kevin and, if nothing else, it was pretty damn clear how much he loved that boy. I could tell he was the most important thing in the world to Matt.

That was the main reason I was there. I could see how much Matt loved his son. That alone was enough incentive for me to work this thing out for him. I wanted him to keep his son. He deserved that much after everything he had been through. To be honest, I thought Kevin deserved that much, too.

With a sigh, I walked over to the bed again, leaving the door slightly ajar. I sat down on the edge of the bed. It had only been two days, but I already felt like I was getting in too deep. I was more emotionally invested than I would have liked to be, particularly after everything that had happened with Matt. After all of it, I just wanted him to be happy. That didn't absolve him from everything that went wrong between him and me, though.

When I was still studying law, I had a professor who

was one of the strictest people I knew. I never saw eye to eye with her but I could admire her skills as a lawyer. She knew what she was doing and she was not just good at her job – she was fantastic at it. Sure, she was only a professor, but there was a time when she dominated the courtrooms. As far as I knew, she had won ninety percent of her cases. That was one of the highest win rates I had ever come across.

Her name was Marianne. She was a British lady with high cheekbones and spectacles older than I was, often perched on the very edge of her nose. As stern as she looked, that was reflected in her personality. In her case, you could definitely judge the book by its cover. The exterior matched the interior.

Even though we weren't always in agreement, I spent a lot of my free periods in Marianne's classroom. She used to offer me tea and biscuits and a word of advice. I felt like I was her favorite student, but I also felt like that was because I was the only woman in my class she seemed to take a liking to.

Although I did not fully understand her fondness for me, I could not blame her for not liking the others. Most of the girls in my class were more interested in boys, cheerleading, and partying. I had always treated my studies with a level of utmost care and importance. As a result, I didn't have very many friends left by the time I was out of school. In fact, the desire to keep my grades up was the only reason I broke up with Matt when we were still in college.

Honestly, it was probably my biggest regret about college. Even though I was the one who ended things, it still hurt like hell. No one ever told you about that part. Being broken up with sucked and it hurt, but it was no easier to be the one to end things. Studying consisted of peppermint chocolates and tears on my papers for a while after that.

They weren't pretty memories to think about.

If there was one piece of advice Marianne had given me that I took to heart, it was to never get involved emotionally. She drilled it into me that the moment I let my emotions get in the way; I had already lost the case. I argued with her for a long time. If you were not invested in the case, was it truly worth winning? Eventually, I started to agree with her. It was possible to be invested and to believe in something without getting emotional. It was tough as hell, sure, but it was still possible. And, above all else, it was necessary.

There was a reason that Marianne had won as many cases as she had. I felt like an idiot for disagreeing with her. I remember emailing to tell her as much and, for the first time, we saw eye to eye.

That was after my third professional case. I could still remember it like it was yesterday. It was the worst one I had ever taken. Many tears were shed, many nights were devoid of sleep, and many dumb ideas were formed. I was lucky that I had won the case at all. Several years later and I still felt that I didn't deserve to win, which was a pretty weird stance to have since I felt like my client *did* deserve to win.

I did not want to be stuck in that sort of position again. Worse yet, I didn't want to put my client in that position. I had to face the facts. That was what Matt was. He was my client. It ended there. Nothing was going to happen between us, even though being around him was waking up all sorts of feelings inside me.

Matt deserved to win. His son deserved to win. I didn't want to screw that up for them. My emotions need to stay down. The more I thought about it, the more I realized that it was impossible to shove them away. Hell, I had taken a flight to the middle of nowhere at the drop of a hat. I wasn't so sure I would have done that for anyone else, even if it did involve the terrible fear of losing one's child.

It was too late to try to put my emotions away, but I had to do my best.

From outside the room, I could hear Matt's voice. He was back inside the house. I stayed where I was, trying not to strain my ears to hear what was going on. I felt like I was nosey but I really couldn't help it. I was in their house. It was impossible. With every other case I had ever taken, I didn't live with my client. We met and went through the case together, we went to court together, and then we went our separate ways. They got to work through their side of things and live their life as they usually would have. Of course, whenever they went home, the case was bound to be entangled in their lives. It was the same with me – the only difference was that I stayed on my own and I had other things to deal with outside of the case. They probably had family and friends to talk to who were all dealing with the case alongside them.

Since I was in their house, I saw things from the other side of the coin. I was seeing the effects of the case they were fighting. To be honest, I didn't want to be seeing any of it. It felt wrong and it was none of my business.

"I wish my mom was here!"

The words reverberated through me like a physical force. I felt the wind get knocked out of my lungs as Kevin's voice sounded through the house, and I could only imagine what impact they must have had on Matt. I stood up and went over to my door. I'd opened it just in time for Kevin to storm past my bedroom on the way to his own. He glanced at me as he passed by, his face pink and wet with tears, before slamming his bedroom door behind him. It tugged at my heartstrings to see a child so sad and angry. He had an expression of utter betrayal on his face.

It wasn't like a typical tantrum. Kevin was going through real pain. It was tangible.

I had been where he was, though even I was older than him when I lost my mom and dad. He was only a small child. He was young enough to feel everything a little bit more, but not so young that he wouldn't be able to remember this time of his life one day. I could only imagine what he was going through. Being back there, in that small town, everything came rushing back to me. It had been so long since I was in that town. I was only a few miles from our farm, from what was left of their house, and from the place where I had grown up.

On the drive to the ranch, I knew Matt thought I was probably upset with him. While I wasn't exactly happy with him, the truth was that I was staying so silent because I was taking it all in. It had been so many years since I had visited my hometown, yet I felt like little had changed. The post office, the local pub, and the grocer all sported the same outdated signs and stood in the same places I remembered them.

There was a fountain in the middle of the square, but it hadn't been active when Matt and I drove through. When I was younger, little kids used to throw their coins into the water and make wishes. My parents never allowed me to do such a thing. They felt that it was disrespectful. It was some kind of memorial for one of the founding fathers of the town who died in the military, serving our country. I couldn't help but think of Matt. I felt a tremendous amount of relief wash over me every time I thought about the fact he'd been in the military himself.

He came back home. I had to stop myself from ending that sentence with, *to me*.

I had always loved going to town with my parents. I didn't get to go out or interact with people often. The trips we took to town, rare as they were, always felt like adventures. I was sixteen the day I met the grocer's son. I could remember it like it was yesterday. It was too bad that it all turned sour in the blink of an eye.

I brought myself back to the present, shaking away all the feelings and memories. I couldn't afford to feel bad about all that. I had been carrying the guilt and shame for years. In a way I hadn't even thought possible, it was all coming back to me stronger than before. Old wounds were opening up and I honestly didn't like it. They were wounds only I knew about.

Any other time, that would have been my cue to get the hell out of there. I would have run for the hills. I was notorious for backing out of things when they got to be too much. I wasn't ordinarily ashamed of that trait, but I would have hated myself if I did that to Matt. Worse than that, I would have hated myself if I did it to Kevin.

That little boy needed me. And although he didn't know it just yet, he needed his father, too.

TWENTY-FOUR

MATT

The door slammed and everyone stared at me. Bile threatened to rise. I wanted to throw up. I gulped. The entire situation was suddenly overwhelming and my heart was racing in my chest. I could feel my chest rising and falling rapidly.

My grandmother stood in the doorway of the dining room with a plate in her hands. I guessed she was still cleaning up from breakfast, even though she didn't need to. We had people for that, but my grandmother had trouble giving up control of her ways. She didn't grow up wealthy and her past had humbled her. She still wanted to do dishes the good old-fashioned way – in a sink, by herself.

Mikey had come out to see what was going on, too. He had been down the hallway. When I made eye contact with him, he turned around and walked back the way he'd come. It was like he didn't want me to know that he cared or something.

It was Kayla that caught my attention in the end. Her door had a slight creak to it. I hadn't heard it before that moment. I made a mental note to oil it for her. She looked sad as she watched from over the banister. She didn't look away when I caught her, not like Mikey had. Instead, she gave a small shrug of her shoulders that felt strangely sympathetic.

My vision was blurry and I could barely make out their figures. The edges were black. It hit me all at once, like a bucket of bricks. I bolted into the hallway, threw open the guest bathroom's door, and dived in. I landed on my knees in front of the toilet. As lovely as the breakfast had been, it was awful coming back up.

There was a knock on the door behind me.

"Matty, honey," Grams said gently, "are you okay in there?"

I heaved first before I was able to answer, as if that wasn't an answer all its own.

"I'm fine. I'll be right out," I called, but even I could hear the way my voice shook.

There was no response and I could almost feel my grandmother's hesitance to leave. Finally, I heard her footsteps walking back up the hall toward the dining room. I sat back against the wall. The wood was cool against my skin, somehow comforting against the thin layer of sweat on my skin. I felt feverish and my hands shook.

In my mind, I was no longer in the house I grew up in. I was back in the field. My brothers in arms and I were all breathing heavily, our backs against the short wall, and our bodies wet with sweat. I remembered pulling my knees up to my chest. I had to resist the urge to curl up in the fetal position – that was how scared I was.

The dust was blowing not from the wind but from all the gunfire of moments before, bullets flying through ruins of old buildings and spraying through the air. We couldn't complain. The dust was doing a pretty good job of covering us. We'd managed to escape under its cover, hunched and marching until we found something we could hide behind. Our attackers probably thought we were still running because they released gunfire into the air ahead of us, making us flinch. One of the men had to cover his mouth with his hands in an effort to remain silent, desperate to scream out in the fear that gripped us all. In a few moments, we might use the cover of the dust to make a run for it once again. We were hiding in it, trying to stay as still and quiet as we could.

I closed my eyes as tightly as I possibly could, forcing everything to go black.

It had been a good few months since my last *episode*. I hadn't needed to go back to the psychologist at that time, although I was supposed to go every month and sometimes twice a month. The business just kept me so busy that I forgot to schedule appointments and without any episodes or breakdowns, I lost track of how long it had been. I never expected it to go away, but for a while there, I forgot it existed. My life had been full enough that it kept me distracted from the thing haunting me.

PTSD. Post-Traumatic Stress Disorder.

That was a term thrown around a lot by people outside of the military but barely spoken about on the inside. We all had to have counseling, mandatorily assigned, but no one had ever used the term in one of those sessions. At least, they hadn't in any of my sessions. Everyone was worried about it before I signed up, but that all faded away after a while. I would come home between deployments and everyone would think that I was so happy and well. How could I have PTSD when I was acting like everything was fine?

Few people considered the fact that I was happy to see

them or that I didn't want them to see what was going on inside me. It was for such a short period that I didn't want anything to spoil it. I made an effort to enjoy every single second because I knew I only had so much time. Beyond that, I didn't know when or if I would get the time again.

Sometimes, I wondered if Jenna would have left me if she had known the way I suffered. I couldn't be sure. I knew that having James there for her when I couldn't be definitely did not help the situation. Things changed so much between us in the last days of our marriage. I could sense it, even in the letters she sent me. I could be glad that she never sent me a Dear John.

While I sat there in the bathroom, plagued by all the memories, I lifted my butt off of the floor to reach into my back pocket. I pulled my journal out. It was small and thin but I knew my tiny writing was scribbled on every inch of spare paper. I'd kept the journal while I was in the military and I'd filled the pages with everything I felt and thought. It made me feel better to let it all out in some way or other. I had one of the military counselors to thank for suggesting that I get one.

It was the only thing that got me through, along with Jenna's letters and the two small photos I had of her and Kevin. I opened my eyes and pulled open the book. It fell open on a picture that I kept on a special page. It was the most read page in my entire journal because I read it whenever things got tough out there. By then, I'd read the page so many times over that I could practically recite it. I could remember the details of the dream as though I'd just woken up.

The photo of Kevin was taken when he was only three years old, a few weeks after we'd picked him up. We were having a picnic in the park. He looked so happy, staring up at the camera. His cheeks were chubby and his green eyes were shining with joy. He was laughing. I was the one who'd taken the picture. Jenna was entertaining him by blowing bubbles into the sky above his head. Sometimes I wished that it could be that easy again. I would blow bubbles high above his head and bring that smile back to his precious face.

My dream had been of that time. It was after a particularly rough day in the field. We lost one of our brothers – a boy, a *mere boy* of twenty years old. His name was David. That night was probably one of the quietest back at the barracks. None of us knew what to say. We gave David a long moment of silence instead.

When I woke up the following day, it was to find that my pillow was wet with tears. I pulled my journal out from beneath the mattress, along with the pen, and began to scribble every single detail of the dream down. I needed to be able to relive it while it was still fresh in my mind. And so I did, again and again.

Each time we had another day like the one we lost David, and there were more than I cared to count, I pulled my journal out and I read the dream. The day I spent at the park, with my wife and my beautiful little boy. It was a beautiful day and it came in handy on days where I felt like I might lose sight of all that was beautiful in the world. It helped. Later on, I managed to get the photo of Kevin. I asked Jenna to send it to me in one of my letters and I slipped it between the pages of the journal that made the image that much stronger. That memory and the deep desire to make more like it were what got me through those days.

Sometimes I felt like they were the only things that kept me going at all.

Kevin was what brought me home at the end of it all. He was too young in that photo to be able to remember any of it, but we were once much closer than we were now. I couldn't blame the kid for being angry with me. And as much as I wanted to, I couldn't bring myself to resent Jenna for putting me in this position with my own son.

The only thing left for me to do was to try to fix things. It was never too late, right? I stared down at the photo of his laughing face, determined to show him how important he was to me. I wanted to see him with that kind of happiness in his eyes. It wasn't going to happen any time soon but if I gave up, then it would never happen.

I had to keep fighting. A toothbrush wouldn't be such a bad idea either.

TWENTY-FIVE
KAYLA

I wanted to go to Matt after everything that happened, but I couldn't bring myself to leave my room. It was one of those moments where I felt like it wasn't my place. And I was kind of afraid of what might happen if I did.

For one thing, Matt might have chased me away. He might have told me to mind my own business, which was precisely what I should have been doing. Hell, he might have asked me to leave and not return. None of the options sounded appealing to me. So, I turned around and I got back to work.

There were only a few days left for me to get everything in order. Time was running out. The official Will and Testament would soon be released and I had to have a plan by the time it happened. So far, I had formed one or two ideas but I had to see if there was something more that I could do.

That evening, no one rang the cowbell to announce dinner was ready. I lost track of time. Before I knew it, the sun had already set and I was deep in a pile of paperwork. I couldn't help but notice similarities between Matt's case and mine, so I'd ended up unpacking some of my own boxes.

By the time I looked up at the digital clock on the nightstand, it was already ten p.m. I'd switched the light on at around six p.m. I hadn't realized so much time had gone by already. I stood up from the bed and started tidying the place up a bit.

I wasn't drained, so once I'd cleared all the paperwork off of the bed, I decided to head downstairs in search of food. I had the bad habit of forgetting to eat whenever I was busy with work. My tummy started grumbling the moment I started moving around, as if it knew to remind me that it existed while I was up and about.

The house was dark and quiet. It was kind of creepy, actually. Every little sound seemed to be louder than usual. I tiptoed toward the stairs. I didn't know why, but before I started making my way down, I glanced back at Matt's door. It was open, but the light was off. I decided I would go and check if he was all right after I'd gotten something to eat. He might have already fallen asleep. He had a long day.

When I reached the bottom of the stairs, I swiftly changed my mind. I was ready to head right back up the stairs, but I felt my belly grumbling in protest. It read my mind. With a deep breath, I decided to head into the kitchen. I could hear noises and the light was on.

Matt stood against the counter, a glass of juice in one hand and a sandwich in the other. He looked like a naughty little boy who'd been caught red-handed when I walked into the room. His eyes were wide and his mouth was full. He visibly relaxed when he saw it was just me. I watched as he struggled to swallow the food in his mouth.

"Hi," I said, smiling.

"Hey," he said as soon as his mouth was empty. "Why are you up so late?"

"I uh... I've kind of been working until just now."

I always hated telling people how late I worked. Some of my colleagues used to ask me to go out to drinks with them, but I was always too busy working. It was the same in college. I felt like I was judged for it. People often told me I didn't have a life. Sometimes I thought they might be right.

"You don't need to work that late, Kayla."

"I know. I just kind of lost track of time, that's all."

He gave me a look of disbelief and I dropped my gaze, looking down at the floor. "What's that you're eating?"

Matt grinned at me. "The best grilled cheese, tomato, and onion that you will ever taste."

"Oh, is that so?"

Rather than answer, Matt shifted to the side. There was a plate sitting on the counter right behind him. It had one more sandwich on it. I looked from him to it and back again, raising my eyebrows. He inclined his head, a grin still plastered onto his face.

I walked over and stood against the opposite counter. I grabbed half of the sandwich and bit into it. It was still hot and a string of cheese stretched between my mouth and the sandwich. The onion and tomato were perfectly cooked, melting with flavor in my mouth. There was some kind of ranch sauce on the bread that made my mouth water.

"What is this sauce?" I asked. I blushed because my mouth was still full, but I was enjoying the sandwich too much to care.

Matt wiggled his eyebrows at me, looking entirely too adorable for my liking. My stomach tightened and I couldn't stop the corners of my mouth from twitching upward. "That's a secret family recipe."

I took another bite of the sandwich. I groaned in pleasure at the taste, my belly relieved that I was eating.

"Okay, how does one get in on this family because I absolutely need to know this secret recipe?" I spoke with a mouth full of food.

For a moment, Matt simply stared at me. He had a strange expression on his face and it took me a while to realize what I'd said, along with the fact that my sentence was strangely muffled because I didn't bother to chew before speaking. My eyes went wide but Matt didn't seem upset. He laughed, looking happier than I'd seen him since I arrived. He'd had a haunted expression on his face when I walked into the room, as deep into his sandwich as he was. I was glad to see that it was mostly gone.

My cheeks warmed even more and I looked down. I was a total sucker for Matt's smile. He was incredibly handsome when he smiled. The corners of his eyes crinkled more, depending on how genuine the smile was. That was something I'd learned when we were still in college. All those years later and nothing had changed.

"Do you want anything to drink?" Matt asked, breaking me out of my reverie.

Looking up at him, I nodded. This time, I chewed before I answered. "Yes, please."

He smiled and walked over to the fridge. I glanced back down at the floor while he poured the juice. By the time he'd handed me the glass, I'd finished the sandwich. I had doubted Matt when he told me it was going to be the best toasted cheese, tomato, and onion but he'd been right. It was definitely the best – possibly the best toasted sandwich I'd ever had in general.

The juice was cool and refreshing, perfect for washing

the sandwich down. My belly was finally happy with me. "Thank you."

"So, was I right or was I right?"

I smiled. "Yeah, okay. You were right. I still want that sauce though."

The curious expression reappeared on his face.

"What?" I asked. There was something about the way he was looking at me that made me feel warm from deep within my core.

"No," Matt said. "It's nothing."

I didn't want to push the subject, so I changed it. "Why are *you* up this late?"

"Ha. I wasn't working enough, I guess. I got hungry and well, here I am."

"Same as me then," I murmured. "I saw your door was open."

He cocked an eyebrow.

"I didn't go to your room or anything. I just wanted to check in on you. You know, after everything that happened today."

Duh, Kayla. What else would you be talking about?

"I don't know how I am, really. This isn't how I expected things to go down."

"What did you expect to happen?"

Matt shrugged. "I don't know if I actually had any expectations. I just know when I heard the news about Jen, all I could think about was Kevin. I guess I acted without thinking things through."

When I didn't answer, Matt snorted derisively.

"What is it?" I asked, taking another sip of my apple-flavored juice.

"It's just typical of me to do things without thinking

them through. Hell, look at the damage I caused between us."

"Matt..." I started.

I stopped when I saw the look on his face. It wasn't one I was unfamiliar with. His eyes were hooded and sparking with some kind of charge. I bit down on my lower lip. I had been ready to defend and comfort him, but I didn't know what I was going to say anymore – not under that gaze. Before I knew what was happening, Matt took a step toward me. And then another after that. He only stopped when he was standing right in front of me. I had to tilt my head backward to look up at him because of the way he towered over me. I was barefoot because, well, I wasn't the biggest fan of shoes and I thought it would be easier to sneak around in the middle of the night if I wasn't wearing any shoes.

Matt glanced from my eyes, down to my lips, and back up again. The small movement had me sucking in a deep breath. I daren't move. I was afraid I would break the moment, even as anticipation surged through my body. And then, just like when we were in his office the day he interviewed me – it seemed like such a long time ago – his lips crashed down onto mine in the blink of an eye. I couldn't resist him and I didn't want to either.

I reached upward, my hands finding Matt's shoulders. I gripped on to the fabric of his shirt as his tongue slipped into my mouth. I moaned at the contact, pressing my body against his. The next thing I knew, his hands had traveled down my waist until he was cupping my ass. I made a small squeak of surprise and he caught it with his mouth. He lifted me onto the kitchen counter as though I didn't weigh a thing and I wrapped my legs around his waist, drawing him into me.

I didn't even know what was happening anymore. My

body was leading the way and I was only too happy to let it. I could feel that Matt was hard and I moved my hips up against his crotch. The pressure was driving me insane because it wasn't enough. It only made me want to feel him even more. Matt pressed right back against me, breaking away from my mouth.

He trailed gentle, open-mouthed kisses along the side of my neck. I tilted my head to expose more of my skin to his hungry mouth. I had to bite down on my lower lip in an effort to stifle the moans that wanted to escape. There was nothing that turned me on more than neck kisses. I was glad Matt was holding me and that I was on the countertop because my knees went weak. My whole body felt like it was on fire. Every inch of my skin burnt with the touches Matt left on it. And I could feel how wet I was for him.

It was a noise from upstairs that finally broke us free of one another. I didn't know what would have happened otherwise. My fingertips were ready to undo Matt's jeans and free his cock. I might have let him take me right there on the kitchen counter. I didn't get a chance to do that, though. I wasn't sure if Matt had broken away from me or if I had pushed him away; only that we were both breathing heavily and his body was no longer on mine.

Concerned that someone might come downstairs at any second, I hopped off the kitchen counter. I found myself fixing my hair up and making sure that my clothes weren't all wrinkled. Matt didn't bother. He was too busy staring at me. He looked hungry. There was no other word to describe it.

"Fuck," he breathed.

We waited for a while before we did or said anything else. Both of us were expecting someone to walk through the door, but that didn't happen. Finally, it seemed like the noise was nothing more than a fluke. Someone was just moving around in their bedroom or going to the bathroom.

To my surprise, Matt made his way back over to me. He picked me up from the ground once more, his fingers digging into the soft flesh of my ass cheeks, and I cried out in surprise. Matt's mouth covered mine, instantly muffling the sound as he took my lip between his teeth. I stared at him when he pulled back.

"What are you doing?" I asked.

"Shhh," he whispered.

With that, I made a conscious effort to keep quiet. I couldn't help but smile shyly at my noise, my cheeks still flushed with both embarrassment and excitement. Matt started walking toward the stairs. I wrapped my legs tightly around his waist and my arms around his shoulders. He didn't make as much effort to tiptoe up the stairs as I had when I walked down them.

I could feel that he was still hard and the thought drove me crazy. I knew what was about to happen, but I wanted it way too much to try to fight it. There was just something about the man that did things to me. He made all sorts of feelings race throughout my body. They were juicy, delicious feelings.

"So, your room or mine?" Matt asked quietly. The question warmed my core, spreading throughout my body like molten lava and making every nerve tingle in anticipation.

"Yours," I whispered breathlessly.

The image of papers scattered all over my bed flashed to my mind. As sexy as it might have been to clear the surface in carefree passion, before being thrown onto it and taken with wild abandon, I couldn't afford to mess up whatever confused system I'd been working in.

God, I thought. *I'm thinking about Matt taking me with wild abandon.*

Matt grinned at me and turned to walk down the hall toward his bedroom, massaging my ass absent-mindedly as he carried me. He closed the door behind us and I switched the light on over his shoulder. If I was going to let Matt make love to me, I wanted to see him. He sat down on the edge of his bed, holding me in his lap.

We looked into each other's eyes for what felt like the longest time. His brown eyes were deep and dark, like chocolate, but flecked with gold. I could get lost in them forever.

"Do you have any idea how beautiful you are?" Matt suddenly asked.

It was so unexpected that I laughed. Matt watched me, his eyes twinkling slightly in this light. He was looking at me in complete wonder. I knew he meant it, but I still didn't know what to say to him in response.

"I want you," I whispered.

Matt answered with his hands. He grabbed hold of the hem of my shirt and lifted it up, exposing inch after inch of my bare skin. He didn't just tear the piece of fabric off me. He dragged it upward so slowly that I literally ached with anticipation, something clenching somewhere deep inside me. He looked at me while he did it. He was drinking in the sight before him as if he was dying of thirst and I was the only drop of water.

My bra followed shortly after. This time, looking wasn't enough for Matt. He groaned at the sight of my breasts. They sat high on my chest and the sudden chill caused goosebumps to rise on my skin. He cupped my breasts and squeezed the soft flesh between his fingers before leaning in and taking a nipple into his mouth. He sucked it to hardness before repeating the motion on the other side. Soft whimpers escaped my lips at the contact, every sensation shooting straight down to my center.

I rolled my hips against Matt's, pressing myself against his bulge. The friction only made me want him that much more. That seemed to be too much for him because the next thing I knew, he flipped me over easily. I was on my back and he was on top of me. He pulled my shorts off in moments. He paused to take me in again and I felt heat everywhere he looked. When he hooked his thumbs into the waistband of my panties, he met my eyes. I daren't look away as he dragged them down my legs. When they joined the pile of clothes already on the floor, Matt moved back up toward me.

"See," he breathed against my mouth. "Absolutely fucking beautiful."

My belly did a somersault. "Matt..."

"Say it again," he whispered.

I didn't have to think about it. I knew exactly what he was talking about. I didn't think my cheeks could get any warmer. The blush spread all the way across my chest and I felt warm everywhere. I bit down on my lip again.

"I want you," I said once more, breathing the words out in an unintentionally husky tone of voice.

He didn't need any more encouragement than that. He pressed his lips to mine, kissing me deeply. I moved my hips up against him and his hands found my breasts. He tugged and pinched my nipples between his fingers until I felt like I was going to explode.

And just when I thought I couldn't handle it anymore, Matt broke away from me. He got down on his knees on the edge of the bed. My thighs were splayed open, and at the first touch of his mouth against the heat between my legs, I was a goner. I cried out at the sensation of Matt's tongue flicking against my center. It was so unexpected, even though I obviously knew what was about to happen. He flicked his tongue against the underside of my clit and I had to bite down on my lower lip to keep quiet.

There were other people in the house. I didn't know how thick the walls were and neither of us wanted to be heard.

Matt easily slid a finger into my depths. I was dripping wet for him already. He must have noticed as much because he added a second finger almost immediately. My walls tightened involuntarily and he started driving his fingers in and out of me slowly at first, quickly picking up speed as my hips moved ever so slightly up against him. All the while, the tip of his tongue hit my swollen button. My hands moved toward the back of his head, holding him to me.

I wasn't going to last long beneath his expert skills. He knew what he was doing and I gasped for breath. Each time I thought the onslaught would stop, he took me even higher than before. My hips bucked up against his face and suddenly Matt pulled his fingers out of me. I groaned in protest, but it was quickly stifled as Matt's tongue slid into me. He stroked my clit in quick, circular motions before pressing down on it with the same fingers that were inside me moments before. I could feel how wet they still were.

That was it. The building pressure finally exploded. My core was like molten rock, hot and heavy and uncontrollable. My thighs closed on either side of Matt's head as I writhed up against him. I needn't have held him there. He wasn't going anywhere. I was no longer in control of my own body. I was practically riding his face. I came with a low moan, throwing my head back against the pillows.

When I finally came down from my orgasm, I looked

down through hooded eyes. Matt was grinning up at me, but he had that same hungry expression from before. Even though I only just came, I felt my core tighten yet again. Somehow, I still wanted him. I didn't think I could take anymore, but my body had other ideas.

To my excitement, he undressed. I didn't know when or how, but Matt wasn't wearing any clothes. He must have gotten naked while I rode my climax out. My mouth hung slightly open as I looked at him. He was absolutely beautiful. His skin was smooth and his muscles were rigid. He was almost golden with a tan. I had never seen a man stronger than Matt. No one in the world made me feel safer than he did.

And no one turned me on more, either. His cock was long and hard and as equally beautiful as the rest of him was, bobbing between his legs. I never thought that I would ever think a cock was beautiful, but there was no other way to describe Matt's. I wanted it. Desperately.

Matt licked his lips and then climbed up my body. He pressed his lips to mine and I could taste myself on them. I sighed against his mouth, wrapping my arms around his shoulders and drawing him nearer. It felt like we were pouring all of the passion we had for one another into that kiss.

I could feel that Matt's cock was still hard, and I spread my legs, wrapping them around his waist. He took that as a signal and reached between us. He guided himself toward my center.

"Please," I finally whispered, "make love to me."

He didn't need telling twice. He pushed forward, sliding his length into me deliciously slow. I felt my walls stretching to accommodate him. He was big and thick, and he felt incredible. I groaned at the sensation of being filled by him. His mouth closed down on mine once again. He sighed against my mouth. For a while, he stayed entirely still, buried in my depths. He was balls deep inside me. I arched my back up toward him, pressing my hips up against his.

"You feel incredible," Matt whispered.

His words drove me crazy. Finally, he started to move against me. His strokes were steady and slow as he slid in and out of me. I could feel the pressure building up all over again. Matt moved his hands up and down my sides and goosebumps rose in their wake. He cupped and squeezed my breasts between his fingers. I explored his body with my hands. He was strong and warm, all firm muscle and smooth flesh. He rippled with each tiny movement.

The sounds of skin against skin echoed in the small room. We made an effort to be quiet but the gasps and moans rang out in my ears like music. The scent of our sex was in the air, and I gripped Matt as tightly as I could, holding on to him. I never wanted to let go of him ever again.

Before long, his thrusts became more erratic and I could tell he was close. I bucked up against him, meeting his hips with my own. His hands moved from my breasts down to my ass, lifting me off the bed so he could thrust into me even harder and deeper than before. I held on to his shoulders, my nails digging into his flesh.

I tried to hold my own orgasm back, not wanting it to end too soon, but I couldn't. I threw my head back once more, shutting my eyes as it hit me. Matt leaned forward and kissed my collarbone, his tongue flicking out against my bare skin. He rocked me through my orgasm, making it that much more intense, and then I felt him swell inside me.

I could feel each vein and ridge of his cock as he started

to spurt into me. His shaft twitched inside me, filling me with load after load. He held himself inside me until he was completely drained. We were both breathless and spent by the time he finally pulled out of me. I whimpered at the sudden empty feeling.

Matt pulled me into his arms, pressing his body against my back. We lay in silence for a while together. I felt like all my nerves were tingling with him. He felt like he was still everywhere and I loved it.

I wasn't sure when I finally drifted off to sleep but somewhere along the way, my breathing slowed and my eyes grew heavy. He was already asleep and his breathing, the rise and fall of his strong body, was my lullaby. I remembered Matt's arms wrapped around me, safe and warm. He held me tightly against him as if he, too, didn't want to let go of me ever again.

TWENTY-SIX

MATT

The following morning, the sun shining through my open curtains was what woke me up. I blinked and stretched, yawning. It took me a moment to realize what was throwing me off. I'd closed the curtains the previous evening. I wouldn't have...

Oh, I suddenly remembered. *I wouldn't have brought Kayla to climax on the end of my bed with the curtains wide open, especially since the light had been on.*

Just thinking about her made my cock twitch – morning glory or not.

She must have woken up early and opened them on her way out. It was a pity that she'd left my room. I felt like it might have been nice to wake up with her in my bed. She would have been naked and her skin would have pressed against me, soft and warm. Before I ended up with a problem, I decided it was time to get out of bed. My thoughts were getting the slightest bit ahead of themselves there.

I pulled the nearest pair of jeans and a t-shirt on. I didn't bother with shoes. I was in a good mood. I'd almost forgotten about the events of the previous day. Almost.

I was about to head into the dining room, but I heard Kayla's voice. It was coming from outside. The front door was wide open, so I went to see what was going on. I heard her laughing and the sound made me feel light in my chest, like some weight was lifting off of me.

Kayla's voice came from the barn. I was about to walk around the corner when I heard a second voice. He was laughing. It made me stop dead in my tracks.

"How do you know so much about horses?" Kevin asked.

"Well, I grew up on a farm not too far from here. I used to love riding horses but I haven't ridden one for many years."

"So is that how you know my dad? Did you guys, like, grow up together?"

I stood back against the barn. It felt wrong to be there, to listen to what they were saying, but at the same time, I couldn't bring myself to walk away. Kayla made Kevin laugh. It had been such a long time since I heard his laugh that I'd forgotten what it sounded like. And he was speaking more than I'd heard him speak in a long time too.

Just as she had at the breakfast table, Kayla somehow knew how to bring Kevin out of his shell. Thanks to her, he was eating again. And now she was making him laugh.

Teach me your ways, I thought. *How are you so good with him? Have you always been this good with kids? Why didn't I know that before?*

If I'd known Kayla was so good with kids, I might have been honest with her about my personal life from the beginning. Maybe then, we wouldn't be in the position we were in. She might never have walked out of the door of my apartment. We might have been able to share a room rather than sneak around in the middle of the night, trying not to be heard. I was struggling to hide my feelings from Grams as I was.

In fact, I knew I wasn't able to hide anything from Grams. She saw right through me. She always had.

Idiot, I thought to myself. I was such a fool for letting Kayla go.

I turned away from the barn. If Kayla thought I needed to know what was being said in that barn, I knew she would tell me. I didn't need to eavesdrop on her conversation with my son. I decided to head back into the house.

TWENTY-SEVEN

KAYLA

Kevin fed a carrot to one of the horses. He was so short that I had to find a step for him. Of course, there hadn't been one. Instead, I managed to find one of the big metal bowls they used to milk cows into. I turned it upside down and Kevin stood on top of it. He was able to stroke the bridge of the horse's nose at the same time as feeding him the carrot. He didn't look at me while he spoke. He was far too occupied with the horse. His face glowed and he was smiling. There was nothing but love in that gaze.

I smiled. "No, honey. That isn't how we know each other. Your father and I work together."

"Why not?"

"Why not what?"

"Why didn't you guys know each other? You lived so close to each other."

"Oh," I said, realization dawning on me. It wasn't exactly a wrong question to ask. "Well. I was home-schooled, so I didn't know a lot of the kids from school. My only friend growing up was a boy who used to work at the grocer's market."

Kevin looked up at me, furrowing his brow together. "You were home-schooled? I wish I were home-schooled."

"Why do you say that?"

Kevin shrugged his shoulders and turned back to the horse. "I don't know. You did it, so it can't be that bad."

"Don't you like school?"

"Everyone is going to treat me differently now," Kevin mumbled.

He turned back to the horse but the carrot in his hand was finally finished. The horse licked between his fingers and I thought it odd that he was not giggling. I couldn't have a horse lick my fingers without giggling like a little girl.

My heart raced at his statement. I hadn't expected him to be so forthcoming, but it made sense. I didn't know how to respond. I wasn't sure I was the one who should be having such a conversation with Kevin. It should have been his father or his great-grandmother.

I never experienced what it was like to constantly be surrounded by other children, but I knew how mean they could be. At the same time, based on my experience at college, I knew how isolated your peers could make you feel. Sometimes they didn't mean to make you feel so left out, but sometimes they did.

"Why would they treat you differently?"

"Because Mommy is dead," he finally said. He turned and hopped off of the metal bowl.

"Honey," I said softly.

Kevin turned to look up at me and I got down on my haunches in front of him, so that we were looking at one another in the eyes. "Why do you think they would treat you differently because of that?"

"Why wouldn't they? Everyone else does."

"Who is everyone else?"

"My dad, Grams, Uncle Mikey. All of them. Sometimes even you do it and you aren't even a part of my family."

"Do I only do it sometimes?" I asked. I was surprised by that part.

"Yeah," he said with a nod, turning back into the kid he was. He didn't always have to be so serious. "Only sometimes."

"Am I doing it now?"

He seemed to think for a moment before he shook his head. "No."

"Good. I'm glad." I looked into Kevin's eyes. They looked way too sad for a kid who hadn't reached his eighth birthday yet. He was only seven years old. "Kevin, you know you can always talk to us, right? If there is anything that makes you unhappy, you can tell us so. We can try to do something about it then."

Kevin didn't answer. He just stared at me.

"We don't want you to be unhappy, Kevin. We want to help you as much as we can, okay?" I didn't want to push it further than that but I couldn't just leave it. There was more to say. "That means your father wants you to be happy too, Kevin."

He didn't say anything for a while. He continued to stare at me. I felt like he wanted to say something, but he didn't know how to say it or what it was that he wanted to say. Eventually, Kevin slowly nodded his head. I wasn't sure if he was doing it because he understood and believed what I was saying or if he was doing it because he wanted to make me stop. Either way, I had to hug him. I pulled him into my arms and squeezed him tightly. It took a moment, but eventually, he wrapped his small arms around me and hugged back.

"Kayla, do you think you could take me horse riding?"

I pulled back and grinned at him. "I would love to take you horse riding, Kevin. But, not today, okay?"

"Why not today?"

"Well, you have to ask your father if it's okay for me to take you horse riding."

"I don't want to go horse riding with him. That's what he was trying to do yesterday."

"What would be so bad about that?"

"I just don't want to," Kevin said. He crossed his arms over his chest and that was the end of it. It was clear he didn't have anything more to say on the matter.

"Remember what I said, Kevin."

He didn't say anything but out of the corner of my eye, I saw Kevin nod his head once.

"Good boy," I murmured. "How about we go back inside and grab some breakfast? I don't know about you, but I am starving."

∽

Later that afternoon, I couldn't find Matt anywhere. I walked around the whole house, thinking that I was going to get lost at any second. I knew the place was huge but I didn't realize just how huge until I started exploring.

There were two wings of the main house. I had only explored half of the first wing. That alone was the size of an ordinary house. They could've opened a lodge in the ranch and had people pay to stay there.

That sounded like a pretty good business venture to me. There were more than enough rooms and bathrooms. There were three sitting rooms, three dining rooms, and some kind of a game room complete with a pool table that looked older than I was. All they needed was a swimming pool and they would have the perfect little holiday getaway. That would not have been too difficult to arrange. As it was, I would still have paid to stay there just because it was so relaxing to be surrounded by nature.

They could have opened up a horse camp or something. A million ideas were popping into my head. It wasn't that I thought they *should* do those things. My brain's synapses were being set alight with them by the mere shock. What did they even have all this space for?

Maybe they used to let the ranchers hang out inside.

That was the most reasonable guess, until I thought about Matt. He wasn't like me. He had gone to school. If his popularity was anything to go by as nothing but a freshman when he was in college... It was probably the same, if not worse, when he was in high school. I could imagine Matt inviting over plenty of people for parties and sleepovers and hangout sessions. It started to make sense when I thought about it like that.

Not only was Matt missing, but everyone else seemed to be missing too. The last person I'd seen was Kevin and I knew he was content to be sitting on his bedroom floor, playing with some of his toys. It had been good to see him that way. I had no idea where Matt, his brother, or his grandmother were hiding.

I was under the impression that I had discovered everything there was to discover when I came across the library. I was so shocked that I'd had a moment where I peeked into the room, saw no one in it immediately, and popped back out. It was only after I turned away that I could process what I'd seen.

I turned around and walked back into the room with wonder in my eyes. There were books everywhere! It was by far the biggest room in the house. I must have been in between the two wings, at the center. It was only four walls, but the ceiling was incredibly high. Every spare inch of the walls was lined with books. There was a ladder on wheels mounted against each wall. And there were three rows of four bookshelves on the floor.

I felt like I'd just stepped into heaven.

Rather than continue on my quest to find Matt, I began to explore the room. To my relief, each section was labeled. There was a hell of a lot of books and they weren't all fiction.

The lawyer in me was more excited than the reader in me. I made my way through the different sections and I was practically giddy by the time I found the law section. The best part was that it was right beside the psychology section. I honestly didn't think that it got any better until that moment. I started pulling out titles, both familiar and unfamiliar. There were even a few books that I'd always wanted to read but never had the chance to.

I was sure no one was going to complain if I took a few out of the room. There were no seats or anything, which was really the only problem with the library. I would have loved to curl up in an armchair beside a window and read a book. Since that wasn't an option, I took them up to my room. I'd picked books that would help with Matt's case – and mine, too.

I was only halfway through one of the thicker books, skimming the pages, when I came across something. It was one of the very first ones I'd picked so I was surprised. I expected to have to read heaps before I made any progress. I pulled one of the boxes toward me and began matching paragraphs between the pages of the book I was reading and the pages Matt had given me. The next thing I did was pull out a notebook and pen and then scribbled down any correlation I could find.

By the end of it, I was convinced there was no way for James to take Kevin away. It all came down to one thing and Matt and I were simply lucky to have grown up in that state. If it had been a different one, everything would have been so much harder. It seemed like things weren't going to be that complicated, after all.

I fell back into the cushions on my bed, laughing hysterically. I couldn't believe such a small thing could make such a massive difference to the case. But then, I had seen that kind of thing happen all the time. It was one of the most intriguing things about law. As horrible as it was to admit, there was always some kind of loophole.

No law was as airtight as we were supposed to believe.

TWENTY-EIGHT

MATT

When the day finally arrived, I felt a lot more confident about my situation. I didn't know how she did it, but somehow Kayla managed to get me out of the dumps. Okay, well, I sort of knew how she did it. Apparently, all she had needed were the directions to the library.

Unfortunately for me, I was never much of a reader growing up. If I was, I would have known to direct her toward our library. I had no idea that we had such an extensive collection of non-fictional books, though. I always thought my grandmother's library consisted of fiction in its entirety. I might have read a little more when I was growing up if I had known that. After all, I had an affinity for business and computers.

No, I was too busy hanging out with my friends or tending to the farm. I guess I didn't have much to complain about. I loved working with my hands just as much as business and computers.

Perhaps I would make an effort to read more books now that I knew they were available.

It had been a week and a half since the funeral. Jenna's

Last Will and Testament still had not been released. I knew that it would be that day, though. Once Douglas caught wind of what was going on, he made sure that there were people on the lookout back in the city. If any word got out, he would be the first to know it, and therefore so would I.

News just so happened to get around to Douglas in the early hours of that very morning. I'd woken up to a call from him, letting me know that we would either receive a letter in the mail or we would be visited by an official sometime during the day. I thought I was going to lose my mind with worry but of course, that didn't happen.

I was quite calm. If it came down to it, I knew I would take James to court to keep my son. I hoped it wouldn't come to that. I was a little uncertain about it all. I knew I could win the case, but I didn't want anyone to get hurt in the process.

Technically, I knew I could win with nothing but the wallet in my back pocket but I didn't want to just pay my way through it either. I wanted it to be fair. Kevin needed me in his life, just as much as I needed him. I loved my son. I wanted that to be known.

As much as it pained me, I had to admit I didn't know James well at all. For all I knew, he did care about my son. I didn't get that impression, but I started to wonder if that was just jealousy and resent speaking.

"Hey," a voice from the doorway said softly.

Kayla walked into my room. She was wearing her riding gear. She looked damn sexy in it. Her pants were tight and clung to her skin. I knew from having seen her in it before that it cupped her behind in the best way possible. She had boots on and a cute black waistcoat. Topping it off with the riding helmet made her look younger. That might have been more due to the expression on her face, though.

She had a smile on her face and her cheeks were flushed. She was excited.

"Hey there," I said.

Ever since that night she'd come down to the kitchen, Kayla and I had been casual toward each other. We had not spoken about what happened between us. I got the feeling that we were trying to pretend it hadn't happened but I wasn't sure if she was pretending or if I was.

All I knew was that I didn't want to pretend. Every time I saw her, I thought of that night. It was impossible not to, which made it impossible not to get a little turned on. It was more than that though.

There were times where she joined us for dinner – assuming she had not forgotten to eat because she was working entirely too hard – and she brought a little piece of light to the table. That same light also shone through in the way that she interacted with Kevin.

It was pretty damn difficult not to think about Kayla the longer she stayed beneath the same roof as us. I knew I wasn't the only one who loved having her around. Kevin was beginning to come out of his shell. He'd even thawed out somewhat toward me. I couldn't tell you that everything was fine between him and me, but I felt like we might be making some kind of progress.

Grams didn't bother to conceal the fact that she liked Kayla. The two of them were talking about baking a chocolate cake that weekend. Grams often gave me knowing looks. It didn't take a genius to know what she was thinking. I'd seen that look on her face many times before. As a teenage boy, there were few things you forget. One thing I would never forget was the look that my grandmother wore when she knew better than me.

Trust me, she usually did. It took me a long time to

come to terms with that. I had a lot of times to apologize for, but I would never argue with my grandmother that she had always been right when I was growing up. I wouldn't be the man I was if it weren't for her. I thanked her for that every time I looked at her, though I guess I should have started to say it out loud a bit more often. She raised me better than I could have hoped for.

A few days earlier, Grams pulled me aside while we were setting the table. She looked suspiciously toward the door, as if she expected someone to walk in at any second. When they didn't, she turned back to me.

"You better not screw things up this time, Matty."

She had that same knowing expression on her face and I knew what she was talking about. I didn't answer her. What was I supposed to say? I couldn't tell her that nothing was going on between Kayla and me because that would have been a flat-out lie. At the same time, I wasn't sure how I could tell her something *was* going on because I wasn't sure if it was.

Yeah, I thought sarcastically. *That makes so much sense.*

I'd come to the conclusion that Kayla and I needed to get something out of our systems and we had done that. It had been incredible and I was pretty sure I still had more to get out of my system, but that was all there was to it. I couldn't ask her for more.

"What do you think?" Kayla said.

I dropped back down to earth. What did I think? She did a little twirl for me, giving me the full effect, and boy, was it a good one. I smiled at her excitement. She even acted younger.

"You look absolutely adorable in your riding gear," I said.

Kayla beamed at me. "So, are you sure you can handle this?"

I raised my eyebrows. "Handle what?"

"Me taking Kevin for his first time horse riding," she said, utterly oblivious to my dilemma. I tried to adjust myself slightly, without Kayla noticing what I was doing. "You don't strike me as the kind of man who has an easy time relinquishing control, Mr. Cole."

I found myself smirking at the way she used my last name. "Maybe I just need the right person to give control over to."

"And I'm the right person?" Her voice was low, flirty, and husky. I wasn't sure if she even meant for it to sound that way.

Kayla wasn't afraid of asking questions like that. Me, on the other hand? I was pretty terrified of the answers I might receive. The fear of rejection was intimidatingly strong. It was like the moment she told me she wanted to be a part of my family. She had been joking, but I couldn't help but wonder what it might be like to have her in my family. I would have been too afraid to make that comment. What if they didn't want me in their family?

I would be lying if I said there were no good thoughts about Kayla joining my family. There were many.

"You're certainly not the wrong person," I admitted quietly.

"I wish you could come with us," Kayla said, acting like she hadn't heard my admission.

"Yeah, me too. Maybe one day. For now, you're who he wants to go with."

Kayla surprised me when she pulled me in for a hug. Her small frame was warm against mine and I hugged her back. All too soon, we were forced apart by the sound of my grandmother's voice.

"Kayla?" Grams called up the stairs. "Kevin's already run out to the stables!"

"I think he's excited," I said.

Kayla laughed. "You think? Last I checked, Myra wanted to take photos. Do you think I've been up here long enough for his great-grandmother to take all the photos she wants?"

I thought back to my senior year prom. I still cringed at the number of photos there were. I was lucky that I even got to the dance that evening. My date and I were pretty late. Most of our year laughed it off. They teased me about grabbing one too many pre-drinks for most of the night. My date, a cheerleader who had been pretty shallow, was only too happy to let them think that. It was better than admitting she had to pose for more than a dozen photos, even if it was with the quarterback of the school team.

Yeah, my son hadn't stayed still long enough for Grams to take that many.

"Yeah." I laughed. "That definitely isn't enough time. I guess you better go join him before he decides to mount a horse without you."

Kayla's eyes widened with panic.

"Whoa, I'm kidding." I raised my hands in surrender. "But you should probably go meet him."

With a nod, she turned and bounded down the stairs. I went over to my window. Our bedroom windows had a similar view because they both faced the same direction. I could see her as she raced out of the house and toward the barn. It was a pity I'd missed my son running out there. I imagined he would have looked just as excited as Kayla obviously was. I hoped that Grams at least managed to get a few good photos.

Before long, the horses started trotting out of the stable. Kayla was first, on a horse named Midnight, so named because of the deep black color of his fur. She had a line between the horses. A chestnut beauty named Aidan was next. I was shocked to see that Kevin was on a fully grown horse. It was a smaller horse, but still. I thought that he was going to go riding on one of the foals.

I turned around and bolted down the stairs, panic-stricken.

There was no way that I would have given them permission if I'd known that it was going to be so dangerous. He was still a young boy, for crying out loud! What was Kayla thinking?

Grams stared at me as I raced past her. She tried to say something but I missed it. I had only one thing on my mind and my ears were roaring. I had to stop them before they got out onto the field. All I knew was that Kayla had already taught Kevin the basics.

By the time I got there, it was too late. I could only watch as Kevin and Kayla rode out onto the pastures. Calling out wouldn't have done anything. The horses had already transitioned from a trot into a steady canter. I knew what it was like on a horse. Unless they looked back, which they did not, there was no way I was going to get their attention. The wind was blowing and it would have drowned me out – not to mention the sound of hooves on the green ground.

I watched, silently hoping that Kayla might look back, but I had no such luck. I was kind of glad that she didn't look back because she was too busy concentrating on keeping my son safe. She didn't take her eyes off Kevin for a second. It didn't make me any less anxious. There was no way that I was going to be able to catch up with them.

As I stood there, all sorts of crazy ideas began to race through my mind. I wondered if I could grab a horse and catch up to them. They had yet to start galloping. That seemed like a ridiculous idea, though, and I didn't want to upset my son. I knew he would get the wrong idea if I joined them on a horse. He'd been rather clear about not wanting to go riding with me.

The next idea to pop into my head was a little less crazy, depending on who you asked. I wanted to get in my car and go around the pasture. If I followed the road, there was only one place for them to end up. The neighboring farm was a vineyard and while my family had permission to ride on their property, Kayla had voiced her discomfort at the idea of trespassing. No matter how much I tried to assure her that it was all right, she wouldn't accept that. She said that she would only go if I went, too. We both knew that wasn't an option.

The third and final idea was just plain crazy. I was tempted to hop into my car and drive out onto the pasture right behind them. I would catch up in seconds. It was clear – there were no steers or anything to get in my way. I had asked the field to be cleared just for Kevin and Kayla. The cattle were happily grazing in the opposite field.

There was nothing to stop me, except perhaps common sense.

My grandmother was standing on the porch, watching me from the doorway of the house. I didn't want to turn to face her because I already knew what she was thinking. I was acting crazy. That didn't stop the thoughts from going wild. Eventually, however, I knew I had no choice. I couldn't stand there all day. They were going to fade from my sight anyway.

Kayla and Kevin were getting smaller and smaller the longer I stood there. We had woods on the outskirts of our land. We were that deep into the country. They were the same woods that Kayla and I drove through on our way into the ranch.

There was a quiet trail that they were going to follow. I'd shown it to Kayla a few days before. That was when she first told me that Kevin wanted to go riding, as he put it, *for real*. They had slowed down to a trot. At least, I thought they had. It was hard to tell from where I stood. They seemed like they were moving slower, but it could have looked that way just because I was so far away.

With a sigh, I decided to leave them be. Kayla knew what she was doing. She would never endanger Kevin. I had to trust her. I turned to head back into the house. My grandmother had her arms crossed over her chest and she was leaning into the arch of the front door. One eyebrow was raised questioningly.

TWENTY-NINE
KAYLA

We were on the trail in no time. I was glad that I'd asked Matt to show me where it was or I might have gotten lost. I wasn't the best person to go to when it came to directions. So, not only did I ask Matt to show me where it was *twice*, but I'd also written it down and drawn myself a map. I might not have panicked so much if I was riding the trail on my own but with Kevin there, I felt like I had to be extra responsible. There was no way that I was going to get us lost.

If nothing else, an overprotective great-grandmother was more than enough to keep me in line.

Kevin was eager to get the horses into a gallop but I was a little more nervous. Every morning that week, I had made time to go to the stables with Kevin. We had completed every cue over and over again. I knew that he knew all of them. The kid practically studied everything I told him about horses. Even at his age, he was eager to learn and learn well.

Still, he was on a fully grown horse. He had insisted on

riding Aidan. I wanted to argue with him, but when one of the ranch hands told me that the foals were not ready to be ridden, I had no other choice. I couldn't bring myself to tell Kevin that he would not be able to ride a horse for a few more weeks, especially not when he was so excited to get out there. I didn't even know if I was going to be around long enough for that.

We picked the smallest horse and I thought that would be okay. I had ridden adult horses as a child but my father was diligent about my safety. I never rode an adult horse for my very first horse, though. I'd had plenty of practice riding ponies. I tried my best to take the same approach my father did with me. There was a line of rope between his horse and mine and if Aidan went too far ahead or got too rowdy, I only needed to pull on the line to give her the necessary signal.

It was slightly comforting but I was still nervous. I wanted to make sure the boy was safe. It was harder since I wasn't Kevin's parent but I did my best. I wished that Matt was there with each lesson I taught him. I hoped that the day he could accompany us would arrive soon. Matt looked so sad when I left him behind. He was trying his best to hide it, I knew that, but I could see through him.

Slowly, Kevin was beginning to come around to his father. Sometimes, I caught him watching his father maintain the ranch and I thought he wanted to go to him. There were other times where Kevin spoke to his dad, usually to ask a question about something he didn't understand, and everyone was momentarily shocked. Thankfully, Kevin seemed oblivious. We needed to get our reactions under wraps. Often, if Kevin caught me looking at his dad, he would duck his head in embarrassment.

I knew he wasn't quite ready to forgive Matt but he was getting there – albeit slowly.

I had a picnic planned for Kevin and me. The basket hitch was tied and everything hung off the saddle. Unfortunately, that left me unable to ride bareback, but I was stuck with a saddle either way. I couldn't let Kevin ride a trail without a saddle. I was pretty sure that Matt would have killed me or something.

It was for his own safety. I was comfortable riding bareback but that was because I learned how to ride a horse without a saddle. It was so long ago that even I was nervous to get back on a horse without the stirrups. Besides, it wasn't like anyone rode a horse bareback because it was comfortable. It was just freeing somehow. It took a lot more effort and a lot more strength.

To be honest, I wasn't sure that I had it in me anymore. Kevin and I had been trotting up and down the barn for a good while and my muscles were definitely feeling it. That was *with* a saddle. The mere thought of how sore I would have been after riding bareback made me shudder.

"What's wrong?" Kevin asked.

I laughed. "No, it's nothing. I was just thinking about how I used to ride horses bareback."

"You mean without a saddle?"

"Yeah. That's how I learned to ride horses when I was younger."

"Whoa," Kevin murmured. "Can I try it?"

"Sometime, sure."

Kevin beamed, straightening his back. He was trying to look like a grown-up and I found myself grinning at the cuteness of it all. He held on to his reins and we trotted along quietly. I didn't want him to know how cautious I was being, but I watched the way he sat religiously. His feet were seated correctly in the stirrups and he was using them as an anchor just the way I'd shown him. He had pretty much mastered all of the cues.

Somewhere along the way, I started to relax and enjoy myself. The freeing feeling of being on a horse again returned to me and my body buzzed with joy. I felt like I had returned home in more than one way. I wanted to laugh with giddiness.

Either Kevin sensed my happiness or he was enjoying the ride just as much as I was. He kept looking over at me with a smile on his face. I couldn't tell but I didn't mind. That smile was all I needed. I had been wondering if it was a good idea for me to take Kevin riding, even after Matt gave his permission. His smile told me that it definitely was.

The trail was not dense like some of the ones near the farm my parents had owned. We were surrounded by trees so tightly knit that it was dark and cold. I could still feel the cool air coming off of them but it was airy and open. The sun shone down on us, illuminating the way. It was peaceful. I could hear birds chirping from the top of the trees.

Soon, the trail opened up into a clearing. It had a meadow feeling but with fewer flowers. The grass was bright and green and speckled with colorful wildflowers. I could see daisies breaking through the earth here and there. The air smelled sweet.

"This is so pretty," I said.

"Maybe we should stop and have our picnic here!" Kevin said excitedly. He looked at me with anxious eyes. "It looks like a good spot."

"You know what, Kevin? I think that is an excellent idea."

The boy gave a giggle.

"Whoa," I murmured, pulling on Midnight's reins.

He came to a steady stop and I watched as Kevin did the same thing with Aidan. I could have tugged on the line between us to stop Aidan but I wanted to give Kevin the chance to do it himself. I knew that he would have wanted to stop his horse on his own too. I was feeling pretty proud of him by the time Aidan slowed to a stop. I could see that Kevin was feeling pretty proud of himself too.

I got down off of Midnight and walked over to Aidan, holding onto the line that connected the two horses. I didn't want Midnight to wander off. I helped Kevin out of his stirrups and he held onto my shoulders as I lifted him off the saddle and onto the ground. He still struggled to get off on his own but that was to be expected. He was riding a horse much bigger than he was supposed to be.

Kevin wanted to set up the picnic on his own so I helped him undo the basket hitch and passed him the wicker basket. It was one that his great-grandmother had made. It was quite beautiful actually. He carried it over to a spot near the center of the clearing and pulled the blanket out. He threw it out onto the grass and then began to lay the picnic out.

While he set up, I turned to the horses. I untied the rope from between them and they shook their manes out. I spoke quietly to the horses, one at a time. I ran my fingertips along their withers and stroked the bridge of their noses with my opposite hand. They neighed and whinnied appreciatively.

"It's ready!" Kevin called out. When he saw what I was doing, he walked over to me. "What are you doing?"

"I just like talking to them after a ride. It helps soothe them."

"Do they need soothing?"

"Sometimes. It depends on your horse and the ride. You

have to remember that it takes a lot to carry us. We're heavy and horses go for a long time with us on their backs." While I spoke, I did not stop petting the horses.

Kevin furrowed his brow, looking at me thoughtfully. "Huh. I guess that makes sense. Can I do it?"

I smiled. "How about you do it when we get back home?"

"Okay!"

I tied the line to one of the trees, loosely. It was long enough that both Midnight and Aidan could wander a bit. I didn't want them to feel trapped but they seemed quite content to remain where they were. Aidan moved backward and forward a bit but he was a younger horse so I was not surprised. I followed Kevin over to the picnic that he'd laid out.

Myra was the one who prepared the food for us. I was shocked by the amount that there was. How much did she think we were going to eat? We were only two people and one of us was a child! I had to stop myself from laughing as I sat down on the blanket.

There was more than enough food. There were freshly buttered rolls that sprayed flour everywhere as you tore them open, cuts of cold meat, and cherry tomatoes. There was a small container of fresh fruit. I thought Myra packed that container mostly for me as she knew I preferred having fruit for dessert most days. She had packed two slices of apple pie though, just in case I felt like something else. It looked mighty appealing and I made sure to save enough room for it. Myra went all out for us.

I told Kevin to help himself to whatever he wanted. In only two weeks, his eating habits had changed completely. In fact, I could hardly recognize the little boy in front of me.

I felt like he was even more comfortable eating in front of me than anyone else. I couldn't help but feel special.

When I arrived on the ranch, the last thing that I expected was to fall in love with Matt's child, but I knew it was happening. The boy was like a little glimmer of light and he gave me more hope than ever. I had always wanted to be a mother. Kevin made me feel like I could be. He quelled all those little doubts sitting at the back of my mind, the ones that told me I wouldn't be able to do it on my own.

If this little boy liked me that much, surely, I couldn't be so bad? I had a chance at motherhood. I had spent the better part of my adulthood believing that it wasn't possible. Spending time with him made me think otherwise. I couldn't wait for it to come to fruition.

Kevin was enjoying the food so much that I had to tell him to slow down. I didn't want him to overeat. We still had to get back to the ranch house. I hoped Myra wouldn't mind if either of us skipped out on dinner because I was pretty sure that we had all but spoiled our appetites by the time we were done eating lunch. There was still leftover food.

With a sigh, Kevin lay back on the blanket. He rubbed his belly with one hand. It was pushed outward. I had to laugh at the sight. He looked over at me and, seeing what I was laughing at, continued. I'd always loved the way children wanted to make you laugh.

I decided to lay back and do the same thing, heaving a sigh of my own. The sky was a bright blue. It was so clear that it looked like a cartoon, with puffy white clouds drifting over it. I remembered trying to name the shapes the clouds made when I was a child. My mom would do it with me and we would make up the most ridiculous animals that we could think of, like a half seal and half unicorn creature.

Kevin raised his head when I sighed, looked over at me,

and started giggling at the sight of me rubbing my belly the same way he was. I did it some more, pushing my belly out as far as I could. He laughed louder. I couldn't help thinking that it was the sweetest sound in the world.

"This is nice," I murmured.

"Yeah," Kevin agreed quietly. "It is."

THIRTY
MATT

I was sitting at my desk when I got the call. My grandmother had given me a lot to think about. There was no way that I had room to argue with her. Then again, when it came to Grams, there was almost no chance to argue. Ever.

Any hope I might have had of being able to walk past her without a hitch was a pointless one. That did not stop me from trying. I walked slowly, calmly, as if I was afraid of setting off some kind of alarm. In a way, it reminded me of trying not to set off mines in the military. This was mostly due to the fact that I knew I had probably overreacted and I didn't feel like getting lectured. Grams let me pass by her without a word, made me believe that there was going to be no talking, but of course, it wasn't going to be so easy.

"Where do you think you're going, young man?" she said.

As old as I was, she was always going to be my grandmother. And that meant she was probably the only person in the world who could stop me from taking another step further by simply saying that one thing. Her voice carried all the authority in the world. Billionaire CEO or not, I stopped dead in my tracks at being called *young man*.

Kayla may have had the magical ability to make me feel like I was younger but there was a difference between feeling like a carefree teenager and a naughty little boy. That was how my grandmother made me feel that day. I froze and it felt like my whole body sighed on the inside. I didn't sigh out loud. I could only imagine the look on my grandmother's face if I'd done that. I probably would have gotten some comment about how I was not too old for a spanking. We both knew that wasn't true, but it didn't stop her from making the comment – nor did it stop me from feeling the mortification wash over me. Apparently, I wasn't too old to be chastised by the woman who helped raise me.

If I hadn't been so worried about Kevin and Kayla, I might have laughed when she asked me if she could put on a pot of tea for us. I didn't feel like I had a choice, and fifteen minutes later, we were sitting in the living room on either side of the coffee table. My grandmother was old-fashioned. We had an entire tray, laden with a teapot, teacups on saucers, and a pot full of homemade chocolate chip cookies.

"So, do you want to explain to me just what was going through your mind when you ran out there? You had smoke on your heels and you damn near toppled me over."

I sighed. "I didn't know Kevin was going to be riding on Aidan."

She nodded slowly at me. "And you thought you were going to stop him?"

When she put it that way, I could see why she disapproved of my reaction. It was the first thing Kevin had looked forward since I brought him to the ranch. I was pretty sure everyone, including the ranch hands, would have been upset with me if I'd told him he couldn't ride. I didn't even want to think about how Kayla might have reacted – especially now that things were going well between us.

She was finally beginning to come around to me too.

"I couldn't catch up with them."

"That was not what I asked. I know you couldn't, but you would have tried if you could. Am I right or am I right?"

There was the famous Cole question. My grandfather used to ask it all the time. I was sure I had a few times too. I didn't feel like admitting she was right. She knew the answer anyway. Instead, I took a sip of tea. No one made tea better than my grandmother, though it was not my preferred drink.

"Matt, do you know how crazy that was? Not only would you have upset everyone, but there was no reason for you to act that way."

"I just don't want my son to get hurt. Is that really so wrong?"

"You can't protect him forever, Matt. He's a child. He is going to get hurt eventually." She gave a chuckle. "More than that, he's a *boy*."

I took a bite out of my biscuit. I knew where this was going.

"Do you even know how much havoc you wreaked when you were a boy? You gave me half my gray hairs, you know."

"I am pretty sure that Mikey gave you way more than me. I do not remember you having gray hair by the time I was a teenager."

She laughed. "Fair enough, but just because you didn't see the streaks doesn't mean that they weren't there. Goodness, your granddad and I didn't know what to do with you when you were a boy. You were so full of energy and it seemed like all you wanted to do was the most adventurous thing available."

"I wasn't *that* bad."

"Matthew! You broke both your arms when you were seven years old! At the same time!"

I had almost forgotten about that. Admittedly, it wasn't my proudest moment. We were visiting the old dam. It was a family day. Ironically, it was the first day that we all did something together since my parents died, if I recalled correctly. It was the first day that I'd been excited about doing something. That was kind of what this was like for Kevin.

I shrugged my shoulders sheepishly. "And I scared the hell out of you, didn't I?"

"You most certainly did. We had to rush to the emergency room with you hollering in the back. We didn't even know what medication we could give you for the pain." She ran a hand over her face tiredly. "It was terrifying."

"So, then you must be able to understand how I feel about Kevin riding on a fully grown horse. I'm not even there."

"Do you trust Kayla?"

That was an unexpected question. I gulped down a lump that had suddenly formed in my throat. "Implicitly."

"Even with your little boy?"

"Yes," I said slowly. I didn't even have to think about it. "Especially with Kevin."

"Then you need to come to terms with that, my boy. I know it's hard, but you need to be able to let go sometimes."

"Let go?" I sighed. "Grams, Kevin is only a boy. He hasn't even turned eight yet."

"You were the same age as he was when you broke your

arms. And you know what your grandfather and I learned that day?"

She waited for me to answer. I simply shook my head.

"We learned that no matter how hard we tried to protect you, there was only so much that we could do. You were going to fall and hurt yourself and get into trouble. All we could do was try our best to guide you and hope that everything worked out, both before and after the fact."

"What are you trying to say, Grams?"

She gave me a small smile and drained the rest of her teacup before she spoke to me. The steam fogged up the oval spectacles perched on the edge of her nose. "I'm trying to say that Kevin is going to get hurt sometimes and there won't be anything that you can do to actually stop that. As much as you want to protect him, the best thing that you can do for your son is teach him what's right and wrong. After that, you kind of have to hope for the best."

"What do I do if he gets hurt? What if he ends up doing the wrong thing?"

"Oh, doing the wrong thing has consequences all its own. It will be a lesson well served, trust me." Grams shrugged. "He's going to end up doing it sooner or later."

I snorted. "Okay, I sort of get you, but I'm inclined to disagree. You and Gramps were only too happy to ground me even after life served me its lessons."

"What are you talking about?"

"I got drunk at a party I wasn't supposed to be at when I was way too young to be drinking. I would assume that the hangover was the lesson life served me, but you and Gramps still grounded me."

My grandmother gave a chuckle. Her belly shook with it. I found myself smiling at having made her laugh that hard. It was well worth it. We would never have been able to talk about this sort of thing when I was a teenager. It would have turned into an argument.

Hell, I was pretty sure I *would* have been pulled over her lap for a spanking if I was still a teenager. I was finally beginning to see what people meant when they said one day we would laugh about it. So, I guessed this was what it felt like to get old.

"You know that was different," she finally said. She was laughing so hard that she had to wipe a tear away from the corner of her eye.

"Uh-huh. That's convenient." I was grinning. I finished the rest of my tea before it got too cold to be pleasant.

"You do know that he'll be all right, don't you? Whatever happens will only make him stronger. It made you stronger, didn't it?"

There was something about her tone that was so anxious it made my chest hurt. I knew my grandmother wanted me to say yes, but I wasn't so sure that was the correct answer. I was struggling with so much that it was hard to believe I actually was stronger. I didn't want to think about any of my episodes. There was nothing that made me feel weaker than one of those.

"Yeah, Grams," I finally said quietly. "I guess that you're right."

I knew she wasn't convinced by the look on her face but she just gave a slow nod. I felt like we were done and I stood up from the couch. I dusted my jeans off, even though there was no dirt on them. I just needed something to do with my hands. I found myself smoothing the nonexistent wrinkles out of my shirt.

Grams stared off in one direction with a sad expression on her face. I was overwhelmed with the need to comfort her but I didn't know how. I had no idea what to say. I could say a lot, but I didn't want to lie to her.

I settled for pausing in front of her. I spoke gently. "Come here, Grams."

She looked up at me with those same sad eyes. I had my grandmother's eyes, same as my mom after her. They were a deep brown, flecked with amber. They kind of reminded me of a Golden Retriever puppy when she looked at me like that. She stood up from the couch and I pulled her into my body. I gave her a tight hug, even though she didn't feel as strong as she used to feel. She hugged me back, wrapping her arms around my shoulders. I couldn't help but notice how much thinner she felt against me.

My grandmother had always been a strong woman, but I'd been away for so long that I could scarcely believe how much the woman in front of me had changed. She still had that headstrong attitude of hers and a brash personality to go with it, but she was starting to look more and more like her voice. It was soft and gentle in nature. My grandmother had become smaller, thinner, and gentler in appearance. Her hair was entirely gray. The lines and wrinkles on her face appeared so much deeper than I was used to, making her look frail and tired. She was worn and I could see it.

The sad part was that I knew why. She had lost the man she loved and, as much as I hated to admit it, she had kind of lost both her sons too. Mikey at least stayed close to home, even if he was always in the town. I had left her behind. Seeing her now made me feel guiltier than ever.

I pressed a gentle kiss on the top of my grandmother's head. "You know I love you, right? And I'm so grateful to have you in my life. No one could have raised me better than you guys did."

"I love you too, my boy," she said. Her voice was muffled

because she was speaking into my shirt. I wasn't quite sure when I got so much taller and bigger than Grams. "He would have been so proud of you."

The last sentence was softer and I felt the ache in my chest once more. I gave her one last squeeze before I let go. When I pulled back, I could see that my grandmother's cheeks were wet with tears. She didn't look up at me. She always hated being seen crying. She felt that it made her seem weak. I couldn't have disagreed more. As far as I was concerned, it was impossible for my grandmother to be weak. She was the strongest woman in my life. She was certainly the strongest one that I'd ever known.

"I'm going to head up to my study, okay?"

She nodded, still not looking up at me. That was okay. She didn't need to.

I made my way up the stairs. My study was on the opposite wing to my bedroom. It was a bit of a mess because I hadn't been spending a lot of time there lately. I was too busy helping maintain the ranch. It was going to be a long time before everything was in tip-top shape, but it was getting there. It felt good to be managing the ranch again.

Even though it was still relatively early on in the day, I felt exhausted by the time I sat behind my desk. There were papers strewn all over it. They were a combination of papers from my company that either needed signing or approving and papers that had Jenna's and Kevin's names scribbled all over them. I didn't want to have to deal with sorting them out right then.

Instead, I pulled my laptop out and started going through my emails. It was difficult to keep up with emails on the ranch. We never bothered much with technology when I was growing up. Being back there brought back all of the memories and it felt kind of wrong to bother with laptops and phones and all that. Besides, I was always busy with chores anyway. We all were.

My grandmother still had a landline, for goodness sake!

Incidentally, it was the landline that started ringing. It echoed throughout the house because there was more than one phone connected to the same line. The house was too big to only have one phone. We would never reach the left wing in time to answer the phone if we had been in the right wing.

I happened to have a phone in my study. I went to answer it. I didn't want Grams to have to deal with it after having left her in such an emotional state. I knew that she was more than capable but that didn't make me feel any better about it.

I had nearly forgotten all about the fact that I was supposed to be expecting a call or an email or a visit. With that in mind, I was suddenly nervous about answering the phone. All the confidence of that morning seemed to have disappeared. Maybe it was because Kayla wasn't around. After all, she was the reason why I was so confident about the case. Her confidence was contagious.

Still, the phone was ringing and if I didn't answer it soon, then Grams *would* have to answer it.

I sighed and picked up the phone with its curly cord. "Hello?"

The voice on the line was a man's. I couldn't hear what he was saying because he was speaking too fast. He sounded kind of breathless.

"Hello? Who is this?"

"Matt, is that you?" the voice said.

"This is Matt. Are you looking for Myra?"

"No," his voice sounded suddenly clearer and firmer

than before. "I wanted to get a hold of you. You better get down here."

It was Mikey. I stood up, kicking my seat back from the desk. His voice was more serious than I had heard it in years and I was right. He was definitely breathless. But I didn't know why.

"What's going on?"

"Man, I mean it. Just get down here as soon as you can. I need a car and you will get down here way sooner than an ambulance will."

My heart skipped a beat. "An ambulance? What the hell do you need an ambulance for?"

"Matthew!" Mikey shouted angrily into the line. I had to pull the phone away from my ear, but I could still hear him yelling. "Will you just get in your fucking car and come to Old Man Wilks's vineyard? Now!"

Before I could say anything else, Mikey ended the call. I stood with the phone in the air, the dead tone beeping ominously for a moment. I think that I was in shock. Everything hit me all at once and I dropped the phone, letting it slip from my fingertips onto the floor of the study. It clattered against the wood. I raced out of the study and stormed down the stairs.

"Matt?" Grams called, poking her head out of a doorway. I stopped only to grab my car keys. There was no time to explain. "What's going on?"

"I don't know. Mikey called and told me to get down to the vineyard." My voice sounded shaky and my hands were just as bad.

The color drained from my grandmother's face and her eyes went wide. They were still red and puffy from crying. "I'm coming with you."

"Grams," I started, ready to protest.

"Don't even think about arguing with me, Matthew. Get your ass out of my house. You are wasting time."

I nodded and opened the front door. I let her walk ahead of me and shut the door behind me. She was already halfway toward the car by the time I turned around. I unlocked the car doors and she climbed into the passenger seat. I ran the rest of the way over to the car.

We pulled our seatbelts on and I got out of the driveway. Between getting off of the phone with Mikey and climbing into the driver's seat, a million different scenarios had run through my mind. Each one was worse than the next. I didn't know what Mikey had gotten himself into but if what I believed was true, he might have been in a whole lot of trouble.

I could not be sure because we had not had a lot of contact since the day we fought outside the barn. He spent most of his time in the town. He said it was because of work, but I had a feeling that he was not entirely truthful. We knew that there was an apartment above the veterinary office and he paid to stay there during the busy season. Still, I doubted it was work keeping him away.

Ever since our argument, I doubted everything that Mikey said. We were not on good terms. My grandmother wasn't happy about it but our teen years had been a learning curve for her. She learned not to push us. If we were going to work our shit out, we were going to do it on our own. I was convinced that part of the reason that Mikey was staying away from the ranch, away from home, was because he was just as angry with me as I was with him.

The main reason I believed that he was lying, though? That was easy. I was almost certain that Mikey was on drugs again.

I was not ready to confront him about it yet. I had so

much going on in my life that I couldn't afford to think about it. My son came first. I needed to sort the case out first before I could think about handling Mikey. I couldn't tell Grams either, not after everything she had already been through.

Every time I thought about it, I couldn't help but wonder how long it had been going on for. Was it ever since my grandfather died? If it was, it was all the more reason for me not to think about it. I couldn't help but feel partially at fault. My family was falling apart and I'd left.

I put my foot down on the pedal and roared out of there. Grams and I braced our heads as they hit the headrests. I may not have been around, but I was being given a chance to fix things. I couldn't afford to mess that up.

There was a large part of me that felt like I'd betrayed my brother. Few people knew about Mikey's history. Most people just knew that my grandparents had taken him in when he was a teenager. They didn't know about the way he had to go cold turkey in those first few months, about how he had screamed out and cried every single night, the way that he shivered with enough force that he had bruises from his bones jostling against anything and everything, and that his skin was often dripping in sweat despite that. It was so bad that we had to frequently change his bedding because even though he was sweating like crazy, he was always complaining about the cold.

That version of Mikey was one that I had nearly forgotten. He was a completely different creature to the Mikey I knew now. That one had been thin, his skin stretched so finely over his bones that he looked almost grotesque. He was yellowy, too. He had bitten his nails down to stumps, so much so that they always had a thin line of blood at the front.

I remembered being slightly scared of the greasy-haired boy. I never understood why my grandparents would bring him into our home.

It was a month later that I had to clean Mikey up on my own. He was covered in his own sick and he couldn't move. He just did not have the willpower to do it. Until that moment, I had thought of Mikey as pathetic and disgusting. It was a horrible thing to say but it was true. Seeing him there, though, I knew that he needed my help. I was the only one who could help him. My grandparents had gone to town.

In the end, it was because I felt so sorry for him that I helped him. The alternative was to let him wait until my grandparents returned. I couldn't do that to anyone, let alone this poor boy.

Once I was done cleaning him off with a warm washcloth, I heaved him into the bathtub. I remembered being shocked by just how light his body was. It had been a struggle to get him to eat and even more of a struggle to get his body to keep it down. He had put on weight but it wasn't enough. I was much bigger and stronger than he was, especially with all the work that I did on the farm and all the sports that I played in school.

From that moment on, it was hard to separate me from Mikey. I took it upon myself to make sure that he was okay, that he ate, and that he never found himself alone and needing help that way ever again. When he was strong enough, I even took him out onto the ranch and showed him how I maintained the farm. He couldn't help, but he liked hanging around the animals. It was much later that he started taking care of them.

It was the summer so I didn't even have to worry about school. That summer was the first one that I didn't have a ton of friends over at the ranch house. Plenty of people asked because they were so used to me hosting parties but I said no. I didn't go out much, either. I think my grandparents were taken aback but also pretty proud of me.

By the time school started, he was ready to go to school. He was still pretty thin, pretty weak, and pretty quiet. He was a different person though. Over the summer, he had become my best friend. More than that, he had become my brother.

No one started with him at school. He was practically ripe for being picked on. If it weren't for the fact that I stood up for him and no one wanted to mess with me, I was pretty sure he would have had a hard time in school. As it was, all Mikey needed was a second chance. My family gave him one and I gave him one too.

We saw him come out of his shell and he started to thrive. It was that year he found out that he loved the animals on the farm. Every day after school, he couldn't wait to get back out there. A part of me wondered if it was even worth it to send him to school when animals were clearly his first passion, but I guessed my grandparents knew what they were doing. Besides, he wouldn't have been able to study to be a veterinarian if he hadn't finished school.

I truly hoped that whatever he did, he had not screwed up those chances.

The last thing on my mind at that point in time was Kevin.

THIRTY-ONE
KAYLA

I was completely terrified of what was about to happen, but I had to leave it in Mike's capable – mostly – hands. I couldn't believe how badly I had screwed up. Kevin was lying on the floor in tears and there was nothing I could do. The little boy asked me to hold his hand and that was what I did, even though my own hands were shaking violently. My heart was racing and I was sweating, but I was trying my hardest not to cry because I felt like I had to be strong for Kevin. I was sitting on my knees beside him. I could only imagine how he might have reacted if I started crying – and how Mike would have reacted, for that matter.

"It is going to be all right, okay? Just remain calm," Mike said, more to me than to Kevin.

I took a deep breath. There was no way that I could answer Mike. I just had to trust him. It wasn't like I knew what I was doing. The fact that Kevin was on the ground, bleeding, was more than enough proof of that.

"Matt is on his way but in the meantime, I need you to stay calm, Kayla," he repeated. I nodded and he turned toward Kevin. "How are you doing, little man? It hurts, right?"

Kevin nodded. He didn't want to talk and I knew why. He didn't want to make me feel bad. His skin had a green tinge to it and I thought that he might throw up even if he did try to say anything.

"I know, kid," Mike said softly. "I need you to be brave for me, okay? Can you do that?"

I had never seen this side of Mike before. He seemed so angry every time I had seen him at the ranch house. Granted, most of that was directed at Matt but that was beside the point. I'd only witnessed the harsher side of him.

The man in front of me was gentle and kind. He had his hand on Kevin's leg, holding it in a stable position. I couldn't bring myself to look at it. It was bent in an awkward position. No leg was supposed to bend that way. It made my stomach turn just thinking about it. Never mind the way the bone broke through the skin.

Oh, God, I thought. *Breathe. Don't look at it and just breathe. In and out.*

"Is his leg going to be okay?" I whispered to Mike.

He nodded at me but I wasn't convinced. "He's going to be just fine. We just need to get him to the hospital as soon as possible. Don't worry. I have called Matt. He's on his way."

"How long is it going to take him to get here?"

Mike gave me a warning look, his eyes darting over to Kevin. He wanted me to be calm for the kid's sake. That made sense.

I nodded in silent understanding.

"He'll be here soon," Mike said. And then, in a lower voice, "There is nothing more important to him than Kevin."

I couldn't argue with that. I knew Mike was saying it more for Kevin's benefit than anything else at that moment. The little boy needed to know that it was going to be okay. I could only imagine how much pain he was in. He was putting on a brave face.

Against my better instincts, I leaned forward and pressed a gentle kiss to Kevin's forehead. "You are the bravest little boy that I have ever met. Do you know that?"

"It hurts, Kayla," he said, sounding nothing like the outspoken kid I was used to spending so much time with.

"I know, sweetheart. I just need you to keep still, okay? You can squeeze my hands if you need to."

As if he had been waiting for permission, Kevin squeezed my hands. He held on so tightly that it actually hurt. I didn't pull away though. If that was what helped him, then it was okay.

I couldn't believe that I'd been so stupid. It was my job to protect Kevin and I screwed up. I could have forgiven myself if there had been nothing I could do about it, but the fact of the matter was that there was. I had been irresponsible.

After the picnic, we packed up and I tied the basket hitch, reattaching the wicker basket to Midnight's saddle. I was about to hook the line onto the front of Aidan's saddle when Kevin stopped me.

"Wait," he had said. "Before you... Before you do that, could I maybe try riding without a saddle?"

I'd hesitated, but the look Kevin gave me made my stomach twist uncomfortably. How was I supposed to say no to him when he was looking at me like that? Factor in that I wasn't his mom and it equated to disaster. If I said no, none of this would be happening. But of course, I didn't do that.

Nervously, I found myself removing Aidan's saddle. The plan was for me to ride side by side with him. I told him that we would have to take it slowly. Riding a horse with and without a saddle were two very different things. Kevin seemed so excited that I was pretty sure he would have nodded and agreed no matter what I said.

"Okay, so your cues are more or less going to be the same," I told him. "The only difference is that you aren't going to be able to guide Aidan with your feet the same way you did with the stirrups."

"So how do I tell him where I want him to go?"

"You're going to use your legs. Here, I'll show you."

With that, I lifted him up onto Aidan's back. I helped him stabilize himself and I could tell that he was a bit uncomfortable, though not nearly as uncomfortable as I was with the entire situation. He put on a smile for me and I let go once I was sure he could sit on his own. I handed him the reins and stroked the horse's fur gently, hoping my touch might keep the horse calm. There was no way that I was removing the reins. The next thing I did was walk around so that I was standing partially in front of Aidan, letting the horse know that it wasn't yet time to go.

"Are you nervous?" I asked.

"A little bit," Kevin admitted. I admired him for being so brave. "This feels different."

"It can be uncomfortable at first. As you know, it takes a lot of strength to ride a horse. But riding without a saddle takes even more strength."

"I can be strong, Kayla."

I remembered smiling. "You are already far stronger than you know, Kevin."

It was the truth. Though he had his moments, as he obviously would, Kevin was handling things really well.

Not only had he lost his mom, but he'd also taken a massive trip across the country. He was living in an unfamiliar state, in a new house, with several people he didn't know well at all. All circumstances considered, I'd say he was damn strong.

I reached out to gently press against the outside of one of his ankles, pressing his foot into Aidan's side. Aidan took a slow step forward on impulse, but he didn't go any further.

"You see how Aidan still moves when you press? The only difference is that without the stirrups, you need to push a little harder than before. All of your cues are very much the same."

"Oh," Kevin said. "So, if I tap my foot against his side, he's going to go forward?"

I nodded. "But please don't do that yet. I need to ride with you."

"Okay. Are you going to ride now?"

"In a moment," I murmured. "I just want to make sure that you understand a few things."

Little did I know, taking the time to explain a few things was not enough to make Kevin understand them in one go. I should have taken him through everything the same way that I did with the cues when we first started talking about riding. We'd spend days and days going over those until I was absolutely confident that he could handle it – and even then, I never intended for him to start riding anything more than a pony. He was just a kid. I was supposed to be the one teaching him these things. It was my responsibility not to let anything bad happen to him.

I took him through his cues, making sure he understood how riding bareback differed to riding with a saddle. He had to sit in a certain way, he had to try harder to balance his body, he had to hold on tighter to the reins, and each cue needed that little bit of extra pressure.

The biggest problem in pointing out all of these things was that I was going off of my memory and, to be perfectly blunt; my memory was not as fresh as I would have liked. I should have realized that. It alone should have been enough reason to tell Kevin that we could ride bareback on another day, when I was used to it. Instead, I ignored all my instincts because I just wanted to make Kevin happy.

Perhaps I wasn't meant to be a mother after all. There was a pool of blood around him. I didn't know how much blood was okay for a person to lose, I had no experience in that field, but I was pretty damn sure that the amount Kevin was losing was not okay. He needed to get to a hospital.

My eyes burned with unshed tears.

THIRTY-TWO

MATT

The second I turned into the drive, I started to wonder how I was going to find Mikey. There were acres and acres of plants taller than I was. I needn't have worried though. I saw where I was meant to be within moments. I glanced over at my grandmother and I could see my own anxiety reflected back at me. She put two and two together too.

Aidan and Midnight came into sight first and I felt my heart lurch into my throat. What were the horses doing there? Kayla specifically told me that she wasn't comfortable going onto Old Man Wilks's property, so why were the horses she and Kevin rode out on that morning up ahead of me?

I brought my pickup to a halt as close to the plants as I could and then I hopped out. A part of me wanted to open the door for my grandmother, the part of me that she had raised to be an upstanding gentleman, but I knew that there wasn't a second to waste. I slammed the door and raced up the pathway, right past Aidan and Midnight. Both horses neighed quietly at me, shuffling their hooves on the ground.

My heart raced as I approached the small huddle. Mikey was on his knees on the ground and so was Kayla. Both of them were hunched over a much smaller body, and I felt my blood go cold with terror. It was the blood that did it. There was so much blood. It wasn't as red as it was in the movies – it was darker; a deep crimson.

And there was so much of it.

"Kevin?" It was supposed to be a yell, but my voice came out in a whisper.

My feet pounded on the ground and Kayla raised her head at the sound. She met my eyes. I saw her lips move to shape my name but I couldn't hear anything, not with the roaring in my ears.

"Kevin!" I yelled.

"Matt," Mikey said. "Matt!"

It wasn't getting through to me. All I could think about was the boy on the ground. He was holding on to Kayla's wrists so hard that I could see her skin turning whiter beneath the pressure. Apart from that, he didn't seem to have much strength in him. He was significantly paler, his skin taking on a bluish-green shade, and his eyes were only half-open.

"What the fuck happened?" I asked.

"Matt," Mikey said.

He sounded far away but I knew he'd already said my name several times over. I looked up at him and my heart sank. I could see it as soon as I met his eyes and, judging by the look of guilt in them, he knew that I could. His eyes were rimmed with red and his pupils seemed bigger than usual. My brother was high or at least, he had been high very, very recently.

"We need to get him to a hospital," Mikey said seriously.

I didn't have time to call him out or say anything about it. I looked down to the source of blood. It was his leg. Mikey had his hand beneath the boy's ankle and he was holding his leg up. There was some kind of material wrapped around his leg, above the knee. I didn't know if it had been a shirt or a pair of pants – the blood had just about soaked through the fabric. Mikey had made a makeshift tourniquet.

It was the sight below that made me swear beneath my breath. I had never been particularly good with blood. That was Mikey's scene. When the cattle got hurt or gave birth, I was out of there. Right then, the blood didn't matter as much to me as the cause did. Kevin's bone broke through the skin and I could see the sharpness of it. I flinched at the sight and I had to force myself to look back up at Mikey. Otherwise, I would have retched all over the place.

"I've placed a tourniquet on the leg but we need to keep it elevated. And we can't let the leg move much. We risk tearing the flesh further."

I winced again.

"Do you understand?" Mikey asked.

"Yeah," I snapped. "What do you need me to do?"

"I'm going to hold his leg in this position. I need you to pick Kevin up and carry him toward the pickup. We're going to need to have him in the front with us."

"Oh, Christ," a voice behind me swore. Grams had joined us.

I resisted the urge to look at her. I kept my eyes on Mikey. I couldn't afford to look anywhere else. I had too many feelings racing through me and I couldn't afford to give in to any of them. None of them were going to do my son any good.

"Okay. I'm going to lift him," I said. My voice sounded like it came from someone else.

Mikey nodded.

"One... Two... Three..."

I picked Kevin up from the ground and I felt my stomach turn at the feel of warm, sticky liquid against my hands and my biceps. There was so much fucking blood. Breathing heavily, I started taking slow steps toward the pickup truck.

"Dad?" Kevin groaned.

Fuck, I thought. My voice came out in a whisper. "Yeah, Kev?"

"It hurts."

Deep breath. Mikey and I walked slowly, careful not to jostle the little boy too much. I allowed Mikey to guide me because his job was so much harder as far as I was concerned. I needed to be careful. I didn't want to hurt Kevin any more than he was already hurting.

"I know, kid," I said gently. "It's okay. We're going to get you help, okay?"

"Where's Kayla?"

I didn't know where Kayla was. I didn't know if she was following me and, at that point, I couldn't look back to check. I'd left her behind with Grams.

"She's right behind us, buddy," I told him.

I felt Mikey pause for the briefest of moments, probably because I was lying, but he caught himself and kept moving. After what seemed like the longest time, we finally reached the pickup. Mikey used his opposite hand to pull open the car's door and I climbed in, holding Kevin close.

Somehow, we were able to position Kevin in such a way that he was lying over my lap. I held his head up with one hand and, so that Mikey could walk around to the passenger side, I took his ankle from Mikey's hand. Mikey made sure that I held it at the right angle and height before he finally released Kevin.

As soon as he was in the passenger seat, Mikey and I carefully shifted so that he could hold Kevin's ankle once again and Kevin's head rested comfortably, as comfortably as could be anyway, on my thigh. I pulled my door shut gently and turned the key in the ignition. I hadn't removed it when I jumped out of the truck. My grandmother and Kayla appeared and I realized that they'd followed Mikey and me to the truck. Grams's head was at my window and I clicked the button that brought it down so that I could hear her. Kayla was right behind her.

"We'll meet you at the hospital," Grams said.

Behind her, Kayla was silent. She couldn't even look up at me. She had blood on her hands – literally. Her hands and her wrists were stained with my son's blood. Her riding jacket was black, but there were spots of red on the white shirt that she wore beneath.

I could have been wrong, but I thought I saw wetness on her cheeks. She'd been crying. I couldn't bring myself to care. I was too angry with Kayla. My son was the most important thing to me.

"Right," I said.

With a curt nod, I moved to pull out of the property. Grams stepped away and, as we watched, she pulled Kayla into her arms.

THIRTY-THREE

KAYLA

I burst into tears as soon as Matthew was out of sight. He pulled away from the property, his pickup engine rumbling noisily, and I found myself crying into his grandmother's shoulder. He hadn't looked at me once since arriving. I could almost feel the anger emanating off of him.

How could I blame him, though?

"Hey," Myra said gently. She stroked my back, comforting me. "It's okay. He's going to be okay."

"How are we getting to the hospital?" I asked, pulling back to sniff my nose loudly. I wiped it with the back of my hand.

"We need to find Miles."

I didn't ask her who Miles was. I just nodded and Myra slipped her hand into mine. I let her lead me up one of the long pathways between the grapes. I noticed that she was trying to avoid the pool of blood on the ground, but I could still see it out of the corner of my eye. It was like a deep, black hole on the ground and I wanted it to swallow me up.

There was a huge mansion behind the vineyard. I would have been surprised that I hadn't noticed it before if it weren't for the fact that their vineyard was more than four times the size. Myra led me up to the steps of the front porch and only pulled her hand away from mine to bang on the door with the huge brass knocker. It was shaped like a horseshoe, which didn't help the way I was feeling.

It looked like no one was home, but Myra simply knocked again. A few minutes later, the door opened. A tall, elderly man stood in the doorway. At the sight of Myra, his face broke into a warm smile.

"Myra! What can I do for you?"

"I'm so sorry to bother you, Miles," Myra said. Her voice took on a tone I hadn't heard before. "There's been an accident with my great-grandson."

Myra glanced in my direction and I saw Miles follow the movement. He took me in and I watched his expression change. He saw the blood. It was kind of hard to miss, I guess.

"Could you please take us to the hospital?" I blurted out.

"Uh..." Miles looked between Myra and me. "Yeah, sure. Let me just grab my keys."

As soon as he turned away, Myra looked over at me. Her face asked me what that was.

"I'm sorry. I just couldn't wait. We need to get there soon."

She nodded grimly. "Yes. I know we do."

Miles returned a moment later and led us over to his car. It was a sports car, so he had to push his seat for me to climb into the backseat. It was awkward and I couldn't help but think the car was probably bought in some sort of midlife crisis. I instantly regretted the thought.

The drive toward the hospital was mostly silent. Myra hurriedly explained that her great-grandson had been in a horse-riding accident before we left. She didn't have much of a choice. He'd seen the blood and the horses. It was impossible not to.

At least it made Miles drive that much faster.

As soon as we pulled into the parking lot, Myra hopped out of the passenger seat. I was relieved that she didn't wait for the old man to climb out and open her door for her. She came from that sort of time period. By that point, I had figured out that this was Old Man Wilks. I pushed the seat forward and climbed out of the back.

I was hurrying off toward the emergency room before either of them had a chance to shut their car doors. I knew Myra would catch up, but I just couldn't wait any longer. We were already so far behind Matt and Mike.

"I'm here for Kevin Cole," I said when I reached the receptionist.

"Hey," Mike's voice sounded behind me. The receptionist glanced over at him with raised eyebrows. "It's okay. I'll fill her in."

The receptionist nodded and went back to looking at the computer screen. Mike led me over to some open seats in the waiting room. Matt wasn't sitting. I shouldn't have been surprised. He paced up and down in front of the seats, still not looking at me.

"He's already gone into surgery."

"What? Didn't they have to do X-rays and stuff like that?"

"It was pretty obvious that the bone was broken, Kayla."

I had to resist the urge to roll my eyes. "I know that, but they still have to follow procedure."

Look, I was a lawyer. I'd dealt with my fair share of cases that included hospital records. I was bound to pick up a few things along the way. One of the things I was sure about was that even if your break was obvious, they still had to do an examination and have X-rays done and, depending on whether or not there was an opening, the patient would have to wait to go into surgery. It took a while. It didn't just happen as soon as you walked through the doors, no matter how severe.

The town hospital was smaller than most, too. I could probably have counted the number of wards on both hands. Okay, that was an exaggeration, but it definitely wasn't far from the truth.

Mike looked surreptitiously at Matt, who had stopped pacing. I met his eyes and suddenly it became obvious. Of course, Kevin didn't have to wait. People with billionaires for fathers didn't have to wait for anything. I nodded and sat back in the chair, biting my lower lip.

I couldn't escape the angry gaze and at that point, I would have done anything to fade away. Maybe it was a bad idea to follow them to the hospital. Matt clearly didn't want me there. I wasn't sure I could blame him either.

"I'm sorry," I finally said. My voice was quiet.

"You're *sorry*?" Matt snapped. His voice dripped with venom and I winced. "What the *fuck* were you thinking, Kayla?"

"It was an accident, Matt," I said. I didn't want to meet his eyes anymore. I was suddenly very uncomfortable beneath them. "The horse... There were thorns on some of the plants and Aidan just freaked out and ran ahead. I couldn't catch up."

"I thought you had a line between the horses. I didn't see a line between Midnight and Aidan when I got there, Kayla." When I didn't immediately respond, he continued. "Come to think of it, I didn't see any *saddles* on those horses either. So why don't you explain to me exactly what happened out there when you were supposed to be taking care of *my* son?"

I couldn't hold back the tears then. They started streaming down my cheeks, hot and fast. My lower lip was quivering. I looked up at him. "I didn't mean for this to happen."

"You are not his mother, Kayla."

The words felt like a kick to my gut, even though I already knew that they were true. I stood from the seat and walked out of the room. I stormed past Myra and Miles on my way out. She had her arm hooked through his. I didn't stop even when she called after me. I didn't stop until I was standing in the parking lot.

Only then, once I was sure no one else was in sight, did I sit down on the floor and let it all out. I couldn't say that I blamed Matt for it all. I was definitely upset with him, but he was right. I wasn't his kid's mother. I was wrong to act like I had any right.

The events of the day were still playing out in my head over and over again. I tried to pinpoint the exact moment that everything went wrong but there was no way I could do that. After I'd mounted Midnight, we took it slow. It seemed like everything was going fine. I promised myself that we wouldn't ride that way for more than ten minutes. Fifteen was all it took to turn into a disaster.

Somewhere along the way, we'd ended up near the vineyard. Aidan, being a younger horse, spooked a lot easier than most. What I'd told Matt was true. There had been some kind of a thorny bramble that caught him and he moved into a gallop. Up until that point, Kevin had never been on a galloping horse before, let alone bareback. Aidan bucked once too hard and Kevin went flying.

I remembered screaming. Midnight caught up quickly

but it wasn't quick enough. Kevin was lying on the ground, on his stomach. I flipped him over onto his back without thinking. That was when I saw the bone, sticking out of his skin. There was so much blood. I didn't know what to do and I tried my hardest not to freak out.

Lucky for me, Mike just happened to be in the area. I hadn't brought my phone along, because living on the ranch made me forget I even owned a phone, and I didn't know what I would have done if he had not shown up when he did. He ran over to where we were and he led the situation from there. According to Mike, humans were only mildly different from animals. I would have liked to disagree but he knew way more about anything medical than I did so I kept my mouth shut and let him work.

Unlike me, Mike was smart enough to carry his phone around. Once he'd secured the tourniquet, made from the picnic blanket inside Myra's wicker basket, he called Matt. I was told to hold onto Kevin's ankle, keeping is slightly elevated, in the meantime. The next thing I knew, Matt was on his way there.

In truth, the moment that everything went wrong was the moment that I put Kevin onto a horse without a saddle. Now he was in surgery and there was nothing that I could do about it. I didn't feel like I even had a right to be there. I decided to head back inside and call a cab to take me home.

It was a time for Matt's family to be together and I wasn't part of that.

~

There was a guest phone the hospital lobby so I didn't need to go back in, but I saw that Matt was speaking to a doctor. The doctor had scrubs on and he was waving his arms around for emphasis. I should have ignored them and continued with what I was doing but I opened the door so that I could hear what they were saying.

"I'm sorry, Mr. Cole. There's nothing else we can do."

"Don't fucking give me that, Joe. Don't."

The doctor shook his head and he was about to turn away from Matt. Matt was not about to have any of that. He reached out and grabbed hold of the doctor's arm, spinning him back around to face him.

"Please. I'll do anything. I'll *pay* anything."

"Money isn't going to be able to help you. Look, if we could do anything else, we wouldn't even need you to pay more than you have. We need to wait and hope for the best."

"You mean Kevin is going to die," Matt said. There was pain in his voice, real pain.

"What's going on?" I asked, walking into the fight against my better judgment.

I could see the cleft appear in Matt's cheek. It was like a dimple, but it wasn't a dimple. It only ever happened when he was mad. I figured that it was a result of grinding his teeth and by the way his jaw was clenched, I would definitely say that was what was happening. I ignored him and turned to the doctor, my eyebrows raised questioningly.

"I'm sorry," he said. "Who are you?"

"I'm Mr. Cole's lawyer." I extended my hand and, after a moment's hesitance, Joe shook it. "Kayla."

"Right. Well, I'm sorry, Kayla. I'm not obliged to divulge that information with anyone who isn't an immediate member of the family."

"Kevin needs a blood transfusion. He's lost too much blood," Matt said.

I looked over at him, shocked that he was speaking to me. "I don't understand. What's the problem?"

The doctor seemed to take Matt's statement as permission to share the information with me all of a sudden. "We don't have his blood type on hand. We're going to have to wait for it to arrive from a bigger hospital."

I gasped. I couldn't hold it back and I immediately covered my mouth with my hand.

"Yeah," Matt mumbled. "I just had to have a kid with the rarest blood type there is. What did you say it was, Doc? Point six percent?"

"Wait," I said. "Hang on. Is Kevin AB Negative?"

The doctor nodded his head after a guilty glance at Matt. "Yes, he is."

"Can you take blood from me?"

Both men froze, their eyes widening as they took in what I said. I spoke loudly, clearly, so that they knew exactly what I meant. "I'm AB Negative."

THIRTY-FOUR
MATT

For a moment, neither of us moved.

Then, in the blink of an eye, everything happened all at once. Joe realized what Kayla was saying before I did. The penny dropped, all right. It just took a while for me to hear the sound. I could blame that same roaring noise I'd been experiencing since I saw Kevin lying on the ground in Old Man Wilks's vineyard.

"There are forms and waivers that you need to sign before you can do a transfusion," Joe started.

"Fuck the forms," Kayla said.

It was always a shock to my system whenever Kayla swore. It didn't seem like her. This short, brunette beauty always seemed too cute to actually cuss – beneath her breath or otherwise. The woman she was right then was more determined than ever though. I didn't think I'd ever seen the fire shining in her eyes before.

"I'll fill them out afterward. This is an emergency, right?"

Joe looked at me uncertainly.

"Joe," she said. "Don't look at Matt. This is my blood –

not his. I'll sign the forms afterward. Kevin needs my blood *right now*."

"Right," the doctor said. "Right, of course. Okay. Yeah, let's go."

I made to follow them down the hallway when Joe suddenly stopped. It was so sudden that I bumped into his back. He turned to face me.

"Matt, you need to stay in the waiting room. I'll come and fetch you when we're done."

I wanted to argue but one look at Kayla's face made me change my mind. I took a step backward and let them go. She glanced back at me before they walked around the next corner and my stomach twisted uncomfortably. Her face was still red from crying. I was struck with a pang of rather sudden guilt. That was my fault.

With a sigh, I turned to go back to the waiting room. My family was waiting for me to return, along with Mr. Wilks. It didn't skip my notice how close he seemed to be to my grandmother but I didn't say anything. It was none of my business, really.

Instead, I found myself watching Mikey. Apart from what appeared to be a nervous tick, he seemed to be fine. He was jittery and he kept tapping his foot against the leg of his chair. He looked up as I entered the waiting room. We were the only ones there. I guessed that the hospital didn't have very many people to cater to.

"Is he all right?" Mikey asked anxiously.

Grams looked up too. Her head had been resting on Mr. Wilks's shoulder and she looked exhausted.

"He needs a blood transfusion," I said.

"Okay, so are they doing that? When can we see him?"

"I don't know. I assume after the transfusion." I took a

seat opposite Mikey. Everyone was looking at me expectantly. "They didn't have any of his blood type on hand."

Mikey sucked in a breath. I thought that his leg was shaking even faster. "What does that mean? Do they need to wait for it or what?"

"They were going to have it transferred over here from the state hospital, but that would have taken hours. Kayla offered to do it."

"Whoa, wait," Mikey said. I could almost see him working it out in his head.

"Miss Walker has the same blood type as Kevin?" Mr. Wilks asked. He didn't even realize how odd it was.

"Yeah, apparently she is."

"Wow," Mikey said. "Well, that was lucky then."

"That's kind of her," Grams murmured.

Yeah, Grams, I thought. *It is; especially considering how much of an asshole I was just a few moments earlier.*

∾

We were in the hospital until it was dark. Eventually, Mr. Wilks took my grandmother home. Both of them were tired and it had been a very long day. Mikey and I hugged our gran goodbye and then we sat together in awkward silence for another hour and a half. That was how long it took for anything to happen.

"Mr. Cole?" Joe said.

I hopped to my feet. I hadn't even realized that he was in the room.

"Your son is stable. I can take you to his ward if you would like to follow me."

It was strange to have Joe act so formal toward me, considering we had been in the same class in high school. In fact, we'd played football together. I didn't question his professional manner though. He was just doing his job – it took a very long time to become a doctor and his training wasn't something that he could just drop, not even for a friend. I just followed him as he led me to my son's ward and Mikey walked with us.

We didn't say anything as we walked, taking extra-long strides to reach the ward as quickly as possible, and as soon as Kevin came into sight, I went straight past Joe. I practically ran towards the cot. Kevin wasn't awake and there was a drip injected into his arm, but the color had returned to his skin. He looked significantly better. His leg was in a cast, strung up at the end of the bed. I took a seat beside his bed and reached for his hand. I knew that he couldn't feel me holding it but I didn't care. I think I was doing it more for me anyway.

"Oh, thank goodness," Mikey said. He fell into the seat on the other side of Kevin's bed. "Thank goodness."

"You did a brilliant job, Mike. Honestly, I don't think Kevin would have been so lucky if it weren't for you. You gave him enough time to get here."

The corner of Mikey's mouth twitched upward but his smile faded before it even fully formed. "I just did what I could."

Joe smiled. "In that case, maybe you should consider studying medicine for humans. I think you'd make a pretty good doctor."

He's going to have to be able to stay sober for that one, Doc.

The doctor turned away before my brother had a chance to say anything else. He was walking out of the ward. I only remembered at the last second.

"Hey, Joe?"

"Yeah?" Joe said, turning back to me.

"Where is Kayla? Is she okay?"

"Yeah," he said with a small smile. "She's a champ. She just happens to be kind of lightheaded. One of the nurses got her something from the cafeteria but she should be able to come see Kevin soon."

I nodded and Joe left the room.

Mikey and I were silent for some time, both of us watching my son. I could tell that Mike was tired and his eyes were hooded. He seemed to have sobered up quite a bit.

"Hey, Mikey?" I finally said in a low voice.

"Hmmm?" He groaned.

"Thanks for helping Kevin out there earlier."

"I wasn't about to let him... you know."

"Right. Yeah." Why did things have to be so damn awkward between us? This was my best friend, once upon a time. "What were you doing out there?"

He shrugged but I already knew that he knew exactly why he was out there, even if he didn't want to talk about it. The longer we sat there, the more I wanted to ask him about the drugs. Kevin was my first priority and now that I knew he was going to be okay, I was worried about my brother. My suspicions had been confirmed and I wondered if Grams had noticed. I doubted it. She would have reacted; I was sure of it.

I didn't know *how* to ask.

My phone started vibrating and, reluctantly, I let go of Kevin's hand. I stepped out of the ward to answer the call. It wasn't until I did so that I realized Mikey had dozed off. He was sitting back in his armchair with his head lolling over the back and his mouth half-open. He wasn't a snorer.

"Hello, this is Cole."

"Matt, you should check your email at your earliest convenience," Douglas said.

"Has the will been released?" I asked.

"It has. I've viewed it." He gave a sigh and all I heard was static. "What did you say Miss Walker's plan was, exactly?"

"That bad, huh?"

"I don't know, Matt. Law isn't my thing but from what I can tell, if you want to keep your son, you're going to need something solid here."

"She's got it covered. It won't be a permanent fix though, by the sounds of things."

"Will you still be going to court, then?"

"Honestly, I'm hoping that James backtracks," I admitted. I shoved a hand in my back pocket because suddenly I felt very fidgety. I wasn't sure I would, in his position. "If he doesn't want to take Kevin, and I don't see why he would want to take a child who isn't his, then none of this will matter."

"That's a big hope, Matt."

"So, I guess this isn't the part where I tell you that Kevin is in hospital then."

I looked over at Kevin and Mikey, both sound asleep. The drip sticking out of Kevin's arm was probably pumping him full of painkillers. The mere idea made me grimace. I was starting to think that Kevin might have been better off somewhere else. He nearly died today. I was pretty sure that wouldn't have happened if he was with James.

"What?" Douglas finally asked.

"There was a horse-riding accident. He broke his leg." I paused before adding the important part. "Badly."

"Fuck, Matt. This is not good."

"Yeah, Doug, I know it isn't."

"How badly are we talking?"

I sighed. How was I supposed to explain that? "Without all the medical jargon and shit, the bone broke through his skin and he lost so much blood that he needed a blood transfusion."

Silence. Doug didn't respond at all. I pulled my phone away from my ear to check if the call had cut off, but the call was still active, recording each passing second we were on the line for.

"Doug?"

He gave a low whistle. "I'm not often at a loss of words, my friend."

"Right." I sighed again. "Yeah, it doesn't look good at this point, does it?"

"Is he all right? Did the transfusion go well?"

"Yeah, it went great. Kayla gave her blood, because the hospital didn't have any of Kevin's blood type on hand. He's stable now."

"Hang on, what? They didn't have his blood type? What kind of hospital is this?"

I actually laughed – a real laugh. It felt freeing, like a weight off of my chest. I didn't think that it was possible to still laugh after the day I'd had. "It's a small one, Doug. My ranch is in the middle of nowhere."

"Yeah, no kidding. Damn."

I didn't know what else to say. "I guess I should let you get back to your day. I'll view the email soon."

"Matt, did you say Kayla has the same blood type as Kevin?"

"Yeah, they're both AB Negative. Why?"

"Oh, I just found it interesting is all," Doug said. He wasn't wrong. What were the chances that we had two people with the rarest blood type in a hospital that didn't even have any of that blood type on hand? Slim to none. Thankfully, we got the slim end of the stick. "I'll let you get back. Call me when you've gone over everything."

"Sure thing. Thanks, Doug."

I ended the call.

THIRTY-FIVE
KAYLA

Shortly after the doctor and the nurse left, I passed out. I felt too lightheaded to stay awake. At some point, they woke me up so I could eat something, but I went back to sleep right after that. The next time I woke up, Matt was sitting in the armchair beside my bed, looking so worried that I was surprised he wasn't chewing off his nails.

"Hey," he said softly, sitting forward in his seat.

He wasn't looking at me, but I didn't blame him. Anyway, I was half asleep. I turned and stretched groggily. My head felt fuzzy, but it wasn't long before the memories of the day started to return to me.

I sat bolt upright. "Where's Kevin? Is he okay?"

Matt gave me half of a smile. "Yeah, Kevin is fine. Thanks to you."

Oh. "Thank goodness."

I sat back. I felt much better than I had before I passed out. I'd donated blood before but never quite so much in one sitting. It was for Kevin, so it was worth it. Besides, we would not even be in a hospital if it weren't for my irresponsibility.

I stared up at the ceiling. I couldn't bring myself to look at Matt again, but I could feel his eyes on me. I wondered why he was beside my bed and not Kevin's. The blinds on the windows were closed but I could tell that it was evening outside. We had been in the hospital for most of the day.

"Thank you, Kayla," he said softly.

I would have missed it if it weren't so quiet in the ward. Across the hall, I could hear the sound of beeping machinery but there were no other patients in this particular ward. I didn't say anything, because I didn't know *what* to say.

"Did you hear me?" he asked.

I looked over at him and nodded slowly. I still felt guilty. "It was the least I could do."

"No, Kayla," he said. "You didn't have to do it at all. If you weren't here, we would have had no other option but to wait."

I shrugged lamely. If I weren't there, we would not have been in a hospital at all. Of course, I didn't point this fact out. How could I when he was looking at me with so much gratitude in his eyes? I didn't feel like I deserved it.

Matt sighed and reached out toward me. His hand found mine, so much warmer and stronger, and gave it a squeeze. I thought that was all he would do but he stood up and moved closer to the bed.

The next thing I knew, Matt's lips were on mine. His other hand found its way to my cheek, cupping my face as he kissed me. That kiss was nothing like any we'd ever had before. It was slow and gentle. I closed my eyes tightly, afraid that if I opened them, I might ruin the moment.

Matt's lips moved against mine, and then his tongue was inside my mouth. Rather than fighting for dominance, our tongues danced against one another. My heart beat faster and faster and when he finally broke away, I moaned in protest. I opened my eyes to find him smiling down at me. He squeezed my hand again.

"That was nice," I murmured, feeling color rush to my cheeks.

"Yeah, it was."

"You should do it some more."

Matt chuckled and I smiled at the sound. I could live to hear his laugh. I bit down on my lower lip and dropped my gaze. I suddenly felt uncomfortable beneath his eyes.

He must have sensed it because he whispered, "I'm sorry for what I said earlier."

Which part? The part where he said that I wasn't Kevin's mother? Well, he was only telling the truth. I wasn't. I had no right to act like I was. There was nothing for him to be sorry for.

I tried to pull my hand from Matt's, the good feelings of a few moments earlier fading away, but he didn't let go.

"Kayla? Please look at me."

Swallowing the lump that formed in my throat, I did as he asked. Matt looked tired. He'd probably aged that day, which wasn't surprising. His son nearly died, after all.

"I was wrong to say those things," he said.

"It was the truth," I responded.

"It doesn't matter. It didn't need saying. I was being an asshole."

"You were scared and angry."

"That's no fucking excuse and you know it." He reached out and tucked a strand of hair behind my ear, his fingertips gently grazing my cheek. He was still holding my other hand and I felt like my whole body was concentrating on that tiny, comforting feeling. "He loves you, you know."

"I'm not his mom," I whispered.

"That doesn't matter. He's still allowed to love you."

"It feels like I'm betraying your wife's memory."

"*Ex*-wife."

I rolled my eyes.

"Excuse me," Matt said. He pulled his hand from mine. "Did you just roll your eyes at me?"

"Yeah, and? What are you going to do about it?"

The look on Matt's face made my core tighten. I don't know why, but I just got the feeling he wasn't thinking remotely innocent thoughts. His eyes dropped down to my lips and then he met my eyes again.

"Maybe I ought to do something about it."

"Go on, then," I said. My voice came out breathy.

Matt smirked. "Maybe once we get you home."

I gave a frustrated groan and he laughed again. The sound made me feel so much better about everything. "Do you want to see Kevin?"

"Yes, please."

~

Relief washed over me at the sight of the boy. He was in a bit of a state, especially with his leg strung up like it was, but he was okay. His skin no longer had that sickly green hue to it and that was all the comfort that I needed.

"Oh, Matt," I whispered.

"Yeah," he said. He squeezed my hand. "He's okay."

Mike was sitting in the armchair beside Kevin's bed. I couldn't help but think that Kevin wouldn't be here if it weren't for Mike, either. I was so lucky that he was around. I wasn't sure *why* he was, but that was irrelevant on the larger scale of things.

Surprising all three of us, I went over to Mike and I

hugged him. When I pulled away, both men were looking at me with wide eyes. How could I tell either of them how grateful I felt to Mike for being there? There was no doubt in my mind that without him, Kevin would not be lying in bed. I couldn't say any of that though. Instead, I shrugged my shoulders and went back over to Matt. His hand found mine immediately and I noticed Mike look down between us with raised eyebrows. He didn't say anything.

It wasn't long after we got there that Kevin woke up. He was groggy. "Dad?"

"Hey, kiddo," Matt said. He went over to Kevin and I took a seat in the second armchair. "How are you feeling?"

"Weird," Kevin said. He clicked his tongue like it felt weird in his mouth. I guessed that he was probably on a lot of pain meds. They were enough to slur his speech slightly. "Whoa!"

My eyes followed Kevin's as he spotted his leg strung up in the air. "Yeah, you did a number on yourself."

He looked over me, his cheeks reddening in chagrin. "I'm sorry."

"Oh, Kevin, it wasn't your fault."

"Yes, it was. I was the one who asked if we could ride the horses bareback. It wouldn't have happened if I had a saddle."

Both Matt and Mike turned their heads toward me. I felt my heart swell for that little kid. I stood up and walked toward him. I pressed a gentle kiss to his forehead. I didn't have any words to say to him at that point. I just sat on the side of his bed, holding onto his arm gently.

Matt stood close behind me, close enough for me to feel his head. When he spoke, it was low enough that only I could hear it. "I understand why you said yes."

I turned my head to face him. "How could I say no?"

Only Matt heard me and he nodded. I knew he understood.

THIRTY-SIX

MATT

"Dad! I'm like a robot!"

Leave it to a kid to make light of a very serious situation. It was one of the things that made kids great. Kevin was allowed to leave the hospital the following morning, his leg in a cast and crutches beneath his arms. Grams was happy that she wouldn't need to go back to the hospital. It wasn't her favorite place after Gramps passed away.

Kevin had a titanium rod inserted into his leg, a plate against the bone, and he was going to have to walk with a pair of crutches for a few weeks. If there were no complications, he would be able to get it removed at a later stage. Kevin didn't know what the plate in his leg meant. When I told him that he would not be stuck with it forever, he looked upset. He was only too happy to be part-robot, part-cyborg, part-metal man. I had to smile.

As soon as we got home, Kayla ran down the stairs. She met us at the door and swooped in to give Kevin a hug. She was wearing a frilly skirt that was cut halfway up her thighs, giving me an ample view of her legs, and I couldn't help but look. She was feeling a lot better, though the good Doctor

Joe recommended we have some steak for the next few days to get her iron levels back up.

When she kissed his cheek, my son blushed. "Kayla!"

Kayla winked at him but that only embarrassed him further.

"I'm going to find Grams," he grumbled suddenly, trotting out of the room with his crutches. I watched him to make sure that he didn't need my assistance.

Both Kayla and I chuckled. As soon as Kevin was out of sight, my hands found her waist. I pulled her petite body against mine and leaned forward to kiss her. Kayla wrapped her arms around my shoulders, kissing me back. The front door was still open behind me but I didn't care if anyone saw. The only person we were worried about was Kevin.

It hadn't been long since his mom passed away. He knew that I hadn't been married to his mom for quite some time, but we were unsure of how he would respond to Kayla and me as a couple. Besides, I wasn't even sure what was going on between us. The previous evening, when we got home from the hospital, we spent the night together.

No, nothing happened. We simply shared a bed. It wasn't until the morning that something happened between us.

∼

Neither of us had wanted to leave the hospital but they had visiting hours and rules to adhere to. Kevin needed sleep, as the doctor said. So, reluctantly, the three of us left. The drive home was a quiet one, but I felt like Kayla's glances said a million things even if she didn't.

I was pretty sure that Mikey noticed something was going on. He didn't say anything though. I figured he was still pretty exhausted, anyway. Kayla and I had interrupted his little nap when we walked into Kevin's ward. A few times I met his eyes in the rearview mirror but he turned to stare out of the window. I think he knew that I knew... about the drugs.

When we got home, we all went our separate ways. Mikey went upstairs to his very unused room, I went to mine, and I heard the water turn on as Kayla climbed into the shower a few minutes later. Despite how tired I'd been, I couldn't fall asleep as quickly as I would have liked. I was lying in bed, twisting and turning, when I remembered the email I was supposed to view.

I never got the chance to check on that email. There was a knock on my door. When I opened it, Kayla was standing in front of me. Her skin had a slightly pink tone from the heat of her shower, her hair was slightly wet, and she was wearing nothing but a white t-shirt, barely covering her ass, and a pair of pale blue panties. She looked equally adorable and sexy at the same time. My cock twitched in response.

"Can I come in?" she asked.

Well, what was I supposed to say? No?

We ended up lying in bed together, her body pressed up against mine. I was hard as all hell but it didn't seem like Kayla was there to do anything about it, so I simply held her body against mine. I wasn't the cuddling type, but Kayla brought out a nurturing side in me. After the day she had, I figured she could use a little nurturing anyway. It didn't hurt that her small, warm body felt amazing pressed against mine. The vanilla scent of her hair was directly under my nose and as we lay there, I felt myself drifting off to sleep. Her presence seemed to act as a lullaby all its own. My restlessness vanished.

That morning was another story entirely. I woke up to find Kayla's ass pressed against my crotch and I had the most glorious of morning glories. She seemed to push back against me on purpose, but she was still asleep. That didn't make it feel any less amazing.

I'd woken her with soft kisses on the back of her shoulder. She was slow to wake but when she did, it was with an appreciative moan. I took that as encouragement and moved to kiss her neck. Kayla sighed in pleasure and I knew she was fully awake. She turned and grinned at me.

"Morning," she whispered.

"Hey, gorgeous."

"It seems like someone is happy to see me this morning." She bit down on her lower lip and looked me up and down.

I was topless, as I had been when she knocked on my door the previous evening. I was wearing boxers and there was no way of hiding the tent in them. The way she bit her lower lip drove me insane. Every time she did that – every single time – I wanted to bite it. At that moment, I didn't feel like resisting my urges. I growled and pressed my lips against hers. I took her lower lip between my teeth and tugged gently until she gave a cute little whimper before I kissed her. She kissed me back, her tongue instantly slipping between my lips and her hands moving to the back of my head. I felt her thighs open up.

I moved between them, pressing against her perfect center, and I felt her hips buck up against me. God, she was so welcoming. I groaned against her mouth, my hand sliding underneath the cotton tee that she wore. I felt goosebumps rise where I touched her. She was delectably responsive. Her skin was incredibly smooth and my hand found one of her soft breasts. I squeezed the mound softly and she moaned as she broke away from my mouth. She was breathless and I looked down at her flushed face as I manipulated her nipple, tugging lightly on the tiny bud.

Kayla gave a gentle whimper and I removed my hand, only to grab the hem of her shirt. She raised her arms so that I could remove it and I felt my cock twitch once more at the sight of her. Her breasts were firm and perky, heaving with each breath she took. I leaned in and took the same nipple I'd been playing with into my mouth, swirling my tongue around it. Her hips bucked and I felt her pussy press against the bulge at the front of my pants.

"Fuuuck," she hissed. "Matt."

"Yes, Kayla?"

"Move."

I raised my eyebrows. "Move?"

"Yes. Get off of me."

Kayla didn't wait for me to move. She pushed me away from her and I lay on my back, staring at her. I was utterly perplexed. That went away, replaced with a surge of overwhelming desire, as she stepped off of the bed, tugged her panties down over the soft curve of her hips and dropped them on the floor beside the bed. I tilted my head to see the soft curve of her ass. All those Pilates classes in college had paid off – probably the horse-riding too – because she had the nicest butt I'd ever had the pleasure of looking at.

She saw me looking and gave me a grin as she wiggled her behind. I took a deep breath as her cheeks bounced. I reached for her, wanting to touch it, but she stopped me.

"No. No, no."

I sighed. "Okay. I'll bite," and I had to admit, I truly wanted to. "What are you up to?"

Rather than answer me, Kayla climbed back onto the bed. I stayed dead still as she started crawling up toward me, stopping between my legs. She reached upward and tugged the waistband of my boxers down, freeing my cock. I raised my ass off the bed for her and soon, I was completely naked, my dick standing at full attention. There was a drop of precum on the pink mushroom head and, to my shock, Kayla leaned forward and dragged her tongue across the head, licking the precum off of it.

"Oh, fuck," I moaned.

Kayla met my eyes as she took me into her mouth. Her mouth was hot and wet and when she sucked her cheeks in, I gasped. It felt amazing. I wanted to throw my head back and close my eyes, but I didn't want to break my gaze from the sight of Kayla going down on me. It was the hottest thing I'd ever seen, especially since she was completely naked. Besides, she was looking directly into my eyes and I got lost in the green-eyed innocence on her face. She was anything but innocent. She was a naughty little minx.

She started to bob her head up and down, her tongue flicking against the underside of my shaft and causing me to buck upward further into her mouth. She didn't even gag when the head touched the back of her throat. It was my turn to bite down on my lower lip. I knew that I wasn't going to last long in her mouth and when she cupped my balls in her hand, I had to hold back a cry of pleasure.

They tightened in response and I could swear she smiled around my dick in her mouth. As if she knew that I was struggling, Kayla suddenly increased her efforts. She started bobbing her head faster and I found my hands curled in her soft hair. I bucked up into her mouth, unable to control myself, but she didn't seem to mind. In fact, I saw her other hand move between her legs. Her moans were muffled by my length but they sent the most delicious vibrations through me.

"Kayla," I gasped. "Fuck, you're so hot."

My breathing became erratic as I felt my balls tighten once more, the only warning I got before I started to shoot my load into her mouth. Kayla didn't pull back. She pushed her head down as far as she could, her nose pressed against my lower abdomen, and I could feel her throat pulsing against the tip as she swallowed. That time, I did throw my head back, shutting my eyes and groaning as I reached my climax.

Kayla didn't miss a single drop, swallowing almost constantly. The feeling of her throat tightening around my cock as she swallowed drove me mad and eventually, I found myself tugging on the beautiful dark curls to pull her head off of my cock. I could feel my dick pulsating with the sensitivity. Everything was tingling and I felt like my balls were exhausted.

The little minx peeking up at me had a grin on her face, looking for all the world like the cat that got the cream. Literally. She even went so far as to lick her lips.

I gave a chuckle at the sight of her, breathless and spent. "God, what am I going to do with you?"

"Hopefully a lot," she said softly.

The question surprised me and, despite the fact that I'd only just orgasmed, I could feel my dick beginning to stir once again. I took a deep breath. "Keep speaking like that and I just might."

I was hoping that Kayla might continue the banter but instead, she climbed out of bed. I watched her butt bounce slightly as she walked over to the closet. "As much as I would *love* that, I think you need to get downstairs and make some pancakes before your grandmother hunts me down for keeping you away."

"What are you doing?" I asked, furrowing my brow as she dug around in my closet.

"Well, I can't exactly go out in nothing but my panties, can I?"

"I mean... You're wearing a t-shirt too."

She looked back at me, giving an exaggerated roll of her eyes. "Uh-huh. And we're just going to ignore this?"

To emphasize what she was talking about, she wiggled her behind at me. The t-shirt barely covered her as it was but when she wiggled it, the hem brushed her pale skin until the waistband and a portion of her back was revealed to me. I felt my cock growing harder. "No, that's pretty difficult to ignore, actually."

Kayla managed to find a pair of old pajama pants and pulled them up her beautiful legs, concealing them from my view. I tried not to let the disappointment show on my face but when she walked back to the bed to plant a kiss on my lips, I grabbed her behind and pulled her onto my lap. The pajamas were extremely loose on her nubile body and my hands slipped into the waistband easily. I enjoyed the way that she squirmed in my lap, her crotch pressing down on my cock. It was as my fingers made their way into Kayla's panties that we heard a knock on the door.

The beautiful woman in my lap broke away from my lips and we both froze, staring at one another with wide eyes.

"Who is it?" I asked.

"Matthew?" Grams voice sounded from outside the door.

"Oh, fuck," I whispered.

Kayla reacted a lot quicker than I did, jumping off of my lap and diving – literally – over the bed and onto the other side of the bed. I flinched at the sound of her body tumbling onto the wood but Grams called for me once again and I was forced to divert my attention. I hopped out of bed and grabbed the nearest pair of jeans, tugging them on before I opened the bedroom door.

"Hey, Grams," I said, trying not to let on that I was breathless from hopping around to get into my pants. "What can I do for you?"

"I was wondering when we would be able to go fetch Kevin? I'd like to come with you for the drive. Joe said he should be ready to check out today," Grams said, glancing behind me with a furrowed brow.

It was obvious that my grandmother was confused, but she didn't seem to realize Kayla was in my room. Then again, I may have been optimistic. I was almost certain I could see that twinkle in my grandmother's eyes – the suspicious one that told me she knew way more than she was letting on. I wouldn't have been surprised if that was the case. I looked over my shoulder just to make sure that there was no sign of Kayla anywhere. There wasn't.

"Okay, why don't you go on and I'll get ready? Are we going to have breakfast first?"

"Sure," Grams said. She looked as though she had something more to say but then must have thought better of it. "I'll see you downstairs. Breakfast is ready and waiting."

And off she went, back down the hall. Grams waited until she was standing at the top of the staircase before glancing back over her shoulder. "Say, you haven't seen Kayla anywhere, have you?"

"No," I said in what I hoped was a nonchalant tone of voice. "Why do you ask?"

The corners of Grams's mouth twitched the slightest bit upward. "Oh, I was just asking. Maybe she was just sleeping too deeply to hear me knocking on her door this morning."

If Grams stuck around, she would have noticed that for the first time in a very long time, my cheeks flushed. But she didn't stick around. She turned and continued walking down the stairs. I almost forgot about Kayla until she reappeared at my side.

"Well," she whispered. "That was different."

"That was us nearly getting busted, you mean," I said.

I turned to look at her and any sign of worry faded away when I noticed her hair was standing up in every direction. I remembered the way she'd dived over the bed and suddenly burst into a fit of laughter. Kayla stared at me in shock before she started hushing me. I'd only just managed to rein myself in when we heard Grams calling me.

"Time to go eat breakfast," I said with a shrug.

I resisted the urge to lean in and kiss Kayla. We hadn't spoken about what was going on between us and I didn't want to seem presumptuous. Grams nearly caught us, although that was better than Kevin catching us. I didn't know how the kid would take it.

I almost wanted to tell Kayla I owed her one – for the fact that she'd swallowed my load and I didn't even get a chance to get her off. I didn't say anything though. Still, as I took the stairs two at a time, I couldn't help but picture the day I'd have her writhing beneath me again. I wanted to make Kayla scream. It took a lot to clear my head of those thoughts before I saw Grams.

I predict she sees right through me.

THIRTY-SEVEN
KAYLA

As soon as Matt was gone, I went back to my own room, hoping no one was around to see me walking around in his pajama bottoms. They were so big that I had to hold the waistband up for fear that they would slide off of my slender hips. The memories of the way his hands slid beneath the waistband, the way he felt my ass up, made my center throb.

Once I was changed into my own clothes, I checked my phone.

"What the hell?" I murmured, scrolling through the call log.

There were over a dozen missed calls from a number in Georgia, but no messages. Someone had been trying to get a hold of me since we got back from the hospital the previous evening. I could already hear the sound of Matt's old pickup engine starting up and walked over to the window to watch as he and Myra pulled out of the driveway.

I hit redial and listened to the phone ring until a disembodied voice told me that I'd reached voicemail. With a sigh, I redialed the number. I could only think of one reason why anyone would want to contact me so badly and my heart raced faster with each sound of the dial tone.

"Hello, this is Sasha."

"Mrs. Williams?" I asked, surprised to hear her familiar twang.

"Kayla? Kayla Walker? Is that you?"

"Yes, it's me. I saw that you were trying to contact me. Is something the matter?"

"Dear, are you still looking?"

"I am," I breathed into the line, clutching the phone so tightly that my knuckles turned white. "Have you found anything?"

"I have. I think I might know where he was adopted."

"Oh, my God," I murmured.

Wherever she was, Sasha gave a gentle chuckle. I was struck with the thought that she *sounded* like a mother. "I thought that might be your reaction. Do you have a pen and paper?"

"Hold on." I scrambled off of the bed to grab the nearest piece of paper from the nightstand. It was in a pile of the documents I'd been going through for Matt. With a pen in my hand and something to press on, I sat back down. "Okay, I'm ready."

"It was a small town in Litchfield Hills, Connecticut."

"Wait, what? Are you sure?"

"Yes, dear," Sasha said. "Why? Are you familiar with it?"

"It's... It's where I gave him up."

"Oh, Kayla," Sasha murmured. I could hear the sadness in her voice even if I couldn't see her. "It seems as though he somehow found his way back home."

"Yeah, that makes two of us. I'm in Cornwall right now. Is the town Cornwall?"

"No, I'm afraid not. It's in Norwich."

"Do you have any contact details for me?"

"I do, indeed."

As Sasha spoke, I started writing down everything she said. It wasn't until after she was all done feeding me the details that I realized I'd just written along the back of Kevin's birth certificate. At least it was only a copy.

"Thank you so much for looking into all this for me, Sasha. You have no idea how much it means."

"Trust me, honey," Sasha murmured. "I know exactly how much it means."

She couldn't see me, but a small smile came to my face. My eyes watered slightly. "Thank you again."

"Go find your boy, love."

The call ended.

THIRTY-EIGHT

MATT

Unfortunately, I didn't get to see Kayla much more after I got back.

"You look like you're going somewhere," I said.

Kayla shrugged, smiling demurely up at me. "I mean, I *am*... if you'll let me borrow your pickup."

I raised my eyebrows. "Where are you headed? Can I drive you?"

To my surprise, Kayla shook her head. I took a step back and all of a sudden it became quite evident to me that Kayla was nervous about something, but I didn't know what. The longer I stared at her, the more stressed she appeared.

"Is everything all right?" I finally asked.

"Well, if everything goes well today, things might be better than ever."

Her stressed expression turned into one of wide-eyed hope and I had to smile at her. I pulled my keys out of my pocket and handed them over. "Okay. Here you go."

"Oh, thank you!" Kayla smiled brightly at me, looking entirely too pretty for her own good.

She wrapped her arms around my shoulders, hugging me tightly, and I pulled her nearer. She smelled amazing.

"No problem, Kay," I said, testing a nickname I hadn't used since we were in college. When she pulled back, she was smiling. She tucked her hair behind her ear. "Let me know when you get to where you're going?"

"I will!"

Before I could tell her to drive safely, Kayla was racing past me and out of the front door. She climbed into the driver's seat of my pickup and gave me one last wave before she started it up. I wanted to give her a hundred and one warnings about the truck and how she drove but, coming from the country, I figured she knew the drill all too well. I watched until the pickup's tailgate was out of sight before I headed back into the house.

~

The day was spent with Mikey and Kevin. My son was finally excited to join me on the farm. If nothing else, it seemed like his horse ride with Kayla had given him a newfound love for nature. I thought he might never want to ride a horse again, but I was proven wrong. He seemed like he couldn't wait to get back on the saddle. I'd never been particularly fond of horse-riding – not the way Kayla was – but it made me smile to think that my son had found something he loved about the country.

Needless to say, the day was charged with optimism. I was beginning to think things could finally work out for us. Once we won the case against James, my son could stay on the ranch and we could work on the family business together. I thought that if my grandfather was still around, he would have been proud to see us. It was the first time since I'd gotten back that Mikey had taken a day off. He told me that he wanted to be around the animals.

Though he wanted to, Kevin couldn't help with much in terms of working on the land. Instead, he sat back on one of the milk buckets Mikey and I carried out for him to use as a makeshift seat. We were working on the fences – just me and my brother. I could have asked a few of the ranch hands to help us out, but I didn't want to do that. The only real problem was that I couldn't talk to my brother without arousing suspicion from Kevin. I was pretty sure no one in the family wanted him to know about Mikey's past, at least not until he was older. We worked mostly in silence until my kid started getting cheeky.

"You missed a spot," Kevin said. Both Mikey and I turned our heads in his direction. Kevin was grinning at us.

"Where's the spot, kiddo?" Mikey asked, arching his brow.

"Over there." Kevin pointed at a spot on the fence.

We looked over to see that he was right. We had completely skipped over a part of the fence where the wooden slat was warped to the point where it would probably split by the time the season was up.

"Nice spot, kiddo," Mike said.

His uncle went over to apply the new slat. We went like that for a good while, until the sun was so high in the sky that Mikey and I were sweaty and tired. From afar, it didn't seem like we'd made much progress, but that was okay. It was a massive perimeter and we were only two men. As therapeutic as I found working on the fences to be, I decided I would ask the ranch hands to join us next time. It was around the time that Mikey and I collapsed on the ground next to one another that Grams walked out of the front door of the house, calling Kevin's name.

"That's your cue, little man," Mike said.

Kevin gave a groan of protest.

"Hey," I said sternly. "Go see what Grams wants."

"*Okayyy* okay," he said.

He put his hands up in mock surrender before he grabbed hold of one of the crutches. I was watching him to make sure that he didn't need any help but I didn't go anywhere near him. I knew all too well what it felt like to have everyone around you make you feel like you needed help, no matter how small the issue was. I was pretty sure everyone who had ever joined the military knew what that was like. Feeling helpless was bad enough without everyone around you think like you needed help.

"I'll see you guys later," Kevin said when he managed to gain his balance. With a crutch beneath each pit, he started making his way back to the house. I looked back to see Grams standing on the porch.

After he was gone, it seemed quieter than before. Mikey and I were staring at the clouds like two kids who tried to make shapes out of them. As it was, I couldn't think of anything. They just looked like blobs; ordinary boring blobs in a blue sky. We weren't even in a room but it felt like an elephant was looming over the top of our heads, something I felt rather ironic all things considered. I wasn't the one on drugs.

"When did you start taking again?" I blurted out finally. I couldn't bring myself to look at him but I could see him turn his head to face me out of the corner of my eye.

"I figured you knew," Mikey finally said, quietly. "I had only just taken some when I saw Kayla and Kevin."

"You were... Jesus, Mike," I muttered. "You'd *just* gotten high? I thought that you were already coming down from it by the time I got there."

"Nothing sobers you up like seeing your nephew bleeding out, man."

My heart skipped a beat at that. I could only blink up at the sky in shock. What exactly was I supposed to say to him?

"Look," Mikey said with a sigh, cutting off anything I might have said. "I know I fucked up, Matt. I know. But I'm not going to do it again."

"How long has it been? Don't even try to tell me that was the first time. I've suspected you ever since I got back."

"Of course, you have."

"Are you going to answer?"

"I think I need a second to process all of this."

He had to process this? My brother and I had never had a conversation like this one before. I felt like I was way out of my depth. "I don't understand why you do it, bro..."

"Of course, you don't. And unless you've done it before, you wouldn't."

"But I've been through the shit you've been through too. It never made me want to stick a fucking needle in my arm," I snapped.

My brother laughed, but it was nothing like his usual laugh. It was devoid of humor and full of mirth. "Oh, really? Are we just going to forget about the first sixteen years of my life? You weren't there when I went through all of those."

His words felt like a kick to the gut. He was right of course. I wasn't there. Hell, I don't think I had ever even asked anyone what happened to him. He just showed up and I went with it, once I'd gotten past the initial disgust of him being there. Suddenly, I felt disappointed in myself for never showing an interest in where Mikey came from. What had happened to him? Why did my grandparents take him in? When did he start taking drugs?

"Okay," I said slowly. "You're right. I don't know. I've never asked."

"Yeah," he said in a tone that sounded very much like it was meant to end the conversation.

"I'm asking now. What happened? Why do... *did*... you do it?"

"Do we have to get into this right now?"

"Why don't you want to?"

"You know, you get everything. And I get it. I'm not their real grandson, but I never ever felt like I was anything less until Gramps died."

"You aren't any less, Mikey," I whispered. "Our grandparents have always loved you. I love you. Gramps definitely did not love you any less than I did."

"How do you know that? If that were true, why did you get the ranch instead of me? Why didn't he leave it to both of us?"

I sat up on the grass, staring at him. Mikey didn't move. He continued to stare up at the sky as if I wasn't even there. In fact, I started to wonder if I *was* there to him. I was speechless as all the dots started to connect. I couldn't deny I'd considered it a possibility that Gramps dying was what set Mikey off, but this information pretty much confirmed my suspicions. I opened and closed my mouth but I couldn't find the words I wanted to say. Nothing sounded right.

"Don't worry about it, Matt. Really. Like I said, I won't do it again."

"Do you want to be a doctor?" I suddenly asked.

At this, Mikey finally looked at me. He was obviously confused by the question. "What?"

"You're good at it. You love medicine. You helped Kevin."

"Where is this coming from?" Mikey asked, sitting up on the grass too.

"I was just thinking about what Joe said at the hospital. He said you would make a good doctor and I'm inclined to agree with him."

Mikey raised his eyebrows. "Yeah, I guess being a doctor would have been a pretty cool career path to follow."

"So why didn't you do it?"

"I wanted to be around animals. Nothing else occurred to me. The animals saved me so it only seemed right to save them too."

In spite of myself, I smiled at that. It was such an unexpectedly sweet thing for him to say. "You know I love you, right, Mike?"

"Not when you call me Mike, I don't."

I chuckled, but it wasn't long before the haunting feeling returned and I had to ask him the serious question. "Are you sure you're never going to do it again?"

"Yeah," he said softly. He was looking down at the grass, where his hands were ripping blades of grass out of the soil absent-mindedly. "This isn't exactly a split-second decision. I wasn't using like I used to. Trust me; I wouldn't be able to sit here in front of you if I was."

"What does that mean?"

"Do you remember when you met me? I'm not that bad, am I?"

"Yeah," I murmured slowly. "I had been wondering about that."

"I'm not going to go into the details of being an addict, Matt. I just want you to know that the sight of Kevin... Well, it nearly killed me. I was so scared about what might have happened if I was too high to help him. I'm never going to put myself or anyone else in that position again."

"So, you're not interested in being a doctor then," I said with a smirk.

"Even if I did, it's a bit late for me to try and win a scholarship now."

"It's never too late to go to school, though."

"Maybe one day," Mikey finally admitted, caving in.

I decided to leave him alone after that. It was obvious he didn't have much more to say. Besides, Mikey had never been particularly fond of talking. I think that was one of the reasons he preferred animals; so he didn't have to talk to anyone. All animals could do was make noises at you.

Before long, we heard Grams calling us into the house too. It turned out she'd called Kevin to help her out with food. I gave the fence a longing look. We still had to stain the wood.

THIRTY-NINE

KAYLA

Norwich, known as the Rose of New England, was nearly two hours from Cornwall. Despite the thoughts going through my mind, the drive was a peaceful one. I was surrounded by greenery on either side. I didn't know how many farms were in Connecticut, but I knew there were a lot. Even so, Norwich was a totally different world compared to the one I grew up in. Cornwall's population was close to two thousand lovely beings who pretty much all knew one another's names whereas Norwich had a whopping forty thousand and something.

Just thinking about the difference in size made me anxious.

If it weren't for GPS, I wasn't sure I would have been able to find the Adoption Services building. Everything in Cornwall was basically within walking distance. When I pulled up to the building, it was outside the hustle and bustle of the town. The building was all brick and there was no one around as I walked up to the stairs toward its intimidating front doors. The road was quiet too.

I had to take a deep breath before I headed in. It seemed

like I was about to cross the threshold from one life into another. I'd been searching for my son for several years and now that it seemed I might be about to find him, I was beginning to get nervous. I'd considered what it might mean, but it wasn't until I was standing just outside those doors, my hand hovering over the handle that I thought about what it might *not* mean.

In my mind, I had replayed the idea of meeting my son over and over again. I thought about what it might be like to get to know the people who raised him. Would he like me? Would I be able to spend time with him? Would his parents want me to be a part of their lives once I told them the truth about why I'd given him up?

I didn't know the answer to any of these questions. All I knew was that I had never considered the answers to them. What if he didn't like me? What if his parents didn't want me around? What if they wanted to send me far away and I would never come knocking on their door ever again?

Finally, it wasn't me who had to open the door. The handle was pushed down, pulled out of my grasp before I had the chance, and someone from inside pulled the door open. I jumped backward, nearly stumbling in my high heels, and the person walked out.

"Oh, I'm sorry!" the woman cried out.

My heart raced as I took her in. She was slim, tall, and dressed in a grey pantsuit. It was paired with a pair of sandals that revealed her cracked heels. I realized she worked there. She was taking a smoke break, cigarette in hand. As I stared at her, her head tilted to the side and she looked worried.

"Are you okay, sweetie?" she asked me.

Her voice was raspy and the look on her face revealed she was a lot older than I initially thought. Her lips were cracked from what I presumed was the smoke, there were one or two streaks of grey in her hair, and the corners of her eyes revealed crow's feet. Her skin was dark, like chocolate, and she had long red nails. I took all of this in without saying anything. I was so silent that she had to ask me if I was okay a second time.

"Oh," I said. "Uh, well—"

"Do you smoke?" she asked.

I shook my head.

"Of course not," she said with a laugh. "Just look at your skin. Why don't you hang out with me for a little while, honey? We can get rid of those pesky nerves of ours together."

"Okay," I said, moving away from the door.

The lady sat on the steps of the building. I went to sit beside her. There was something about her that seemed very welcoming. She had a kind smile, reminding me of my mother. She always had a way of making people feel comfortable.

"So, what brings you here, doll? Are you looking to adopt?"

The inside of my mouth was dry and moving my tongue felt uncomfortable but I forced myself to say, "No."

The woman lit her cigarette and took the longest drag, blowing it out in the opposite direction before she looked back at me. "Are you sure you're okay?"

I gave a nervous titter. "I don't think I said that I was okay at all, to be fair."

"Oh, right! No, you didn't." She had a cockney accent and she was smoking her cigarette way too fast. Soon, her smile faded and her voice grew softer when she spoke to me. "So, if you can't talk to me out here, how do you think you're going to be able to talk to anyone in there?"

The words hit me like a pile of bricks – as though the building behind us fell apart. I licked my lips. "That's a very fair point and I hadn't considered it before now."

"What are those papers you have there?"

I looked down at my hands. There was a folder in them, filled with all the relevant information I had on the boy I'd given birth to. I bit down on my lower lip and pulled it onto my lap, opening it up. The wind nearly blew the top paper out of the folder and my fingers grabbed it out of the air just before I had to run out onto the road after it. It was the paper I'd written the details on. It wasn't until I nearly lost it to the wind that I realized what it was.

Kevin's birth certificate.

Thankfully, it wasn't the original. It was just a necessary copy that I needed for the case. I had to do a double-take as I stared down at the other side of the document though; the one with Kevin's details. Just to make sure I wasn't seeing things, I ruffled through the other pages in the folder. I could feel the woman from the Adoption Services staring at me but at that point, I didn't care. I was preoccupied with something else.

"Holy shit," I finally breathed when I found what I was looking for. "This has to be a coincidence."

"What is it?" the woman asked me.

Glancing over at her, I noticed that she'd finished her cigarette and was inspecting my folder and over my shoulder rather intently. I wasn't sure if she could see what I could but I stood up from the stairs anyway.

"Have you finished smoking? Are you still on break?"

The woman looked up at me, raising a pair of perfectly shaped eyebrows before she stood up. "I am ready to go inside when you are, darlin'."

"Great," I said with a smile. "Let's go."

~

We walked into an entrance hall that spoke of age in the marble floors and the wooden stalls, similar to those at banks and post offices. Behind them sat two receptionists, answering calls and filling out forms. There was no one in the waiting room and I didn't get a chance to see much more than a collection of old leather chairs, the cover chipping off of the upholstery, and a wooden coffee table stacked with outdated magazines before she was leading me down a hallway to the left and into an office.

The office was crowded and small. There was a dusty ceiling fan that looked older than I was and a small desk in the center of it, with two mismatched office chairs on either side. There were several filing cabinets behind her and many of them were open, papers and names sticking haphazardly out of them.

"Please, have a seat," she said, gesturing to the scratchy chair across from hers. She smoothed the wrinkles in her suit as she sat down. "I'm sorry about the mess. I haven't had a chance to clean yet. I only recently moved into this office."

"Oh. Where were you before?" I asked, pulling my seat out and sitting.

"I recently got promoted. I was working in a different branch." The woman smiled at me. The cigarettes had yellowed her teeth slightly. "So, what can I do for you?"

"I'm honestly not even sure," I admitted.

"How about we start with the basics? My name is Genevieve." She stuck her hand out across the table.

"That seems doable," I said with a smile. I reached out and shook her hand. "I'm Kayla."

"There now. That feels better, doesn't it? We aren't total strangers anymore."

I couldn't help but smile at her. She was doing the thing where she made me feel welcome again. Rather than speak, I decided to let the papers do the talking for me. I had to push myself to get into my lawyer's state of mind. Lawyers didn't need to do a lot of talking because their evidence did it for them. At that moment, my documents were my evidence.

Even though I'd practically memorized every detail on the page while we were sitting on the steps outside the building, I still gave Kevin's birth certificate a cursory glance. I still couldn't believe what I was seeing. It didn't seem possible to me.

"Okay," I said once I had laid all the papers out for Genevieve. I took a deep breath, knowing I was going to need it for everything I was about to say out loud. "I'm looking for my son. I gave him up when I was a teenager. I've never stopped looking for him."

Genevieve didn't say anything for so long that I had to look up at her because it just didn't feel like her. I know I had only met the woman a few moments before but the idea of her being a quiet person had never struck me. And I was a pretty good judge of character.

I licked my lips. "Are you going to say anything?"

"I was trying to figure out *what* to say, to be honest with you. I didn't expect this. We don't usually get cases like this."

"You don't? I thought that you guys would have people looking for their kids all the time."

"They don't usually come to us directly."

"Oh," I said. "Well, I guess that makes sense."

"You know that we aren't allowed to give out details, right?"

"Look... I know I'm no one to you. I'm just another

woman who came back for a kid that she gave up. But I need you to know that isn't all I am. I never wanted to give him up."

Genevieve clasped her hands together. "Why did you give him up then?"

"Because I couldn't afford to keep him," I said. "I was a teenager and I was alone. I didn't have anyone. And it wasn't like I could have gotten a job and worked on it either. I was in debt at the age of sixteen. My parents died and I was left with it."

As I spoke, I could hear and feel my own voice growing thick with emotion. I was able to hold back the tears. I thought about it every damn day of my life. I guessed after a while, I started getting used to it. Still, something about saying it out loud always got to me. Genevieve reached out and grabbed a tissue from a box I had not even noticed before, handing it to me.

"Thank you," I said, wiping my eyes gingerly.

"Sixteen is a very young age to fall pregnant, honey."

I snorted. I couldn't help it. "I'm a lawyer. Trust me; I know it is. And I know that it gets worse than that."

She didn't seem to want to push any more than that, nodding kindly. "Okay, well, where would you like to get started? I see you have quite a bit of documentation for us to sort through here. Fill me in."

"I didn't give him up here. I had him in Cornwall."

Genevieve pulled out a notebook and wrote that down. "That's not far from here, is it?"

"No, it's part of the state. Litchfield County. It's about two hours from here."

"Interesting. I don't suppose you know how he ended up here?"

"I actually might. He was in the system for the first four

or five years of his life, moving from foster home to foster home."

She wrote that down too. "But he isn't anymore? Do you know what his name is?"

My eyes flitted down to the birth certificate in front of me. "I didn't think I did. But now I might and I want to make sure that it is him before I start asking questions."

"What do you mean, Kayla?"

"Well," I started. "It's a long story."

FORTY

MATT

Kayla didn't return home that evening. She didn't answer any of my calls throughout the day, either. When she asked me if she could borrow the pickup truck, I assumed that she was probably going to go as far as the town or perhaps the next town over at the furthest. I was beginning to worry about her by the time dinner rolled around and she still hadn't returned. The only reason I'd put her out of my mind before was because I didn't feel like I had any right to be asking where she could be – other than the fact that she was driving my pickup truck, that was.

"Where's Kayla?" Grams asked as we sat down at the dinner table.

"I have no idea," I admitted.

All eyes turned toward me. Even Kevin looked at me with wide eyes.

"Is she all right?" Grams asked carefully.

"I'm sure she's fine. Wherever she is, she is too busy to answer her phone. I'm sure she will call when she has a moment."

I started slicing into my steak and after a moment, my

family joined me. I wasn't sure any of them believed me and the air crackled with a sense of unease, but I needed to try to convince myself that was the case too. If I didn't, I would have lost my mind with worry. The truth was I couldn't handle Kayla being away for so long and the following day, we had a meeting with James and his lawyers.

The arrangement had been made at the last minute. I got a text from my assistant, almost immediately followed by none other than James himself, and forwarded everything to Kayla. The fact that she had sent her confirmation to attend the meeting was possibly the only reason why I was able to stomach dinner. If she was able to respond to an email in mere seconds, things had to be all right. Right?

After dinner, Grams and I went to the kitchen to clean up. It was Mikey's turn to help Grams but Kevin had asked his uncle if he wanted to watch a movie and no one was willing to say no to Kevin at the moment. We were certain that Kevin had no idea how serious his incident had been. I was sure he knew that he could have died but I don't think he understood how serious that was. He was just happy to have a metal rod in his leg. It was quite the story to be able to tell. And I was convinced that he was going to keep the cast – already filled with several signatures, including my own – for the rest of his life.

Then again, I didn't have the casts I'd worn when I broke both arms. Hell, I didn't even have the shirt I'd worn on the last day of high school. It had been a white shirt that ended up so full of words and names that you could barely tell it was initially been white by the time I walked out of those doors as a *free* man. Little did I know that life was about to give me a whooping.

At least the first whoop to hit me was Kayla. I couldn't complain too much.

"So, you don't know where Kayla is?" Grams asked me while she scrubbed plates and I dried them.

"No clue. She asked to borrow my truck and I let her. That is the extent of my knowledge."

"You're very defensive, you know."

"Yeah, but I also know that makes no difference to you."

"Oh? And why is that?"

I grinned at Grams as I took the next mug from her hands. "I already know that you can tell when I'm lying, no matter how defensive I am."

Grams paused to look at me with raised eyebrows – or what was left of them. I was struck again with the realization of how old my grandmother had gotten. "You're damn right I can."

"And, am I lying?"

She rolled her eyes, turning back to the soapy dishwater. "No, ya' smartass. You're not lying."

"Thank you," I said, bending at the waist and giving an exaggerated bow.

"I really like her, Matty. I think she's good for you. And I think she's good for Kevin too."

I already knew my grandmother liked Kayla. It wasn't exactly something she hid, but then it wasn't something anyone else hid either. I was starting to think that it was impossible for people not to like Kayla, not that I blamed them.

"I think you're right, Grams," I said.

What I wanted to say was that I thought I was falling in love with Kayla. Every second spent with her brought me an overwhelming sense of pleasure I never thought I would ever experience again. Not to mention a sense of warmth that started in the center of my chest and spread outward through the rest of my body. As a guy, most people wouldn't expect me to admit that sort of thing but I couldn't help it if it was the truth and that was the case. The only real problem was that I didn't know if she felt the same way I did, or if she was in this for something more casual.

I had to look at things practically. Kayla wasn't going to be staying with us forever. She was only here because she was working on a case and very soon, she would be returning to the city. If things worked out the way I wanted them to, I would not be going back to the city and neither would my son. I already knew that a long-distance relationship wasn't going to work for either of us.

"What are you thinking about so intently?" Grams suddenly asked. We were done with the dishes and I'd just put the last one in the cupboard.

"I was just wondering what will happen when this case is over."

"It's about to start, isn't it?"

"Yeah," I said, clenching my jaw.

My grandmother reached out and gently squeezed my bicep. It was comforting and it distracted me from the direction my thoughts were headed in. I was thinking about James and his overly smug face and how hard I wanted to punch it. I needed to learn to control that side of me. God forbid I attacked my opponent in the courtroom. That would definitely lose me my son.

"You said you have an excellent case, right?" Grams asked me. "Kayla found the loophole?"

"She did, but it might only be a temporary fix. I guess we'll have to see what happens."

"Why does James even want to take Kevin? I've spoken to Kev. It isn't like they're close or anything. Honestly, this whole thing just seems fishy to me. Jenna never seemed like this kind of woman."

I sighed. "Yeah, Jenna didn't seem like a lot of things but I've started to realize that I didn't know her very well at all."

"I'm sorry, Matt," Grams said quietly.

I didn't respond. I didn't know how to.

"I'm gonna head to bed. We have a big day tomorrow so you probably should too."

"Night, Grams."

She surprised me by pulling me in for a hug. I froze for a moment before returning the embrace, pressing a gentle kiss to the top of her grey-haired head. Despite her frailty, my grandmother still gave some of the best hugs around. They were so tight that it felt like she was trying to glue every cracked piece together.

I followed a short while later but before I could head upstairs, I heard Kevin's voice coming from the lounge. The lights were off and I would never have noticed that he and Mikey were still sitting there if he hadn't called me. The light from the television glowed off of their faces and Kevin was covered in a blanket, the cast sticking out from under it.

"Do you want to watch the movie with us?"

Only a few days earlier, I would never have imagined Kevin asking me to join him for a movie. How could I say no? I went to sit next to him on the sofa, delighting in the way his face lit up with a smile.

I half-expected Kayla to call me before I eventually fell asleep but that didn't happen.

FORTY-ONE
KAYLA

Genevieve and I ended up going through the file cabinets in her office, which I learned she had absolutely nothing to do with, to find any details we could. By the time I left, I was pretty sure I knew who my son was. It was such a shock to my system that I found the idea of making the two-hour drive back to Cornwall impossible. Instead, Genevieve gave me directions to the nearest hotel and I checked in.

It felt weird not going back to the ranch house. In the short time since I'd arrived in Cornwall, it felt like home to me. It was not simply the place either – it was the people. I didn't know how I was going to be able to return to my own tiny, lonely apartment in the city. Grams wouldn't be there with a delicious meal at the end of a long day, Kevin wouldn't be there to hug, and I wouldn't be able to climb into bed beside Matt's warm body in the evenings. I didn't want to go home at all.

The following morning was a race.

Marianne's advice came back to me once again, but it was far too late to take heed. I'd been emotionally involved since the beginning. And after what I'd discovered the day before, I was in deeper than I ever expected to be.

"There is no turning back now," I muttered to myself as I started the pickup truck and made my way back toward the place that had become a home away from home.

I'd barely pulled up to the ranch house when Matt walked out. He was dressed in a business suit and it was the first time I'd seen him dressed so formally since the day he interviewed me to be his company's legal representative. My core clenched at the sight of him and a sudden heat overtook my body. I wondered how much fun it would be to peel a suit off of him even as he walked toward the truck. It was cut incredibly finely, outlining and defining each muscle. My eyes traveled as low as his crotch and I wasn't sure whether to be disappointed or relieved that the pants he wore didn't quite outline his rather sizable package. I knew from experience that they still made his butt look nice.

Nothing suited Matt quite like his casual getup did because he just seemed the most natural in it. I could always tell that was the real him. It was a true sign of the cowboy within, the one who'd grown up on this very ranch, but there was something about him in a suit that threw me. He was also fresh shaven and he had hair product in. He was so attractive that for a second, I forgot all about everything else and admired him.

When he climbed into the truck, he brought the delicious scent of cologne with him. I was glad that I'd taken the time to shower at the hotel that morning. I hadn't taken any of my clothes with me because I hadn't expected to spend the evening in Norwich. But as soon as I woke up, I made my way toward the hotel's boutique and picked out the most professional-looking outfit I could find – a button-up white blouse, grouped with a black blazer and a black pencil skirt. Their choice of stockings was too sheer for my tastes. With the same heels I'd worn the day before, I left the boutique feeling like I was walking off the scene of a movie and my rich lover was about to take me to a crowd of businessmen when I was totally unfamiliar with the business world. In some ways, that was true.

"Hi," Matt said as he opened the driver's seat door and I moved.

"Morning," I mumbled. I felt guilty about not returning or even calling Matt and as I stared at him, I knew that I would have to talk to him as soon as all of this was over. As it was, we had to get through this first. "How are you?"

"Where were you last night?" He ignored my question of courtesy completely.

"Look, I don't want to talk about it right now, we have a bigger matter ahead of us, but I promise that I'll explain all in time," I said with a sigh, wanting to convey to him the fact that I was tired. It wasn't a lie, the driving and the constant worry that had built up inside of me was exhausting.

Nothing. Matt stared straight ahead, seemingly seething about the situation.

"Matt," I spoke louder, showing him that I wanted a response.

"Why didn't you answer my calls though?"

"I...just please don't be mad." I rested my head against the window, not wanting to look at him.

Matt started to drive, heading away from the ranch and up the track.

"I'm not mad, I just was worried about you. I didn't know where you were, and you only briefly replied to that email."

I bit my lip. "I know. It looks bad."

"I don't know where I stand with you, I know that's not what we should be focusing on right now, but that's the truth of it."

My eyes flitted over to his stiff body, hands gripping the steering wheel so tightly that his knuckles were turning a strange white color.

"You're right, it's not what we should be focusing on right now," I muttered. The truth was that I had no idea how to reply to him.

"Just remember that I'm not mad at you," he reinforced, and it eased my mind. But only slightly, the looming prospect of the fact that I'd still have to tell him about where I'd been and what I'd found out giving me a headache.

I jumped slightly at the feeling of something brushing against my hand, settling back down upon realizing that it was Matt's hand. I let him take mine in his, holding it gently as though I were a piece of delicate china, unable to stop the smile that was tugging at my lips.

It was no longer a gesture of comfort, I no longer needed that. Although it reminded me of the time that we'd first driven into the town. How much such a small display of affection could fill a hole that would, in turn, lift my overall mood.

This time, the gesture was shattering through the awkwardness that had amalgamated, although it was technically my fault that this had happened. It confirmed to me that he wasn't mad, or if he was, he was saving this anger for later. Now we had more pressing matters to concern ourselves with. The main one being that the longer we sat in the truck, the closer we were getting to seeing James.

I shouldn't be nervous. I couldn't be. There was too much riding on this, both with my career and with Matt's custody battle. Especially after all of this new information, although my mind was overwhelmed, there was still a clear cut path ahead of me that dictated what we had to do.

The drive wasn't too long, but it felt better to not be the one behind the wheel and staring out at the long road ahead of me. I'd done enough in the past day to last me for a while. Yet for the remainder of the drive, it felt good to hold onto his hand tightly. It kept me grounded, easing my thumping heart as we neared our destination.

"Are you ready for this?" Matt asked with a sigh, although I felt that it should have been me asking this. I was the professional, after all.

"I guess so." He let go of my hand as the car came to a stop.

FORTY-TWO
MATT

We pulled up to a rather lavish-looking restaurant in the depths of Cornwall, the décor oozing with grandeur before we'd even stepped out of the car. I had to let go of Kayla's hand. There was no point walking into that building and professing to everybody's eyes that we had more than just a professional relationship. It would only give James more ammunition for the case.

The building itself was crafted from strong white bricks, even the sign seemed as though it had been procured from some room in the Vatican. The cursive writing complemented by a small painting above it. Although it was clearly an upper-end restaurant, I couldn't help but notice how homely the place felt.

I could sense Kayla's nerves, and although I chose not to say anything, it was definitely concerning for a lawyer like her to be worried about this. *We were going to be fine*, I kept telling myself.

As soon as we walked inside the restaurant, I spotted James, sitting in a lonely corner of the room. A quiet and inconspicuous-looking booth, it would give us enough privacy.

"Matthew." James nodded, his greeting was curt, and he barely turned to look at Kayla. He was accompanied by two men, one on either side of him. All three sat as though there was a rod down their back.

"James," I replied, not wanting to be too emotive in my responses. One of the men looked familiar, elderly and thin, despite the fact they all sat down, I could still tell that he was much taller due to his posture and height. He was the lawyer from the funeral, his face a pale grey that reminded me of some kind of grotesque caricature, a version of the living dead.

"Look, I'm going to cut out all of the courtesy stuff and just get to it. I want to strike up a deal, one that I think we'll both benefit from."

"I'm listening," I spoke slowly, carefully, upon following Kayla into the booth. I stared intently at James the entire time, not once breaking eye contact. This would be as much a psychological war as it would be a war of words. I didn't pay any attention to the other man, choosing to consider him as only there to ensure that they were richer in numbers. A tactic of intimidation.

"I'm willing to wipe the slate clean, to forget and move on from everything that has happened and simply go our separate ways with our lives," James said.

"What's the catch?" I knew that deals such as these don't work out when they're merely one-sided.

"You can have that if you hand over custody of Kevin to me," James explained, face deadpan, the muscles barely moving. The cost of this deal wasn't even up for discussion in my eyes, it was a no brainer that I would never give up Kevin, no matter what it cost.

"Okay, this is where I'm going to have to step in." Kayla sighed from next to me, she leaned forward further over the table. I had to stop my mind from wandering, the way her breasts were perched on top of the wood, their voluptuous shape visible through the white blouse.

It was a shirt that I didn't recognize. Instantly, my mind flitted back to the many questions of where she had been yesterday.

"To put it plainly, you've not got enough on Matt that makes this deal worth taking. There isn't anything that we need dropping this instant." There was a glint of fire in her eyes when she spoke, something that sent the blood rushing to my cock, a feisty side of her that I only wanted to explore more. "Jenna and Matt adopted Kevin in Connecticut."

"What's your point?" the grey lawyer questioned, his eyes narrowing, showing the first signs of life in his expression.

"Connecticut is the only state where a guardian and parent can share full custody. If you go up against Matt, you know that he has the stronger leg to stand on here."

There was a silence that hung over the table, Kayla unable to hide the triumph from her face. I continued to stare at James, cocking an eyebrow up as we awaited the response from their side.

"Well?" Eventually, I had to prompt them, it was somewhat amusing to watch the way James squirmed. I could see that he wanted so badly to turn to his lawyer for advice, yet his stubbornness wouldn't let him break our small staring contest.

"I uh, I think we'll need to think about it more." He eventually spoke, pondering over what Kayla had said as though it was an offer.

"You can see that there's nothing here that we want

from you," I said, the blunt edge of my voice hanging in the air as James finally turned away to speak to his lawyer.

Although there wasn't much space between us, the table was a sufficient width to deny us the luxury of listening in to the incredibly hushed discussion. I had other matters to worry about upon feeling Kayla's hand take my own under the cover of the table. The three men in front of us couldn't see a thing; however, there was too much of a risk, so I pulled away.

"Before we leave," James began, the two men at either side starting to rise from the table. "I want to have a word with Kayla."

"She's right there," I spoke with a shrug, wanting to show that I could be just as stubborn, my petty business ego shining through.

"Alone."

I didn't bother to fight back, knowing that there was no point. Surely, there was nothing he could say to her that could be that bad.

"Don't be too long," I warned, stepping out of the booth with the other two gentlemen, but I kept my distance. They were also wearing suits, looking incredibly professional, but it was hard to imagine that they had a life outside of this.

I'd always tried to maintain a balance, not to swarm myself with too much work, these men had clearly dived in headfirst and had never returned from the murky waters of the business world.

I didn't dare try to strike up a conversation once we were outside, there was no point, and I didn't want to give anything away to the case that they could use against me.

The two stood close together, their lips moving, but I couldn't quite hear their conversation. Like two penguins huddled into a corner of the building. I had to commend them on their incredible ability to whisper, imagining that they would prosper on having a gossip in the library without anybody hearing them.

My worry turned its attention to Kayla, I could see the back of her head through the window, not giving me any insight at all as to what her reaction was going to be. Although the smile on James's face was as clear as day through the window, despite the shadows, regardless of my reflection marring my view through the glass. The smile on his face was malicious, cold and only pleased because it must have something to do with his own personal gain.

FORTY-THREE
KAYLA

This wasn't good. The way that James's attention was now solely focused on me. Sure, it was all in an attempt to get us to agree to his rather weak and pathetic deal, but there was something about the way that he smiled. He knew something.

The thought left my gut heavy with an uneasiness that I didn't know what to do with. He was waiting for the three men to leave the vicinity, and he only broke eye contact to follow the three figures out of the door with his eyes.

I shuddered when he wasn't looking at me, feeling a slight warmth return now that I wasn't under his icy gaze. No, I had to be strong, I reminded myself. Rolling my shoulders back and staring at him, my lips drawn in a straight line to not give anything away.

"So, what's this about?"

"It's about the deal, of course." He chuckled, shaking his head and sitting back for the first time.

"What about it that you couldn't say in front of the others?" I wasn't in the mood for games. I still had the issue of who my true son was at hand, and this was just another bump in the ever-growing long distance of road ahead of me.

"Because it only applied to you." He shrugged, the air of nonchalance beginning to grind down on my patience. "More specifically, your past cases."

His words piqued my interest. Involuntarily, one eyebrow cocked up at the realization of what James knew. Wracking my brain as I knew that there was only one thing in my past history of cases that would be worth talking about like this, I just couldn't understand how he knew about it.

"I have an excellent success record."

"I bet you do." He chuckled, a hint of sarcasm in his voice.

"What's that supposed to mean?" I wasn't going to hint at what I knew in the same way that he was, not wanting to get too comfortable and let it slip before he spilled what he knew. There would be nothing worse than thinking one thing while James was thinking another. To reveal such compromising information by accident would be a disaster.

"Perhaps I'm not clear enough." He cleared his throat, sitting forward and coming toward me. Over the table, our faces were closer than before, although it wasn't in a way that suggested any kind of attraction. More along the lines of intimidation, he was using almost every textbook tactic to wear me down and try to break up what little composure I had left.

Underneath the large table we were both now leaning on, my sweaty hands were gripping one another tightly, trying to keep a lid on the overwhelming anger that was threatening to boil over.

"I'm talking about that third case, Kayla." A glint formed in his eyes upon seeing the way my entire body caved. I winced, probably visibly too, because the words hurt so much more out loud than I'd anticipated. It hadn't adequately occurred to me that he actually knew about my past, that he knew what I'd done and was going to use it against me in this case.

It was my worst nightmare coming true, the one thing I'd always thought I'd gotten away with, yet now it was coming back to haunt me. With a vengeance, may I add.

"I'm afraid...you're going to have to elaborate on that. I can't quite recall which had been my third case," I said but he could see through my lie as though I was made of glass.

"Oh, really? You truly can't sift through your memories, cast your mind back to the time that you spent on that case?" James provoked me.

"Nope." My response was curt, blunt as I swallowed down the bile that had risen in my throat. I wasn't proud of what I'd done by any means, but I didn't want Matt to find out what had happened. He would fire me as his lawyer in an instant, and I didn't know where that would leave us. The thought terrified me.

"Well, I do believe that it was one of your hardest. It was an impressive win, don't you think?"

He wasn't wrong. It had almost destroyed my career before it had barely begun. "What's your point?"

James continued, "I mean, it just seemed odd, there was a lot of evidence against him that expressed how he could have easily been guilty. But you managed to counter all of it, it was all of it, wasn't it? You must know that withholding evidence is a felony."

My breath caught in my throat, leaving my body as I felt frozen to the seat of the booth. This was ridiculous, how my entire world and career was going to come crashing down around me because of one mistake.

"He was innocent," I countered, eyes narrowing, blood boiling and freezing simultaneously as it filled with adrenaline.

"I didn't want it to come to this, Kayla, and let me just tell you, this is nothing personal. I just asked a few people to do some digging, wondering what they might be able to unearth." His nonchalance was back, except this time it was urging me on to throttle the wormy man. However, I held my nerve.

I had to keep going. "So when you say that you will forget everything, you were talking about this?"

"Unfortunately, yes." He sighed, trying to act as though he was upset that it had come to this. But I knew the reality, he was probably thrilled when he learned there was more to me than met the eye.

"In exchange for full custody of Kevin..." I said, moving away from the table to sit back in the booth, an immense sense of deflation settled over me.

"Yes," he replied simply, all efforts to appear sympathetic seemed to have evaporated. "So much about having the stronger leg to stand on in court."

"I may not, but what's to say the next lawyer Matt hires won't have a stronger leg?" I thought that I'd got him, that he was just going to continue destroying people's careers until he got what he wanted. However, that was where I'd made the unfortunate mistake of underestimating him.

"I'll find something on them." There was a new determination in his eyes, something that hadn't been there before.

"You're crazy."

"No, Kayla, I'm just a good businessman. If I want something, I'll get it."

"Why do you even want Kevin so bad? Are you even

that close to the kid?" There was a pause as James eyed me carefully. I managed to resist the urge to shrink further back in my seat, although there wasn't much further back that I could go.

"I have my reasons." He coughed. There was no affection when he thought of Kevin, at least, none that was evident on his face. It didn't even seem as though he wanted to talk about Kevin. "Anyway, back to the part where you withheld evidence."

"This is blackmail."

"This is business." He was swift to reply. As he coldly stared at me with that icy glare, to him, I was no more than a mere appointment on his calendar. To me, this case meant everything. If Matt lost, it would ruin him to not see his son.

"This is wrong. You could get that man thrown into prison after all of these years." It was true, the man was completely innocent, yet when they had stacked up against the evidence, I knew we wouldn't be able to cope. I covered some up, withheld it to make his story look slightly straighter.

It was by no means a highlight in my career. That day, I went home and sobbed. Albeit a victory, there was always something nagging in my mind that it would come back around to haunt me. That part of my mind had been correct after all.

"You would go to jail too, Kayla." His tone was warning me, yet it also held a glint of daring. As though he was daring me to pull away from this deal and to defy him, he had this card tucked up his sleeve, with his other hand on it and ready to pull it out if need be.

"You're disgusting. I don't care if I go to jail, but you can't send somebody innocent. That would be taking things too far." My voice resembled more of a snarl, leaving me unsure as to where this sudden bout of courage had sprung from. "I don't care if I never work again as a lawyer, because if you leak that information, then that would most definitely be the case, but I will fight until the end to make sure you don't get Kevin."

It wasn't exactly all true. There was a huge part of me that was utterly terrified of what fate awaited me. A lawyer that couldn't even keep herself out of jail, nobody would want a mess like that to represent them in court. I would never let James take Kevin, but I wasn't sure what would await me once everything was said and done. I'd be utterly ruined.

He moved closer again, this time walking around the table to sit on my side of the booth, but there was nowhere for me to move to, I felt cornered. Like a wounded animal, preparing itself for the kill, I felt that he was going to deliver the fatal blow.

"So what's it going to be? Kevin? Or your career?" he asked.

I sat there for a moment, trying my hardest not to cringe at how close James had gotten. I could feel his breath on me as I met his eyes. My own blockade against his various intimidation tactics had crumbled in an instant, leaving me embarrassingly exposed. This wasn't what should happen to a lawyer, we were supposed to be sharp, not show much emotion and keep a level head.

I was breaking almost every rule in the book, but I couldn't help how much this new revelation had compromised me. I felt like a spy who had been found out. A felon, I would no longer be a lawyer, but a criminal.

"I need more time to think." I was using his line from previously, how I wished more than anything that I could go back to that moment and revel in the knowledge that we had the upper hand. Poor Matt still thought we did.

"I'm not a very patient man, Kayla," he warned, licking his lips as I watched his eyes dart down my body. The gesture was oddly perverse and left me wanting nothing more than to kick him in the teeth, but I had to show etiquette. Especially in such a fancy restaurant. Perhaps that was why we'd come here. It was to make sure nobody stepped a foot out of line, to maintain a conversation instead of kicking off.

I couldn't imagine responding to his blackmail with violence would look particularly good in any case, let alone in making a plea that I was innocent in this.

"I'll give you some time," he finally concluded, coughing slightly and moving out of the booth. I moved back over, taking up the entire seat so that he couldn't change his mind and try to get that close again. Out of the window, I caught Matt's eye.

Even from across the room, I could see the frown on his face. He would be grilling me on this just as much as he wanted to know about where I'd been the previous day too. The lies were eating me up, causing me so much pain that it was beginning to make my heart ache.

I knew I couldn't give up Kevin for Matt, and I guessed that I'd been steering down this path for a very long time. Sooner or later, something was going to give. A captain was going to have to go down with his ship. It was just a shame that not everybody on board was guilty.

"That man was innocent, completely innocent," I insisted.

"Tell that to the judge." James took his coat and made his way toward the exit.

This seemed to catch Matt's attention, as moments

later, he was storming through the door. "What did he say to you?"

"N-nothing, he just wanted another professional's opinion on the whole matter and—"

"Bullshit." He was furious.

I gasped at him, realizing that a couple of people in the restaurant were beginning to turn around to see what all of the commotion was about. I was glad James had picked an off-peak time, less of a crowd in case anything had gone too wrong to handle.

The way that James had left me so suddenly had brought them on. Tears. They were rising and welling in my eyes before I could even try to react and stop Matt from seeing them.

"Why are you crying?"

"It doesn't matter. Come on, let's just go," I grumbled, moving past him and heading for the door. From the reflection of one mirror, I could see that Matt was following behind me, keeping hot on my heels. But I chose to continuously walk at a fast pace, not bothering to thank any of the waiting staff as I pushed the door open, quickly moving out into the fresh air.

It was then that I realized the tears were already rolling down my cheeks, the cold catching them, the coolness of the wet feeling suddenly amplified.

"Kayla, you promised that you would tell me everything," Matt spoke sternly; however, I continued to walk until my hand was wrapped around the door handle of the car.

"I'll tell you everything, I promise, just...once we get on the road." I wasn't convinced the three of those worms had slithered off completely, terrified that they would record me admitting to what I did. Nobody could deny something as tarnishing as concrete evidence like a recording.

"All right, go for it," Matt spoke once we'd barely turned out of the quiet parking lot of the restaurant, yet he was already too curious to hold it in.

"I'll start with today." It felt as though I were glancing between two options that weighed down the judging scales; equally, both were such deep secrets that I never thought I would be able to tell Matt. "James's lawyer has been doing some digging on me, and it's not looking good." There was no way that I'd be able to sugar coat it; instead, the words poured out of me in a sea of regret. I told Matt every detail of the case, how I'd come to realize that my client was completely innocent, that somebody was manufacturing evidence to make it seem as though he were guilty. I continued on about how I'd then hidden some of the final pieces of evidence before they had been handed in and recorded as part of the case.

Withholding evidence would easily land me in a nasty jail cell. I wasn't sure how long for though. It wasn't an active case anymore, and I felt as the judge might add on a few years if James were to whisper in his ear.

As the words poured, tears and sobs fell free too. All of the bottled-up emotions that I had kept sealed away were rising to the surface, and fast. I wanted to know what Matt was thinking, but the entire time, he kept his mouth pursed closed.

"And now my stupid past mistakes have put the custody of your son in jeopardy, I'm so sorry, Matt, I truly am."

"You have nothing to apologize for, if you say your client was innocent, then I believe you." He spoke with a clenched jaw, leading me to believe that it wasn't easy for him to say this. "But it doesn't change the fact that we are now in a pretty tight situation."

"I know." I rested my head back, wishing the past few hours had been a nightmare and I'd wake up soon hopefully.

"There's more at stake here than simply my case, though, this is your entire career on the line." The gravity of the situation was beginning to sink in further for Matt. "You could be in serious trouble."

"I know, so could my client. I don't just mean another-visit-to-court kind of trouble, not even a lose-my-job kind of trouble, I'm talking about jail, Matt. James said that he would put me in jail if we don't agree to the deal."

"But we can't." He groaned, hands gripping the wheel tighter as we sped down the road, I didn't bother to question the speed at which he was going, knowing that if he was this pent up, there was no point arguing. Although even in such a dire situation, tears staining my cheeks and my chest shaking heavily, I still couldn't deny how hot Matt looked when he was angry.

However, it wasn't as lovely as it had been in the past, not when there was so much riding on our next move. If it were chess, it would be getting into the crucial stages where any move could lead to your last.

FORTY-FOUR

MATT

"Why don't you just go and take a rest? You've been through enough today." I put my hand on the small of her back as I led Kayla into the house. A grimace taking ahold of my face as I tried to avoid making eye contact with my grandmother. There was nothing anybody could do or say to console us.

"Thanks again for driving." Kayla sniffled, I'd never seen her looking this vulnerable before. There was something about her that just seemed different this time. A deflated look about her, like by letting out her secret, it had punctured a hole in her.

"It's all right, you go on upstairs. I'll bring you up a hot drink if you'd like?" I didn't know why I was so nice, her biggest secret might have just lost me the custody of my son. I think it was spooking both of us that I was acting so out of character.

I had been raging in the car, gripping on to the wheel to try to control the anger surging through me. It seemed to all disappear once we'd reached the ranch, the anger flowing out of me as I crossed the threshold.

I waited until Kayla had gone upstairs and was confidently out of earshot. There was no way that I wanted her to hear my phone call.

"Matt?" Doug answered.

"Hey, Doug." I winced, knowing that this conversation was going to be uncomfortable.

"Is everything all right? Is there anything that I can do for you?"

"Actually, yes, I need you to do some digging for me."

"Digging? On who?" I could practically hear Douglas's curiosity overshadowing his logic even through the phone.

"On my lawyer Kayla." My voice was suddenly very stiff and I had to choke out the words. I could hear him take in a deep breath. "I'm not sure what you're supposed to be looking for, but there's something else going on. Something that she keeps dodging around." I began to tell him about her worst case, about the fact that James knew and whether or not he had any advice on how we could fix this problem.

"Damn, he's definitely got you in a corner there," Doug spoke, clearly impressed.

"I don't know what it is, but it's definitely personal, more so than my case."

"How do you know?"

"She was crying, Doug. I don't know, I just feel as though there was more to the reason why she was upset than she was letting on."

"Were you with her while James threatened her?" Doug's question caught me off-guard.

"Well, I watched from a distance. I was outside the restaurant when it happened." I frowned, not understanding what was meant by his question.

"And you say that you have no idea where she was yesterday?"

"No, she just took off, but she promised that she'd tell me."

"And has she?" There was a pause. Doug was always good at getting to the bottom of things for me, it was why I'd hired him.

"No," I replied bluntly.

"Well, if James is in town, did you ever consider that maybe—"

"Are you saying that she was with James yesterday?" My anger returned, as though it had merely been hiding around the corner. There was a pause on the other end of the line and I could tell that Douglas knew I was angry.

"I'm merely suggesting it," he said in response carefully.

"I'd never thought about it that way."

The more that I thought about it, the more it began to make sense. The way she was continuously avoiding the question, even choosing to tell me about what happened with James over where she'd been for the past day. Perhaps there was something else James had told her when I'd stepped outside. I'd been so naïve to think there couldn't have been anything else that they were talking about.

"You say she lied about things, who's to say she isn't lying to you? I'm sorry, Matt, I know it's not what you want to hear, but before I dig, just make sure you've thought about every possibility of what could be going on here," Doug pointed out.

"You honestly think that she's been seeing him?"

"I think the only person who could tell you that is Kayla herself."

I sighed at his response, admiring the way that he knew how and when to keep a distance from a situation, merely offering advice instead of his opinion.

"Well, thanks for your time, Doug. I'll get back to you if

I need to follow up on the digging, but first I'm going to ask Kayla straight up what's going on. If I feel like she's lying, then I'll come back to you, okay?"

"Sounds good to me." With that, I hung up. He was used to my spontaneous phone calls by now.

My grandmother had wandered into the other room, luckily unable to hear any of that conversation. I slowly ascended the stairs, gulping down my fear that these thoughts could be true if she was seeing him, then she was out straight away.

My hand knocked against her closed door. No response. I knocked again, hearing a sniffle and a short, "Come in."

I pushed the door open, unable to wipe the anger off of my face. It seemed to sink into every crack, every wrinkle of my skin. Settling on my expression as though it were permanent paint.

"Kayla, I know you're upset, but I need to talk to you." My voice held no warmth, I watched the way that she cringed at my words. I'd caught her just before she'd started to change out of her professional outfit, heels kicked off and discarded across the floor.

"About what?"

"You never told me where you were yesterday." I tilted my head to the side as she stood up from the bed, although I didn't know why she did it. I still stood tall, towering over her small frame.

"I told you, I don't want to talk about it at the moment. I promise I'll tell you, just not now."

I groaned at the answer, storming out of the room without looking back. She was driving me crazy, but I was so angry. Too angry.

I only managed to get to the landing by the stairs before I turned around, storming back inside, pushing the door roughly. Kayla jumped at my sudden entrance, her eyes wide as she could clearly see the anger written across my entire stance.

"I can't believe you would lie to me! You've been with James!"

"What? No, I haven't!" she shouted back, snapping as her own face seemed to go up in flames.

"Don't lie any more than you already have. I'm not an idiot, and I see what you've been doing. I want answers!"

"Well, you are an idiot, Matthew! You've got it completely wrong, I hate James, especially after the dirt that he's dug up on me."

"Then tell me where you were!"

"Or what?" she was calling me out, I could sense it. The way that her nostrils flared, she wasn't ready to back down. I began to realize that taking her as a lawyer was probably not the best idea. "What will you do? Kick me out?"

I couldn't kick her out, no matter what she'd done, I was too emotionally involved. Also, there was a large part of me that didn't want to kick her out. This part seemed to crave her touch, her attention, her body. It was the part that looked forward to seeing how she would cover her body each day, how each outfit would highlight her curves deliciously.

"N-no." I looked down, knowing that there was no way I would want her to leave. She was right, I was an idiot.

"I didn't see James yesterday, please believe me about that."

"I do." I'd given in too quickly, let my guard down and was literally melting at her pleas, she wasn't even trying that hard. Although fresh tears threatened to spill in her eyes.

"Thank you." She breathed out in relief.

"But I need to know, I won't judge or anything, but please, Kayla. Tell me where you went yesterday."

There was a long silence between us, her arms wrapped around her chest as though they would protect her from something. Eventually, she gave in.

"Fine." Kayla sat on the bed, gesturing for me to follow her lead, perching down next to her. "This is a story that stretches back to when I was only sixteen. It wasn't just about yesterday, this is something that I've been hiding from almost everyone."

"Does James know?" I had to ask.

"Not that I know of, if he did, the case truly would be done for, I think. There would be too much personal attachment."

I frowned, not understanding what she meant, but waited for her to carry on nonetheless.

"When I was sixteen I was homeschooled, but there was this guy down at the grocer's, his father owned the place so it was almost a guarantee every time I went there that I'd see him. We seemed to catch each other's attention until one night he helped me sneak out. My parents were so strict that it was hard for me to see him outside of going down to the grocer's with the excuse that we needed more supplies."

"What was his name?" I don't know why I asked, but I felt as though I needed to put names to these stories, to make sure that she was telling the truth. Although a part of me knew I already trusted her.

"Damian." I could see the pain in her eyes at the memory. "We were just kids fooling around in bed, not using protection but not realizing the consequences. We could hear my parents stirring, Dad was calling out to me through the wall, wondering what all the noise was. So we jumped down from the second floor to sneak out. It was painful but what my eyes saw was worse. A fire had broken out on the lower floor, spreading swiftly and enclosing the house almost in a matter of seconds. Damian ran straight in, shouting at me to stay there, that he would save my parents."

"You don't have to continue." I placed a hand to her cheek, wiping away the stray tears that had begun to fall.

"No. I need to get it out." She sniffled, sitting up straighter and moving out of my grasp. I felt as though we both instantly missed the contact. "Damian never came out of the house, the roof collapsed, and he died along with my parents."

"I'm so sorry, I had no idea."

"Well, the fire was only the first of my problems, you see, my parents were up to their ears in debt. It was all they ever talked about, but I thought that it was all adult stuff, that it would just go away and I could begin to move on with my life. That was all the therapist kept saying to me after the entire ordeal. They said that I just had to keep moving and looking forward. It was kind of hard to do with crippling debt hanging off my back."

"But you've gotten through it? You've managed to pay it off and thrive." I tried to flip the mood, still not seeing how it matched up with her disappearance yesterday.

"Yeah, I guess. A couple of weeks after the fire, I found out that...I was pregnant. With Damian's baby. I had no home, the people that ran the place I stayed in, a caring place for unwanted kids, they said that I couldn't keep the baby." She was crying properly now. Instantly, my arm was around her, pulling her close to comfort her to the best of my ability.

"I'm so sorry, Kayla."

She didn't try to wriggle out of my arms this time, instead choosing to hold me too, her dainty hands holding onto my arms, as though she might fall or fly away if she let go. "I've got you."

We stayed in this position for a long time. I'd lost track of how long—that seemed to happen a lot when we shared moments like this. Her body drowned my senses, I couldn't tell if ten seconds had passed or ten minutes.

"I wouldn't have been able to get a college scholarship, pay off the debts, and work my way back up if I had kept the baby, but not a second goes by where I still don't regret that decision."

"I think you made the right choice. Think about the fact that you gave that baby a better life," I offered, knowing enough about the adoption system myself to understand that there were many positives to it.

"I know for a fact that somebody gave my boy a good life." There was a knowing smile on her face, but I had no idea what she was getting at.

"What do you mean?"

"That's where I was yesterday, I went to the adoption center to work out where my son is. I've been looking for four years now and it's been eating me up inside the entire time." The moment felt so raw, Kayla was exposing so much of her life to me. "That's why I had to break up with you in college. There was so much that I had to do. I was looking for him and using almost all of my extra time to do so."

"How did I never realize?" I asked myself in disbelief.

"But now I know who my son is." She smiled, moving off the bed to grab a folder, flicking through the various plastic wallets in search of something. Finally, Kayla retrieved a piece of paper. It looked to be some kind of official document.

"That's Kevin's birth certificate. What are you doing with that?" Confusion flushed through my mind. It wasn't working fast enough to connect all of the dots.

"I went to the adoption center yesterday in—"

"Norwich. You went to Norwich." I stated, the pieces beginning to align.

"The date matches the date that I gave him up," she explained, moving closer to me again. "But you never told me that Kevin was adopted."

"I know. It's not something that we bring up often, he gets a bit...funny around the subject."

"But he does know?" She seemed desperate. This was the boy who had spawned her search that had lasted over many years.

"Yes, he was four when we adopted him, so he has a few memories of the various foster care places he was in before that." I felt awful, a lump in my throat for even considering that Kayla would go against me. I could see the way that she winced at the fact that her son had spent the first four years of his life in care. "Don't blame yourself."

"There's nobody else to blame." Her words came out under a chuckle, although I knew that she was laughing to cover up how hurt she was inside.

"You did the best that you could. In my opinion, you made the right choice. You wouldn't be a lawyer, you would still be crumbling under all of that debt, and Kevin wouldn't be in the most stable of positions, would he?"

"I know, it just hurts to think about all of the time that I've lost with him. He doesn't even know that I'm his mother."

I moved closer to her, our faces merely inches apart. "Jenna and I never told him much about the adoption. We didn't want it to be the thing that defined his childhood. But

I feel he should know about you, he has a right to, and after all of this time, you have a right to tell him."

"Thank you." Her voice was a whisper, coming out hoarse and croaky due to the tears welling up yet again. I hugged her tighter, placing a kiss to her forehead, before moving down until our faces were merely inches apart.

"No, thank you. It means a lot that you've told me this." It was true. There was a part of me that felt relieved and I no longer had to question her motives or whereabouts.

Finally, I closed the gap, tenderly pressing my lips against hers, the gesture positively surprising her. Yet her body betrayed her, both arms moving to wrap around me as she twisted until she was on my lap.

I could tell that the position was slightly uncomfortable for her, due to the lack of elasticity in her skirt, although I didn't let this hinder our movements, roughly pushing the material back so that she had a better position straddling me. There was a groan that left my lips as her hips brushed against the growing bulge in my pants. Her mouth against mine managed to muffle the sound slightly.

"Matt." She groaned, moving her hips again, I could feel the way that my cock was twitching at the contact, a low growl leaving my lips as my hands dug into her hips.

I felt as though I couldn't take it anymore, the heat of the moment getting to me, that if Kayla continued with what she was doing, it would make me explode. Instead, I moved her back, my body shifting until I was hovering over her, not wanting to hurt her in any way or cause her discomfort. I wanted this to be about showing my appreciation.

FORTY-FIVE
KAYLA

I was a panting mess beneath him, not sure how he managed it, but he always made it feel as though my body was made of pure electricity, sparking at his mere touch. His hands wasted no time in popping open each button of my shirt, moving erratically to rid me of all clothes as though there was a timer on.

His hands then hungrily reached around my back, unclipping the clasp of my bra. A short gasp leaving my lips at the rushed way that he was acting. Yet I couldn't deny the amount of heat and wetness rushing to my core. It only seemed to increase as his hands wandered lower down my body, cupping my breasts as his mouth broke away from mine to pepper kissing down my jaw.

The sensation of his lips as they greeted my neck was incredible, eliciting a chorus of moans from my mouth as his teeth nibbled at a particularly sensitive spot. I could barely control myself as my hands pulled him closer, playing with the hair at the nape of his neck to try to ground myself, to pull myself out of his lustful haze.

"Matt," I breathed out again, alluding to the fact that his

name seemed to be the only word that I could remember how to say. However, he suddenly pulled away, causing my eyes to lock with his in a frown. I didn't know what he was doing or why he'd swiftly moved.

"I want to make this special," he murmured, moving back down, slower in pace this time. Lips pressing so gently to mine that he was acting as though this was our first kiss. I knew what it was. It was all a ploy to comfort me, to make me seem as though I was special in his eyes.

His hands had moved down to my sides. I was thankful I wasn't ticklish or it would have completely ruined the moment. Instead, his fingers danced over my stomach area, paying closer attention as his mouth moved in their direction too. You would have thought that I was pregnant by how he was acting.

"I can't believe that you might be Kevin's mother," he whispered. He didn't say it in a bad way, his wet kisses causing goosebumps to rise on my skin in their trail. He spoke with positive disbelief, as though he was thankful the whole thing had worked out in the way that it did.

"Neither can I, after all this time that I'd spent searching..." My voice trailed off as I felt Matt's hands beginning to travel lower, gaining confidence as they pulled down my skirt.

I helped him by kicking the fabric onto the floor once it had wriggled down my legs, a part of me felt incredibly anxious at what was to come. This seemed so much more stripped back, and it made me feel even more exposed than the other times I'd been naked around him, the only addition being that my secrets were also laid bare in front of him. I gasped in surprise, feeling Matt's lips pressing against my core through the thin material of my panties. The sensation was nothing I would ever be able to get used to, something that felt incredible but still sent a wave of fire burning through my veins.

"I'm so happy that it's Kevin. There wouldn't be any other way that I would have it," I added, smiling warmly as he sat back, beginning to take his own shirt off.

Matt seemed to have nailed the concept of taking a shirt off quickly and with ease, his smart trousers following afterward. Once they were gone, it gave me a better view of all of him, his cock more defined through the tight material of his boxers. It was easier to see this now than it had been with the slightly looser trousers.

"Tell me what you want." He spoke huskily, his eyes much darker than before. There was a glint of lust shining through.

"I want you," I breathed out, my hands running down his toned chest, exploring each corner of his body before ending up in the area that I needed him most. "I need you."

This seemed to be all the confirmation he needed, his hands ridding my body of its final article of clothing, the thin lace dropped delicately to the floor like a feather. There was a liminal moment between us, my hands hovering over his waistband, as though there was still time to turn back now. But neither of us wanted to. There was no point in prolonging the inevitable, after all.

I let my hands lead. They quickly pulled down the final piece of material, revealing his hard cock, which once the boxers had been discarded, I took into one hand. The instant I had my fingers wrapped around his length, I heard a gasp come from his mouth, the pleasure that only my hand could bring him was remarkable.

"Fuck, Kayla." He groaned, unable to help the way his hips bucked involuntarily into my hand. I continued to pump at a slow pace, if he truly wanted to take this slow, then this was what I had in mind. However, after a few moments, Matt's hand had wrapped around my waist pushing me off. "You're such a tease."

"I thought you wanted to take it slow." I smirked mockingly, leaning back as he groaned again.

"I just meant that I wanted to appreciate you more, to pay attention to all of you." His mouth was back on my body, kissing around each breast. I could feel his hard dick against my thigh—it was so close yet so far. However, I chose not to tease Matt further about wanting to take it slow, I was happy he was showing so much care toward me.

Finally, his lips met with mine again. He had a hand on either side of my head, holding me up as I moaned into his mouth. After what seemed like a long time of making out, his tongue pushing into my mouth as if he couldn't help but assert his dominance, one of his hands finally moved down to my clit.

"Matt." I moaned out loudly, causing his mouth to attach to mine instantly. He knew we would have to be quiet as we weren't the only ones in the house, and this was his way of reminding me. "Oh, God." I couldn't help the words tumbling out of my mouth, my body responding heavily to Matt's actions.

"Does that feel good?" I couldn't reply, merely nodding as my eyes screwed shut, rendering me useless as I simply basked in the pleasure. Somehow, I managed to get my hand to move back down, tugging on his length once again, eliciting more moans from Matt. "Kayla, I said don't, or I'll be finished in an instant."

His words made me smile, yet I did what I was told, moving my hand away as Matt suddenly slid a finger into me. His forehead was now resting on mine as I panted heavily, my hips moving in time to meet his finger's movements.

"Matt, please."

"Please, what?"

"I need more." I groaned, not wanting to release under him on his fingers. There was no way this was all I was going to get. There was a moment of silence and an emptiness as he finally pulled away.

This void was filled not a moment later when I felt the head of his cock at my entrance. Matt pushed himself in with long and incredibly drawn-out sighs escaping both of our lips. There was nothing better than the toe-curling feeling of him stretching me out, pushing my walls and filling me completely. A slightly squeaky sound came from my throat as I attempted to suppress my moans and be as quiet as possible, no matter how badly I wanted to scream Matt's name at the top of my voice.

The room was filled with the sounds of our skin hitting each other and our hushed moans that managed to seep between the cracks of kisses and bit lips. Matt was still moving relatively slow, clearly keeping to his word that he would take this slowly. It was as though he was savoring every movement, wanting to keep it all bottled up and conserve it for later.

After a while, Matt finally began to pick up the pace of his thrusts, something to do with the fact that I was meeting his thrusts perfectly, urging with my body that I was craving much more than this. My mouth formed an O shape when he slightly shifted the position we were in and the adjustment of angle allowed him to go deeper. Pushing further into me and reaching a spot of pleasure that wasn't usually found.

A string of curse words left my mouth as he persisted in pressing into this spot, pushing it and bringing me closer to my high. His hand then moved down my body, stopping at my stomach once again, perhaps to highlight the importance of this latest revelation.

After all, it would mean that I was Kevin's biological mother, and Matt would still be Kevin's legal father.

"Matt, oh, God. I feel like I'm close." My words were spoken in between thrusts, whenever it was convenient and only when my shortness of breath would permit it. It seemed to encourage him to move even faster, his thrusts becoming sloppy due to the lack of energy that his body contained. I could tell he was coming to his end too, his cock twitching against my walls whenever I accidentally clenched, the action causing him to bite his lip.

It didn't take much longer, and soon both of us had reached that moment of euphoria, moving through it together as one as the waves of pleasure continued to roll over us. My senses were incredibly overwhelmed by the many sensations that were running through us, nerve endings feeling as though after this overload, they could be numb forever.

Neither of us said anything. I didn't feel as though there was anything that we could add to the ambiance around us, filled with our labored breaths and hammering hearts. Finally, Matt pulled out and flopped down on the bed next to me, his arm still protectively wrapped around my middle, pulling me close to him.

"That was incredible," I whispered, my hand coming down to squeeze his as he pulled me even closer to him.

"It was," he agreed, groaning as he finally sat up and looked back over at me, a small smirk working its way onto his face. "I just want to say as well that I'm sorry about what I accused you of. I was just incredibly angry and didn't know what to think."

"Matt, I'd never want to be with James." My voice came

out in a sigh. A look of disappointment had washed over my face, and I didn't know how to react to his apology.

"I know, I just wasn't thinking about it logically, and now that you've told me where you were yesterday, it all makes so much more sense."

I felt glad to know that he trusted me, although it still hurt to think that he assumed so low of me. "I understand how it must have looked suspicious, though." I moved over to kiss him, sitting up as a frown settled over his face suddenly. "What?"

"I just have to make a phone call."

I was incredibly confused, watching as he dressed, however I felt it was for the best. There was going to be suspicion from everyone if we were in my room for too long. I didn't exactly want to discuss our sex life with people, especially not explaining it to Myra. That would be awful.

FORTY-SIX
MATT

I walked out of the room with a sigh, not wanting to leave Kayla on her own, especially after what I'd just found out. It hurt to think that she'd been carrying around the burden of knowing that Kevin was her son for almost an entire day without telling anyone.

I took out my phone and redialed Doug's number, needing to confirm to him that everything was fine and there was no need for him to do any digging on Kayla.

"Hello?"

"Hey, I'm going to call off the dig."

"All right, I was just about to start it. Caught me in the nick of time." Doug spoke with a sigh, although I was sure that he was thankful to have been offloaded from something today.

"Yeah, I spoke to her, and she told me the real reason why she'd been absent yesterday." I went on to explain that she thought Kevin was her biological son.

"That's...incredible," Douglas breathed out over the phone.

"Listen, Doug, do you know anybody that would be able

to check over to see if a signature is forged?" The idea had only just come to me, that perhaps there was something wrong with the will, that somebody else had been signing it off.

"You have a suspicion?" I could tell this was the kind of gossip that Douglas lived for, although he'd never admit it. He was able to keep professionalism at the forefront of his work better than I would ever be able to.

"I do, matters concerning the will."

"Yes, I think I could contact an old friend and see what she could do," Doug replied shortly.

It was moments like these that I treasured, proving that sometimes it wasn't what you know, but who.

"Thanks again, Doug. I knew that I'd be able to count on you for this."

"It's all right, and I did have second thoughts over my suspicions as to where Kayla was yesterday. I'm just glad I had been wrong in my assumptions." It was strange to hear him admit this. Although his tone was still professional, I could tell he was genuinely sorry for planting the idea in my head.

"It's fine, Douglas, you helped me get to the bottom of it regardless. Have a good day."

Upon exchanging curt replies, the two of us hung up the phone. I stood on the landing for a moment, fearful that we were going to find out even more lies weaved around the family. Although it was only as I hung up that I began to wish I'd questioned Doug as to who this old friend was. He said he was going to be sending her over to the ranch to observe the will.

I was sure there was something else going on. It didn't make sense. James was beyond obsessed with the idea of getting custody of Kevin. Even though I had never suspected they were close in any way. A sigh left my lips as I walked downstairs, and my grandmother looked confused.

"I heard shouting. Is everything all right?"

The concern in her voice touched me, but I didn't feel as though this was something that she should know just yet. I wanted Kayla to be the one to tell people, on her terms and not on my own.

"Yes, everything's fine now." I nodded at her, smiling stiffly and trying my hardest to appear fine, although inside I felt incredibly drained. From both the mental strain of being backed into a corner by James and also the physical activity I had been partaking in only moments beforehand. I could tell by the look on Grams's face that she wasn't convinced. So much for trying to keep her out of it. I knew how feisty she could get, and the last thing I needed to do was drag the entire family into this mess.

~

A couple of hours passed, leaving me slightly impatient and desperately wondering who it was that Douglas was sending over. Kayla had joined us downstairs finally, after changing into something a little more comfortable. The loose joggers still somehow seemed to hug her curves perfectly. It seemed as though there was no outfit that this woman couldn't pull off.

"There's a car pulling up." I could hear my grandmother saying from the front room.

"Can you see who it is?"

"Not yet," she called back. Instead of waiting on her description, I walked around to the front of the house, opening the door to the porch to get a good view.

"Who is it?" Kayla wandered over to where I stood,

gasping at the sight of the slightly older lady getting out of the car. "Marianne?"

A rush of relief flooded through me. It was nice to feel as though we were in capable hands. Kayla had told me of the professor's old law career, her high success rate being one of the highest that Kayla had ever heard of. I was happy Douglas had such great connections, ones we would be able to rely on.

"Good afternoon," I called to her, walking down the steps of the house to help her walk, the woman was clearly moving into her older age and looked as though she'd need the aid climbing the stairs. "How are you doing?"

"Great, actually." She smiled up at me, clearly grateful for my help. "I hear that you have some signatures for me to look at?"

"Yes, I think they might be forged," I spoke as we got to the top of the stairs. Kayla had heard what I'd said and frowned, likely feeling out of the loop. "I spoke to Doug on the phone, and he said this could be a good lead in our case if somebody could prove that the writing is forged."

I wasn't sure how they could check; if there even was a way to tell whether or not it was forged. Perhaps these 'professionals' made it up.

"Right, I'll get to work straight away then." Marianne greeted everyone as she stepped into the house.

"It's good to see you here, Kayla." She beamed. I watched as Kayla returned the smile, happy that the woman with precariously high cheekbones had taken the time to acknowledge her. I'd heard how much of a big deal Marianne had been back in the day, in the law sector, anyway, so it wasn't surprising that Kayla still held a sense of awe toward the woman.

"This way." Kayla directed Marianne into the sitting

room, where I had taken the time to set out the document, even digging out a magnifier glass. It was only when Marianne produced a set of almost clinical-looking tools from her small bag that I realized she was more than prepared for the task ahead of her.

There was no need for any more courtesies after Kayla offered her a drink, which Marianne promptly declined. Instead, she chose to sit down and get straight to work, her eyes staring down at the signatures, utilizing a broad spectrum of instruments to formulate some kind of conclusion.

Kayla and I didn't want to, however, we moved into the kitchen area waiting patiently at first, yet after a large chunk of time had passed, I began to lose hope. It was causing me to question her integrity. Although I knew that she was old, I was sure Marianne wouldn't be able to tell whether or not it was forged.

"I'm telling you, she's the best in the business," Kayla spoke. Perhaps she'd been having similar thoughts.

"With detecting forgery?"

"Detecting any kind of lie. She just seems to have this ability where she can see through people and things. She's a lawyer's dream." I admired the way Kayla complimented the woman, although there was something else behind it. It could have easily been envy, jealous that her win rate wasn't as good, or just her overall reputation wasn't regarded with as much respect as Marianne's automatically demanded.

Marianne called us back into the room, claiming that she had an answer for us.

"It's forged. An artist has done an enviable job on it, but nevertheless, it's still forged," she spoke confidently.

"Would anybody like a drink of anything? I'm just about to get one for myself." A small voice called from the doorway. It was Kevin. He seemed shy, yet determined to show off the fact that he could be a reputable host. A chorus of *no*s followed after him, and then Kayla excused herself and made a bee-line for the kitchen.

There had been something different on her face when she'd replied to his offer, an admiration, a closeness that only I could see due to the recent revelation. I could practically feel how much she craved for him to know.

"What does this mean? Would you say that we have a case against James?"

"I couldn't prove it was James, only that it's forged. Like I said, whoever did this is good at what they do. It's virtually undetectable," Marianne explained with a sigh.

"But at least it's something, right?" My eyes narrowed.

"Yes, it's better than walking into a courtroom with no evidence at all." She shrugged with a nonchalance that was slightly vexing.

"All right, thank you for your help. I'm sorry about the drive." I knew I was going to have to pay Marianne significantly for her help. Although brief, it had given us a verification that something else was going on.

We said our chaste goodbyes, interrupting the artwork that Kayla was drawing on Kevin's cast. I'd walked into the kitchen to see him sitting on a stool as she drew swirls along the cast. They had previously been laughing at something, that light, childish laugh of his. There was a glint of happiness in Kayla's eyes I hadn't seen before. We locked eyes for a brief moment, giving me the opportunity to see this.

"Marianne's just leaving now," I explained. Kayla reluctantly got to her feet and moved out of the room to see the old lawyer off.

"Dad, look what Kayla's drawing." Kevin pointed down at the doodles on the crisp white material. It made me wince that he called her Kayla and not Mom. It felt wrong.

"She's gone," Kayla confirmed, walking back into the kitchen and crouching down in an instant to finish up the drawings. I stood there watching the two of them. Of course, there was a connection there, even if Kevin didn't mean to, it was ingrained in his DNA. He was pulled toward his true mother, watching intently as she doodled and drew a rather basic picture of the three of us.

Was this more intended to catch my eye than Kevin's?

"I want to take a maternity test." Kayla suddenly spoke up after Kevin had left the room. It was clear she'd been anxiously waiting to ask this, the way that she'd constantly looked on edge. I didn't min. It was clearly within her right to want this. She had been searching for years, and I wasn't exactly about to step in her way of finding out the truth. "Of course, I'm sure that Kevin is my son. I just want the complete medical confirmation."

"I understand." I nodded, wanting to do everything that I could to help. "There's no way that we could hand Kevin over if he were your biological child. Surely, the legal system would work in our favor if this was the case?"

"I hope so." She sighed, moving in to hug me tightly. It was as though she was a child herself, wanting the comfort of somebody else.

∼

We didn't waste a second, wanting nothing more than to find out and confirm whether or not all of the speculations were true. The way Kayla's leg had continuously bounced in anxiety was stressing me out just as much, and in the end, I had no choice but to place my hand over her leg.

Instantly., she stilled. Although the gesture was not one made sexually, it was used to comfort Kayla. Her breathing was still incredibly labored, leaving the underlying anxiety to simmer beneath the surface of her skin now that it couldn't burst out through the avid action of her shaking leg.

"How are you feeling?" I'd asked once we made it to the clinic. They already had Kevin's DNA on the system, it was just Kayla's that they needed.

"Nervous, I don't want all of this to go to waste."

"It won't." I took her hand, squeezing it gently as we waited together. "You know, regardless of whether or not you truly are Kevin's mother, it would be great after all of this for you to remain in his life."

"I'd like that too." Her face lit up. "But let's get through one thing at a time. Who knows, by the end of this, James could have custody of Kevin."

"I won't let him." My voice was monotonous and ominous. There wasn't much to the threat, with nobody else able to hear it. At least nobody that mattered.

"Matt, we have to think of every option. He could still completely destroy me with this new evidence."

"Then we could get him back with our new evidence," I countered, eyes narrowed as the thought of James winning was becoming more and more awful each time I thought about it.

"There's no way that this could happen without ruining my career." Her voice was small. The idea sounded selfish, but I knew what she meant.

"That would never be my intention." I squeezed her hand again, reassuring her that I would find some kind of loophole. "If all else fails, you could always join my company." The idea was stupid. There weren't any fields in the company that involved law, at least none that would work with a tainted lawyer like Kayla. She was going to have to change fields if this information was to leak.

Almost a week passed by. Kayla was always on edge as she waited for the phone to go, unable to sit still for too long. There was nothing worse than the occasional false alarms; Doug ringing to talk to me about various details, or even cold calls that were more infuriating than the tediousness of the clinic itself.

"Finally." I groaned as the phone rang, noticing that the caller ID was different to ones I'd seen in the past. I let Kayla answer the call, watching her facial reactions as worry and nerves flooded through every muscle.

"Yes." She nodded. "Yes, of course." I could imagine the other half of the conversation, the woman wanting to confirm she was talking to the right person before disclosing this information. "Really? Oh, my God, yes, thank you! Wow, thank you so much. Okay. Yes. All right, goodbye." And with that, she hung up.

"So?"

"He's my son." I couldn't help myself, rushing over to scoop Kayla into my arms and swing her around in happiness. Tears streamed down her cheeks in floods, the joy of the news encapsulating both of us. I kissed Kayla repeatedly, pecking my lips to hers as the two of us became unable to wipe the grins from our faces.

"I'm so happy for you." I smiled widely, pulling away to see that her smile was even wider. I leaned in once more, slower this time, pulling her close to me and entrapping her within my arms. Kayla's arms wrapped around mine, pulling our bodies so close to the point where they physically couldn't be any closer together. I realized at that moment that something deeper existed, deeper because I wasn't just happy for her.

I was happy for *us*.

For what this meant for our strange and slightly dysfunctional group of people, it meant there was solidarity, unlike anything Jenna and I ever had, a genuine connection. No lies in the picture.

I pressed my lips tightly to Kayla's. It became a passionate kiss, one that involved us moving slowly yet with force, both breathing heavily as the adrenaline of the waiting had already begun to wear off. I couldn't place the feeling. It was something more than I'd ever managed to get with Jenna, and I'd barely been with Kayla in this way for that long.

"I think we should wait to tell Kevin," Kayla spoke, suddenly pulling away.

"Why?" I frowned.

"I want to make this special; I don't care whatever legal shit we still have looming over our heads. I want to have an incredible day out and reveal it to him as a grand surprise."

That was when my phone rang.

FORTY-SEVEN
MATT

She had waited patiently for me to get off the phone. The news hadn't been the best and was slightly annoying because Kayla had just begun planning a special day imminently.

"That was Douglas. He says that I need to go back to the city, that I'm needed in the office." I watched as Kayla's face dropped instantly. It wasn't fair on her after the news we'd just had. I understood she was over the moon, but back down on Earth, there was still an active custody case underway. "I'm truly sorry, Kayla, but I promise that we can tell him once I'm back."

"When will that be?" Her voice was fragile.

"I'm not sure yet, hopefully no longer than a couple of days."

"So, two days?"

"Well, I'm not completely sure yet so—"

"But you said a couple, that means two, right?" She was already bursting at the seams to tell Kevin the truth, but I knew that we had to make this special. For it to sink in for

Kevin, it was going to have to be something memorable, the perfect day. It was a lot of pressure on top of a lawsuit.

"Kayla." I sighed, rubbing my eyes. "I'll keep in contact and let you know all of the details as I'm told them, all right?"

"I guess."

I moved over to her, pressing my lips to hers once again. I was definitely going to need to tell her about the way my feelings were growing. It was inevitable that they were going to continue along this path and not subside. However, I felt a few days away in the city could be good to help me organize my thoughts. I wanted to show Kayla that I genuinely cared for her and didn't want to jeopardize this no matter which way the case went.

"I'll be back as quickly as I can. You can count on that," I promised while beginning to climb the stairs, realizing that I was going to need to pack swiftly. Luckily, this was the sort of thing that was drilled into me from my military days, the way you had to be able to quickly gather up the essentials and move off in a matter of minutes was lurking somewhere in my muscles. An old habit I was going to have to dig out of my system.

∼

The idea of leaving Kayla behind wasn't a decision that my heart took lightly. It ached to be in her presence, to have her delicious body underneath mine and these thoughts, these reminders only made it harder to drive away from her. Although I knew that if I were to just ignore the outside world, I could lose everything, including my money, Kevin, and even Kayla if the entire thing was turned upside down.

"Thanks for coming," Doug spoke over the phone once I'd finished the drive. It had been grueling, and my eyes were stinging from continually staring at the road. Focusing on driving seemed to tax more of my energy as the sun began its descent down the sky. The darkness put a strain on both my mental capacity and ability to stay awake. Luckily, I made it to the city with myself and the car in one piece.

"Yeah, no problem. So what time are we meeting tomorrow?" I questioned, flopping down on the plush bed.

"Actually...I was thinking that we could maybe meet at the office right now? I'm still here and wanted to discuss things out of hours."

I had to stop the groan that had risen through my throat, not wanting Douglas to hear my disappointment at going to see him. Of course, I was intrigued, but I was also exhausted.

"All right, I'll see you in around fifteen minutes." I then hung up, groaning as my mind had already begun to get enticed by the idea of changing into comfier clothes that weren't as tight while feeling the satisfaction of lying under freshly pressed sheets. Few things in the world were as enticing as this image in my mind.

I'd specifically chosen to book into a hotel for the night to relax; if I wanted food, it would be brought to me. There was no need to wash up or even cook for myself. But this would all have to be put on hold as I managed to drag myself off of the bed and check my appearance in the mirror. My hair was slightly disheveled—nothing that running my hands through it a few times couldn't fix, but my shirt was incredibly creased, mainly due to the monotonous task of driving.

It wasn't as though I was going to anything official, I

reminded myself, merely shrugging at my appearance and walking out of the door.

I arrived at the office slightly earlier. It hadn't been intended, but I'd forgotten how short of a walk the hotel was from the tall skyscraper that I had ascended.

However, there was something wrong instantly. The lights were off on the entire floor once the elevator had stopped, the doors open to reveal a scene of utter desertion, nobody in sight at all. Tentatively, I had stepped out of the comfort of the elevator, neglecting the easy escape route. It was something else that had become a habit from the military, always making sure there was an easy way out of any situation.

But the further that I walked into the room, the quicker I realized Doug wasn't there at all. There was still something that was shifting the air. Something that wasn't quite as still as the rest of the room.

"Doug?" I regretted calling out the moment that the words left my mouth, giving away my position to whatever was waiting for me on the floor. The darkness concealed whatever secret lay ahead of me to discover. I crossed the room, heading in the direction of the light switch, but something stopped me.

I could hear my heart hammering in my ears, fists clenched as I was ready for a fight. A military instinct that I couldn't get away from. No matter how many years I tried to swamp myself in the world of business, the initial survival training remained.

"Doug? This isn't funny." *Stop talking*, I scolded myself. However, there was a fear that took over me. A fog in my mind that was conjured by my terror of the unknown.

"Try again." A voice cut through the silent tension.

I tensed my muscles to stop myself jumping out of my skin too much, although I was still startled by the sound.

"James?" I whirled around in every direction. By now, I had neared Lydia's desk. One of the prototypes of the products still sat proudly on the wood. I began to formulate a plan, wanting so badly for the product to work and for it to alert Lydia of my location.

I pressed the button, seeing the red light going on. All I could do was hope that Lydia would see the notification and call the police or at least come to see what was going on. I had no idea where she would be after office hours, but there had to be something that she could do.

James suddenly emerged on the other side of the room, his silhouette from the glow of the city proving the only indication of his arrival. I had given up on my attempt to get the lights, not sure if I wanted to see James fully.

"What are you doing here?"

"I didn't want it to come to this," he murmured. There was something ominous in his voice.

"Come to what? What are you talking about?" I could see the object in his hand as he stepped into the light. A gun. "What are you doing with that?"

"What do you think?" he snapped, his voice raised to an uncomfortable level. Every hair on my body stood up on end in apprehension. There was a moment of stillness, where neither of us moved.

I wanted to harness the technique of attacking by surprise, cutting through the air and ducking behind a desk. The gunshot splintered through the air, but it managed to miss me completely. I didn't wait. I launched myself at James before he got the time to aim again, another perk to my colored history being my swiftness and ability to move without being seen.

My body thrust into his, my arm instantly moving to hit the gun from his hand. We both heard the thud of it hitting the ground from somewhere in the darkness. My fist landed on James's jaw, striking into him again and again. However, there was a sudden split of pain that erupted through the side of my head. James had hit me with something rather hard. A warmth dribbled onto my shoulder, and I knew instantly that my white shirt was about to be ruined. This was the least of my worries as James wriggled out from under me, punching my jaw and kicking me in the ribs. I cried out in pain, unsure how well I could see due to the darkness, making it almost impossible to assess the damage of the head injury.

James was shuffling around. I could tell that he was desperately searching for his deadly weapon. I had to find it before he did. However, there was no point letting him move around freely; instead, I focused my efforts on hurting him again.

"What happened to good old law and order?" I barked at him once I had James's head held tightly in a headlock.

"You didn't seem to be scared by my threats. I didn't want it to come to this, but I'll go through with all of my promises."

"To kill me?" My heart was thumping so loud that I was terrified that he could hear it.

"A promise I made to myself." James laughed. Down below us, the sounds of sirens flitted up to meet our ears. The device had worked. There was a commotion from downstairs. Lydia had called the police. "What's that?"

"That's justice, James. Do you actually think that they'll let you keep Kevin after this?" I questioned, realizing this was all of the evidence that I needed, although, my vision was blurring slightly. My hearing wasn't as sharp. There was nothing that I could do to shake the dizziness overtaking my mind and body. *I have to keep a grip on him*, I reminded myself. There was no way that I could let James get away with this.

"This wasn't how it was supposed to be. You should be dead!" His voice was shrill due to the lack of air that I was letting him have.

"Why did you want Kevin? What was it about him that you needed?" There was no response and his hysterics ceased, so I squeezed him harder. "Tell me!"

"Okay! Okay! I wanted him because of his trust fund! The money that Jenna had left for him in a private account. It's for college, it's for when he's older. But I-I—"

"You wanted to take it for yourself," I breathed out. "I knew it wasn't sentimental. There was never that close of a connection for you to have wanted Kevin so badly that you were willing to commit murder."

"Oh, God." The man sobbed in my arms, choking on his own sorrow, as though he was expecting me to give him any sympathy.

Thumping came on the stairs, the sounds that indicated the police were getting closer. Soon they would be upon us. The lights would go on and reveal to them the violent scene around us. Did I look guilty?

"This is ridiculous, James. You did all of this just because of money?" I continued on, feeling that it was better to talk to him than having to listen to the ear-splitting sobs that filled the entire office floor.

The adrenaline still flooded my muscles, causing me to shudder; if there was one thing that the military taught me, it was that there was no way you could relax or turn your back on your enemy. Not until he was secured tightly, unable to escape or attack you again.

"It was a lot of money," James countered, shaking his head as the tears continued to pour down his face, all implications that he was a threat had long since fled, just like the coward he was.

"I don't care, I still don't believe that you would be willing to put so much on the line for a trust fund, and you were going to ruin Kayla's career!" I squeezed tighter again, the images of the devastation on her face after our meeting at the restaurant resurfacing in my mind.

"Police!"

The shout made both of us jump, allowing James a minuscule moment to wriggle out of my grasp and move away from me. The lights flicked on in a flash. I was dazzled, completely disorientated as my eyes continuously attempted to get used to the new brilliance of light. It was exposing, displaying me to the new people in the room.

All I could see was red, somebody close by was shouting. The shouts continued to get louder until they were suddenly silenced by another gunshot. There was nothing I could do but blink. I tried to get up, but somebody was pushing me back down. Shouting was then mixed with an alarm as it began to sound.

"Sir? Are you all right?" A woman's voice was shouting in my direction, but I couldn't respond.

"Can you hear me, sir? We need to know if you're okay."

I sat there, attempting to put a hand to my head again. It felt wet. My hand revealed the amount of blood that I was losing.

The final thing that I remembered before losing consciousness was the brilliantly white light above me. The buzzing noise became incessant. It surrounded me and carried me into the darkness. There was nothing I could do but let it take me.

~

The hospital had been great to me, stitching up the head wound and allowing me to contact Kayla to let her know I was all right.

"Are you sure you don't want me to come down there?" Her voice was laced with worry. It left me feeling warm to the fact that she was genuinely caring about my wellbeing.

"I'm fine, honestly, Kayla," I said with a chuckle. "James is in custody. So there's no way that he'll get Kevin. We've done it, and we're going to win."

"At a great cost. It took you to get injured for us to know the truth."

"And I'd do it again in a heartbeat if it would land James in cuffs again," I responded fast, speaking no word of a lie as I knew I would most definitely put everything on the line to save Kevin.

"I'm just so glad that you're safe now. I can't believe that he had a gun pointed at you." There was a shake in her voice.

"I know. He was willing to go to those extremes to get the money."

"Do you know how much it is?"

"Not at the moment, but James said that it was a savings account for college. It's strange because I didn't know about it, but I'm guessing it must be enough to get Kevin through the years of study without him needing to pay a dime toward tuition fees."

"That's amazing," she breathed out. It was quite a shock

to learn that I was one of the people who had been left in charge of this account. I'd completely missed it in the will.

"I know, right? I'm going to get some rest. The hospital said they can discharge me in the morning and I'm coming straight home."

"You're not driving, are you?" The worry was back in her voice, that uneasy shakiness that reminded me of all of the times I'd been concerned for Kayla instead. It was funny how the tables had turned so much.

"No, of course not. The doctor said I can't drive for a couple of days, at least until the swelling has gone out of the lump." Around the main cut, the skin was raised and as lumpy as the moon's surface. I felt incredibly lucky that the injury hadn't been more severe and would affect me for longer. It was just the initial blood loss that had caused me to pass out. "I'll get the train over there."

"All right, I'll see you soon then." I could tell even over the phone that Kayla was excited to see me. It had barely been a day since I'd returned to the city, but I was already fine with leaving, missing Kayla and Kevin much more than I had anticipated.

Kayla hung up the phone after saying her goodbyes. I didn't want to sleep in the hospital overnight, but the medical staff had insisted that I stay in to make sure there was definitely not any internal bleeding. That last bit hadn't left me feeling the most secure. I would have thought this was something they could diagnose straight away.

"Matt!" I was just dozing off when Doug burst into the room. He seemed genuinely disheveled and quite frightened.

"Doug, what happened?" I questioned, confused as to why he hadn't been in the office.

"Some crazy bastard with a gun burst in and told me to

hide in the other room, he said that if I call for help...he'd shoot me." There was a shakiness in both his voice and in his hands. I could tell that the entire situation of being held at gunpoint had shaken him up tremendously.

"It's all right, Doug. It was James, and he's in custody now."

"James?" He gasped, eyes widening. "Did he try to—"

"Yeah, I managed to get him on the floor and pin him so that he couldn't attack me more." I gestured to the wound on my head, watching as Douglas winced. Although he was an older man, he seemed to still be as fast as though he were in the prime of his youth. His mind ticking so fast that if I were to look inside, I would be dizzy.

"I'm so sorry, Matt. I didn't realize he was going to try and attack other people."

"It's all right. It's over now." I didn't trust Douglas as much physically, it was more his strategies and loopholes that I took more comfort in understanding. This wasn't something I was about to lose that kind of intel over.

"So, you think that the case will definitely work in your favor now?"

"It has to. James is under arrest for attempted murder, premeditated at that," I spoke with a sigh. "No court is going to rule that he is fit to be Kevin's sole guardian." It felt good to say, to know there was no way this could go wrong for us now.

∼

The next day, I made it back home in record time. I wasted no time during the nurse's first few moments of her shift to talk her into discharging me. I was getting restless, being confined to staying in a bed with thin sheets and a blinding light that was beginning to give me more of a headache than the initial head injury.

It didn't take as long as I had thought on the train. I was used to making this journey on the road and hadn't realized how much the railroad could cut down the journey time.

Anxiety fluttered in my gut. I was looking forward to seeing Kayla and Kevin, wanting to finally have this special day that Kayla had begun to talk about before I'd left. I hoped that while I'd been away, she'd planned it down so that we knew what we were going to do.

Finally, the train pulled into the nearest station, and I quickly rushed off and into the first taxi that I could see in the rank, itching to get home as though it were a balm for a rash. My head was throbbing slightly from all of the travel. The nurse had suggested that I just go home and rest up as much as I could, even writing me a note to show to anybody who wanted me to do any work. But I'd put that in the bin the moment I had left the hospital, knowing that I wasn't going to need it.

I was the head of my company, after all. There was nobody I had to answer to whether I wanted to work or not. However, to make sure that I was prepared for any delays, I'd rung up Lydia to tell her that I wasn't going to be in the office any time soon.

"I can't believe that the prototype worked." I sighed, sitting down at the counter with my grandmother and Kayla. They'd welcomed me into the house with open arms and smiles filled up to the brim with relief. I was just as happy to be able to see them again.

Even Kevin had hugged me. It was a surprise due to his rather cold nature that he'd had toward me in recent weeks.

"I'm so happy that it worked, but please never rely on something like that in a life-or-death situation. I wouldn't want you to gamble your life on whether or not a product worked." Kayla smiled, although the feeling was bittersweet.

With the case almost finished, there was no longer a reason for her to stay. But I wanted her here regardless. I loved her. I just had to work out how to tell her.

FORTY-EIGHT
KAYLA

I wanted to kiss him to death the moment Matt stepped through the door, but I refrained from doing so in the presence of Myra and Kevin. I'd never seen the young boy move so fast, especially with the cast hindering his movement. It was incredible to know he was so happy that his dad was home.

"I missed you," Matt muttered to me, moving closer once Myra had left the room. Kevin had requested her to go upstairs, in his room.

"I missed you more, I was so worried." I sighed, placing my hands on his chest to steady myself. I didn't even have a head injury, but his presence alone made me dizzy. Slowly, I pressed a kiss to his lips. It was chaste but meant more because I didn't want the usual sloppy and desperate kisses we were both so used to.

"Kayla, there's something that I want to ask you," he began, pulling away, but his nose was still touching mine, our faces barely apart. "After the case is over when we can return to our normal lives for sure."

"Well, I wouldn't call the way that you live normal," I

countered with a smirk, regarding his abundance of money, the subject he always tries to avoid. I watched as he rolled his eyes.

"Well, you know what I mean. You're going to be going home, right?"

I nodded at his question, although my head moved reluctantly, mentally arguing against the movement because I didn't want to leave at all. I'd left once before in the past, and there was no way I was going to lose him again. "I don't want you to go."

"I don't want to either," I babbled, not wanting to leave what he'd said hanging in the air for too long, feeling as though that would imply a sense of doubt. There was definitely none of that whenever I thought about Matt.

"Then stay. Stay here with me and help me raise Kevin. Together." His words were music to my ears, leaving me speechless and breathless. A smile spread my lips apart, the shock paralyzing my entire body. Only my mouth could move, curving upward into an expression of joy.

"R-really?" My arms wrapped around Matt, pulling him closer to me as he nodded, smiling just as wide.

"Kayla, I've wanted to tell you for a while now about how I feel." He swallowed, and I could tell that this was hard for him. "I-I like you and I've wanted to say those words for so long, but recently another set of words have taken their place. They can no longer satisfy me."

"What do you mean?" It hadn't clicked in my mind yet.

"I love you." His words knocked the remaining air out of me, rendering me powerless to his ways. There was a moment of silence, causing him to raise an eyebrow. I was embarrassed by the fact that I'd failed to respond.

"I love you too, Matt." The words were foreign on my tongue, feeling right, yet different. He pulled me in again, pressing his lips to mine in a passionate kiss. This was faster, filled with a stronger sense of lust that filled me up and made me warm inside.

The thought that he loved me felt surreal, as though I was living in some kind of fantasy, destined to wake up at any moment now. But I didn't. This was truly happening. He loved me.

I knew we couldn't take this too far in the kitchen—anybody could see into the house and even Myra, or worse, Kevin could easily walk in on the two of us. That would be something that could quickly ruin the moment.

"I've planned the day," I spoke, pulling away once I could feel Matt's hands traveling lower. We were dancing on that thin line between what was permitted and what wasn't. I was quick to shut it down, stepping away from him.

"We could do it tomorrow?"

"Yeah. I've invited a few people to come. But only if you're feeling better. You look exhausted." Stepping back had given me a better view of Matt's condition; dark rings hung heavily under his eyes, his complexion was slightly paler than usual, but there was a way that his body was somewhat swaying from side to side that worried me.

"I'm fine."

"Are you sure about that?" I didn't mean to press him, but something definitely wasn't right.

"Kayla, I said I'm fine," Matt said with a sigh, rubbing his eyes, although the action only caused him to sway more.

"Hey, come on. I'll take you up to bed. You definitely need to rest," I said in complete confidence. I wanted to break the news to Kevin, so a slightly more selfish part of me was urging Matt to have a fast recovery.

Matt stopped protesting and let me lead him upstairs.

On the way up, I caught a glimpse of his stitches. They were big, binding the wound together, the nurse had clearly shaven a small patch of his hair to have better access to the injury. It looked as though if James had hit him with any more force, it wouldn't have been guaranteed Matt could have gotten up.

I still didn't know the full story, but a large part of me didn't want to. The fear gripping me as to what it must have been like to be attacked in the dark, held at gunpoint, and told that you were going to die because of a custody battle. Yet Matt seemed utterly unfazed by it, returning home as though the injury had been caused by nothing more than a nasty fall. I was sure it had something to do with his military past. Over his time spent there, he'd clearly become desensitized to violence.

~

The day passed quickly while we waited for Matt to rest up. I busied myself with finalizing the paperwork of the case and also helping Myra with the house.

Matt was still asleep. I'd been in to check on him, but there was nothing else I was able to do to help him recover.

"Kayla, come and see what I've drawn!" Kevin called out to me the next morning. The offer sounded so appealing, I couldn't help but wish that he'd called me Mom. I needed to tell him.

I was going to burst if it didn't happen soon, and by soon, I meant today. I climbed the stairs and followed Kevin into his room, smiling at the mess that had been a consequence of his inspired creativity. Paper was strewn across the floor, and on top of old pieces of newspaper, a set of paints were almost tipped over. Leaning against one another like dominos, however, no paint had managed to mar the furniture or carpet. I was thankful that I'd found him like this before his creativity had caused some permanent damage to the pieces of furniture around him.

"What's this?" I questioned with a frown, looking around at the various pieces of paper.

"It's us," he stated, looking as though it were as clear as day. The strange stick figures were holding hands, although it looked more like flowers that were attached to their arms. There were four of them. "Me, you, Dad, and Grams," he explained, giving me a beaming smile. It felt like a moment of acceptance, a moment when I realized he'd already welcomed me into the family, no matter whether or not we put the label of mother on the relationship.

"Oh, wow. It's excellent," I praised with a smile, crouching down to see the many drawings that were similar to the one he'd shown me. In some of them, it appeared as though we were on a boat of some kind, while in others, we were having a barbecue. "I never realized how talented you were, Kevin!"

"Thanks." He seemed suddenly quite shy, hiding his current drawing with his arms as he continued to work on it, splashing paint all over the old newspaper. "Are you going to stay here forever, Kayla?"

"Would you like me to?" I countered, not knowing for sure, although Matt had expressed his want for me to do so.

"Yes." He spoke with a smile, sitting up only to beam at me. "I'd love it, then we could play and draw and watch movies together all of the time!"

"That sounds like a lot of fun," I muttered, my mind drifting off, still in disbelief that the boy who sat in front of me was the child I'd given birth to all those years ago.

"I'm going to tell Dad all about it when he gets up!"

Kevin declared. It made me smile to think that he was finally warming back up to his dad, especially after the trauma of Jenna's passing. I knew exactly what it was like to lose your parents. It was only going to get harder for Kevin. But that was why I wanted to be here, to help him through something that I'd struggled with. If only I'd had some support, perhaps it would have been easier on me. I would have dealt with all of that ripe emotion in a much healthier way. "I missed him when he went away."

"So did I." I nodded, thankful that Matt's injuries hadn't been more serious. "Kevin, do you want to go on a big family walk today?"

"Sure." He smiled, although it was clear that he didn't actually see why.

"Okay good, because we're going to be having a few guests join us."

"Like who?" Matt's voice caused us both to jump and turn around. He was up and smiling, watching the two of us in delight.

"Oh, I just phoned a couple of people to come and visit. It would be nice to see everyone, like Douglas, Lydia, and even Mr. Wilks out of a professional kind of setting," I explained. Matt walked into the room and crouched down beside us. "Like I said yesterday, I can still cancel it if you don't feel up to it."

"No, no. I'm fine." He brushed it off. Admittedly, Matt did look a little better after the sleep, although I felt this might be a very long recovery. "If I feel any worse, I'll simply call the doctor, but for the moment, I feel like I'm on the mend."

"That's great news. Now go and get dressed." I gestured to his pajamas. "People will be here soon. We don't want you scaring them off wearing that."

Kevin laughed as Matt playfully rolled his eyes and left the room. Leaving the two of us alone to draw some more.

Kevin and I headed downstairs as I heard a knock at the door. It was Lydia and Douglas. They'd traveled in together, walking into the cozy house and smiling widely. Matt came downstairs, freshly showered and somehow shaven too. It was a miracle to me that he'd managed to concentrate so much with a nasty head wound. On top of that, he'd managed to do so without cutting himself on the razor.

"What a nice idea this is." Lydia beamed, her eyes darting around the house, taking in the ranch's style. It was definitely a stark contrast to the sleek, professional environment that she was very used to being in because of the city.

"Indeed." Douglas nodded. Myra walked back into the room holding hands with Mr. Wilks. I hadn't even noticed that he'd entered. Perhaps he had a spare key or something. I'd seen how close he'd grown to Myra, something that definitely hadn't gone unnoticed by most.

"I have an announcement," Myra called, gaining the attention of everybody in the room. "Well, we have an announcement." She blushed at the words, the elderly woman acting as though she were a quarter of her actual age. "We're dating."

"Grams, really?" I could see Matt trying to hide how much the idea was making him cringe.

"Really." She smiled, I couldn't help but be happy for her, after the passing of Matt's grandpa, I'd seen how unhappy she'd been. It was nice to have somebody fill that hole. It felt as though it was what her late husband would have wanted. No man would want their wife to be unhappy for the rest of her days, after all.

"That's great news, Myra." I beamed at her, walking over and hugging her tightly. "I'm happy for you."

"Thank you, my love." She smiled, laughing delicately as she patted my back. "Shall we go outside then?"

The trees stretched out in every direction, lining the planes of grass and causing my nose to twitch slightly due to the overload of greenery. The sun beat down on our small party of people. Even Mikey had joined us, hearing that there were some big announcements to be made.

Kevin held on to my hand as we walked, not talking, but it didn't feel as though it was needed. I was happy in the comfortable silence, basking in the feeling of belonging to a group of people like this. Each of us a jigsaw piece from a different puzzle stuck together in an almost-perfect way, but there was no other combination that I would have it in.

"Are we nearly there yet?" Kevin finally groaned out.

"Almost, don't worry, not far now," I spoke up. We were at the front of the group, and Matt walked on my other side. I had to refrain from holding his hand. It felt odd, even though we'd declared our love to one another. We walked on a bit further, until the ranch was far in the distance and a layer of sweat had amalgamated on top of my brow.

"All right, I think we've walked long enough." Matt chuckled, finding a nearby log and perching down on it. "Kayla has an announcement, I think." He smirked up at me, watching as I took both of Kevin's hands and crouched down to his level.

"Kevin, you know you said you'd like me to stay forever?"

He nodded in response.

"Well, I have a confession to make, I'm never going to leave you again. I only did once before because of the pressure put on me. I've spent the last years looking all over the country for you." Tears welled up in my eyes as I spoke.

"But finally, I did the correct tests and found the right adoption center."

"What are you saying?" He frowned. His small mind hadn't yet caught on to what I was talking about.

"Kevin, I'm your mother. Your real mother," I explained, watching the delight that seemed to spread across his face. I'd always wondered what his reaction would be, but I was thankful that I hadn't been disappointed. There was always the possibility it could have gone the other way. He could have been angry or upset. Perhaps that was all still to come.

"You are?" He wrapped his arms around me, practically jumping into a hug. The tears fell freely, landing on my cheeks as I held him tightly in my grasp.

"Yes, and I'm never leaving you again," I added, reinforcing to him that he was safe with me. I felt a presence next to me. It was Matt. He'd crouched down too. Kevin glanced at him for a moment, and then extended an arm out to hug him too. The three of us sat there on the grass, holding onto each other as though somebody was going to be blown away.

Myra had gasped in amazement at the news. The happiness seemed to be infectious. Everyone was smiling, even Old Man Wilks.

"I-I don't know what to say," Kevin spoke with a giggle, but yet again, it instantly became one of those moments where he didn't have to say anything. The silence was just as comforting.

Matt turned to look at me, our noses were practically touching as I laughed slightly. Everyone seemed to be so happy, it was a moment that I wanted to capture forever, to put that feeling in a bottle and spray it all over me whenever I felt down in the future.

"I don't know if I can call you Mom yet," the young boy said with a frown. The thought was strange even to me. I'd never been a mom, unsure if I'd even respond to the name if somebody were to call after me with it.

"That's all right, Kevin, we have all the time in the world," I assured him, smiling widely as he nodded. I knew it was going to take some time to adjust to this kind of way of life, a family. A real-life family.

I hadn't had one of those in years, people to call mine, people who relied on me and loved me as much as I did back.

"I have another announcement to make," Matt spoke, clearing his throat. This seemed to catch the small cluster of people off guard. "But first, I need to speak to Kevin," he said as though he'd suddenly remembered, taking his son's hand and walking off away from us.

I glanced up at Myra with a frown. She merely shrugged in response. Yet there was a knowing look on her face.

FORTY-NINE

MATT

"How do you feel knowing that Kayla is your biological mom?" I questioned him. The two of us had moved out of earshot from the rest of the group.

"I feel amazing. I think she's going to be a great mom." He giggled, I couldn't tell if he was taking the entire thing seriously or not. Thinking that it could be a few years before he'd consider what this even meant. I could tell that the thought of Jenna was still looming in his mind. She'd been a good mom, but she wasn't Kayla.

Sure, she'd had the maternal instinct, told him off when necessary and praised him when that was applicable, but there was always that overshadowing thought that we tried our hardest not to mention Kevin wasn't ours.

"What's this about?" Kevin was growing impatient.

"I want to tell you a secret." I crouched down, my words captivating his interest. "I think I've fallen in love with Kayla."

Kevin gasped, a look of wonder on his face. I didn't want him to ask 'what about Jenna?' and thankfully, he remained silent.

"I want to ask for your approval. What would you think if I married her?"

"Oh, my gosh, Dad!" he exclaimed, putting his little hand to his mouth and giggling wildly. There was something about the way he laughed and did his little celebratory dance on the spot that would make even the iciest heart melt in seconds. "Yes! Are you going to ask her?"

"I am right now," I muttered, rolling my shoulders back, a hand touching the jacket pocket that was bulging slightly. It housed an extraordinary box I'd been keeping a hold of for a while now. The near-death experience with James made me realize there wasn't any point in waiting longer than I had to.

"Come on!" Kevin pulled at my arm, dragging me back toward the others. "Dad has something he'd like to ask Kayla!" Kevin shouted excitedly, moving over to stand by Grams.

"Kayla, I've known you for years, and although we haven't always seen eye to eye, I think the past weeks have made it clear that I love you."

I heard Myra gasp at the comment.

"So while we were on the subject of announcements, and I knew that you wouldn't want a big public display, I figured there's no place more perfect than here with our great friends."

I dropped to one knee, watching the reactions on people's faces change from shocked to elated in an instant, a quick flick as though somebody had pressed a switch. I produced the box from my pocket to reveal the dainty but elegant ring cushioned inside of it. Kevin cheered, but I kept my eyes locked with Kayla's. She was in complete shock, fresh tears rolling down her cheeks with a hand to her mouth.

"Yes," she whispered, her head nodding along with her answer. My heart leaped at the answer. "Yes!" She spoke louder again as I rose to my feet. We halted our elation for a moment to concentrate on putting the ring on the right finger. I was absolutely terrified of dropping it or even worse, losing it in the vast field.

From this close, I could see that Kayla's hands were shaking. There was so much joy in her that it almost seemed as though she couldn't contain it.

"I love you," she said, wrapping her arms around me as we stayed close to each other.

"I love you more," I countered, pecking her lips. Kevin was making immature, sick noises in the background at the kisses, causing everyone to laugh.

"Congratulations, Matt." Douglas smiled, shaking my hand; however, I was never one for such formalities. I pulled him in for a brief hug that caused us both to chuckle. Watching as Lydia hugged Kayla tightly, admiring the stylish ring, I felt the luckiest man alive.

"Well done, my boy." My grandmother pulled me in for a hug too, kissing my cheek in the same way she'd done since I was little. The gesture was kind, one that left me with tears in my eyes. "You know that your gramps would have been incredibly proud." It was these words that set me off. "And anyway, I like her much better than Jenna already."

I heard Mr. Wilks chuckle at the comment. I laughed too, although I didn't want to think about that, instead, choosing to focus on the here and now and the people around me. I was just incredibly thankful it seemed like everything had ironed itself out.

All of the lies, the cheats, the sadness, and secrets, they

had all dissipated. Leaving in their trail a path of love, and an upcoming wedding.

"I love you," she whispered again, the group continuing to chat around us.

"I love you too," I spoke back, tenderly kissing her cheek as Kevin took hold of her other hand.

"I love you, Kevin." Kayla smiled down at our boy. There was a look about him that had been vacant for a long time, even before Jenna had died. It was a look that told me he was already viewing Kayla as a mother figure, but to my surprise, Kevin looked between the two of us and said, "I love both of you."

A NOTE FROM THE AUTHOR

Thank you for taking the time to read my book Boss Daddy. I hope you enjoyed reading this story as much as I loved writing it.

If you did, I would truly appreciate you taking some time to leave a quick review for this book. Reviews are very important, and they allow me to keep writing.

Thank you again for your support, I am incredibly grateful.

Thank you very much.

Love,
Suzanne

ABOUT SUZANNE HART

Thank you so much for reading my romances. I'm an avid reader who lives her dream of becoming an indie author. I enjoy writing about gorgeous billionaires that love to protect their sexy women.
I hope you love my books as much as I do!

Get FREEBIE!

https://dl.bookfunnel.com/rfgslpe5al

- facebook.com/SuzanneHartRomance
- amazon.com/author/suzannehart
- bookbub.com/profile/suzanne-hart

ALSO BY SUZANNE HART

All books are standalone novels.

Click Here for the whole catalogue on Amazon!

Turning Good Series

Rescuing Single Mom

Wanting Secret Baby

Second Chance Ex-Marine

Unexpected Roommate

∽

Untouched Series

Her First Game: A Billionaire & Virgin Romance

Her First Dance: A Billionaire Fake Fiancé Romance

Her Accidental Wedding: A Billionaire Fake Marriage Romance

Her Rough Hero: A Military Single Dad Romance

Claiming Christmas: A Mountain Man Romance Novella

∽

Irresistible Bosses Series

Bossing the Virgin: A Billionaire Single Dad Romance

Bossing My Friend: A Best Friends To Lovers Romance

Bossing My Dirty Enemy: An enemies to lovers romance

Bossing My Fake Fiancé: A Brothers' Competition Romance

~

Irresistible Bosses Box Set

~

Dancing with the Mob

Made in the USA
Monee, IL
18 May 2020